BREAK AND ENTER

CALLAHAN SECURITY BOOK 1

LORI MATTHEWS

BLURB

Callahan Security is on the brink of disaster. Mitch Callahan pushed his brothers to expand the family business into private security, and their first major client is a complete pain in the ass. It's no wonder the man has a target on his back, but nothing could prepare Mitch for how seductive his adversary is.

Love hurts. No one knows that better than Alexandra Buchannan, so she uses her talents as a thief to equalize the scales of romantic justice. Your ex still has your favorite painting? Not for long. Alex's latest job is her biggest challenge yet. Her target just hired a new security company, and the team leader is as smart as he is sexy.

Mitch knows he's jeopardizing not only this job but the future of Callahan Security. If only he didn't find Alex so damn irresistible. Soon their game of cat and mouse explodes into a million pieces. Unbeknownst to them, there's another player in the game, and his intentions are far deadlier.

Break And Enter

Copyright © 2020 Lori Matthews

For Harve
Because the alternative is unacceptable

ACKNOWLEDGMENTS

It's often said that it takes a village to bring a book into the world. This one took a city, not New York sized maybe, but say, Cleveland. My deepest gratitude to all the inhabitants of my city. My editors, Corinne DeMaagd and Heidi Senesac for making me appear much more coherent than I actually am; my cover artist, Llewellen Designs for making my story come alive. My personal cheer squad which I could not survive without: Janna MacGregor, Suzanne Burke, Angi Morgan, Kimberley Ash, Stacey Wilk and the Cheeky Tarts. Thank you all for talking me off the ledge more than once. My mother and my sisters who told me to dream big. My husband and my children who make my life complete. You all are my world. A special heartfelt thanks goes out to you, the reader. The fact you are reading this means my dreams have come true.

CHAPTER ONE

S weat trickled along Alexandra Buchanan's hairline under her wig. Her heart thudded in her chest. She was minutes from her goal, mere seconds from obtaining her objective. She had been planning for months. Her fingertips tingled as the seconds ticked by slowly. She itched under her red velvet Venetian mask. Its feathers tickled her face.

The humid air hung heavy in the grand ballroom. The smell of women's perfumes and men's colognes mixed with sweet scent of the dozens of flowers that were on tables stationed around the room. But none of it could mask the funk of body odor or the even stronger stench of money.

The room was filled with the elite of Venice, of Italy and beyond. Women wore eye-catching costumes. Sequins and jewels glittered in the light from the ornate chandeliers. Men wearing masks and capes flashed jewels of their own on their fingers and their wrists. The room was a swirl of color and sound. Everyone who was anyone was invited to the Santini's spring ball. And this year it was a masquerade. She smiled to herself. She couldn't have asked for a better cover. It was as if the stars had aligned perfectly just for her.

She glanced at her watch. Only another twenty seconds, and the song would be over. And then it was time. As always happened at this moment, her senses heightened. She could hear every voice distinctly, see every small movement. Time slowed down to a crawl.

Finally, the orchestra was playing the last few notes of the song. This was it, the moment she lived for, the moment when she either conquered her goal or she failed miserably. Adrenaline roared through her body. Excitement exploded in her chest.

Alex moved across the floor as dancers mingled, looking for their next partner. She had her target in sight. He was passing his partner from the previous song to another man. He turned and smiled at the woman standing next to him. He took his new partner's hand in his.

She increased her pace slightly so that she was directly beside her target as he swung his other hand around to clasp the woman. She didn't look at him as she jostled him slightly. It was expected in this crowded space. Her fingers deftly performed the task they had done many times before. Quickly, silently she had her prize. She made her way across the floor, smiling as she went. She slid her hand into a hidden pocket, depositing her bounty.

This was it—the worst and, yet, the best moment. Would he notice? Would he yell? Would he point her out?

She kept her head up and her steady pace as she broke free of the dancers and started up the stairs to the mezzanine. Sweat was a fine sheen across her body. She had a fixed smile on her face and nodded to several of the partygoers as she crested the top of the stairs. Walking across the floor, she made her way toward the restrooms but glanced around quickly. No one was close. No one was paying attention. She passed the restrooms and made for the hallway on her left.

She moved down the corridor and made it to the doors that led to the terrace, but she kept walking. The security plan she'd gotten a hold of indicated they were tied to an alarm that would be on tonight. She went a few steps farther.

After making sure the hallway was clear, she did a little dance and slid her crinoline off. She wouldn't need it anymore, and it would just be in her way. She'd bought it from an online shop using a fake account and had it delivered to an office building. She hadn't touched it without her gloves so there were no prints, or at least not hers.

Glancing around she spotted a chair a little farther down the hallway. She put the crinoline on the far side of the chair, so it wouldn't be immediately seen by anyone walking down the hall.

Alex went back to a window at the far end of the balcony and unlocked it. Lifting it silently, she was once again amazed at how many people didn't alarm their windows above the ground floor. Tugging her costume up around the tops of her thighs so she could move her legs freely, she put one foot through the window, ducked under, and brought the rest of her body through onto the balcony. She lowered the window again from the outside.

"Where the hell did you come from?" a voice demanded from the darkness. She froze. No one should be on the balcony. She had planned this heist meticulously, and nowhere in the Santini security arrangements was there any indication that someone would be on the balcony.

A guest then? As she slowly turned in the direction the voice had come, a man dressed in a tuxedo emerged from the shadows. Damn. Security. They were wearing tuxes instead of costumes. But not Santini security. He didn't have the same type of ill-fitting tux as the Santini security guys. His fit him like a glove, like he was born to wear it. Someone else's security. A private bodyguard. Great. She'd been fifty-three seconds from freedom, and she runs into James Bond.

Her mind reeled as she tried to figure out a different escape route. The weight of the watch hidden in her skirt was a thousand pounds heavier. *Don't panic.* She smiled and moved forward a couple of steps, letting him take a long look at her.

The trick was to keep as much space between them as she could without seeming reluctant. She thanked her lucky stars once again that the party was a masquerade ball. For a thief, it was like hitting the jackpot. An *Asset Repossession Specialist Extraordinaire*, she mentally corrected herself.

Her duchess costume, which she'd had made especially for this job, not only showed off her assets but had a few hidden surprises. The security guy's gaze lingered for a moment on her "girls" as she called them. Not her norm to display them so blatantly, but she'd wanted to be sure anyone looking at her would be distracted, even the women. Better to show too much tit than too much of her face.

She took a deep breath. If she was careful, maybe she could still get away unscathed. After all, the mask she wore covered most of her face except for the lower part of her jaw, and the voluminous brown wig hid the rest of her head. Her heart rate started to come back down to earth. She could do this. The fine sheen of sweat had turned into a small river making its way down her back.

"What are you doing here? This area is off limits. No

one is supposed to be up here." He walked closer to her, his stance showing easy confidence. They were about twelve feet apart, separated by an area bathed in shadow. The breeze ruffled the feathers of her mask, but it also brought his scent to her. He smelled of soap and citrus and something wholly male that had her taking notice.

"*You're* here," she said in her most sultry voice. She prayed he wouldn't come any closer. He was bigger than most men, much bigger than her diminutive 5'5". At least six feet, she figured, which wasn't necessarily a problem, but his shoulders were wide. Why couldn't he have been one of the doughy types she had seen earlier? The guys who'd gone to seed years ago. She could have handled one of those guys no problem. Years of kick boxing, Tae Kwon Do, Krav Maga, and general self-defense training meant she could have rendered one of them unconscious soundlessly.

But she had to get the keener who looked to be in fabulous shape. All narrow hips, broad shoulders, and solid muscle. One of the major lessons she had learned was how to assess her opponent, and this one would be tough. Her stomach roiled. A fight with this guy would be loud and painful. Fighting was off the table.

She smiled as she studied him. His hair was a light brown with blond highlights. He wasn't wearing a mask, but it was hard to determine his eye color. There was no mistaking his square jaw though, especially since it appeared to be clenched. He was also drop-dead gorgeous and sexy as hell.

His eyes narrowed and focused on her after casing the rest of the balcony. "Who are you?"

She ignored the question. So, throwing him over the balcony was not going to work. Physically impossible, and besides, she wanted to avoid a scene. The water in the canals would catch his fall, yes, but everyone would rush to see as soon as they heard the splash.

"Who are you?" he repeated as he stepped closer. The Venice breeze ruffled a lock of his hair so that it fell over his forehead.

She gave a girlish giggle while mentally rolling her eyes. Men loved that crap. "Well, doesn't that defeat the whole purpose of a masquerade ball? I can't tell you who I am. It would ruin the mystery."

"Then why don't you tell me how you got onto this balcony? Like I said, no one is supposed to be out here."

She pouted. "Well, *you're* here." Then she closed the gap between them with a sexy stroll. She smiled up at him while caressing the pleats of his tux shirt with her gloved fingers. She needed him to stop asking questions. "All by yourself, I might add." Yes, all muscle. She could feel it through his shirt. Warmth spread through her insides as she peered up into his startlingly gray eyes. She had never seen eyes that gray before. They were like polished steel.

If circumstances were different...she still wouldn't touch him with a ten-foot pole. She'd been down that road before. If she'd learned nothing else in life, it was that the best-looking men were the ones that couldn't be trusted. Not ever. Not even if they were family.

He grabbed her fingers and held them fast. It sent an electric charge skittering up her arm. Startled, she tried to pull her hand back, but he held on. Her plan wasn't working. *He* was the one who was supposed to be distracted, not her.

"You need to leave. Now." There was no sign that he was remotely affected by her presence, unlike her who was totally suffering from their closeness. Her pulse skyrocketed. She was surprised he couldn't see it with her chest on display. Maybe he could. Sweat was now running down her legs as well as her back. This man was sexy as hell, but he was like kryptonite. She needed a new plan and fast.

"Uh..."

"Go for Callahan," the man said as he pressed his earpiece. He dropped her hand. Then, turning around, he walked over to the railing and looked down.

Recognizing her chance, she quickly and silently moved the fifty feet to the other end of the balcony. She took off her shoes and stuffed them into the hidden pockets of her dress. Then she hoisted herself onto the railing. With a quick glance back, she saw the man was still on the other side of the balcony looking down. She quickly stepped onto the small decorative ledge running along the front of the building and, hugging the wall, slid her way carefully to the corner.

She reached up and grabbed the edge of the roof and swung herself around the corner. Regaining her balance, she took a second to breathe and rest her cheek against the building. She took one hand off the wall slowly and wiped it on her dress. Then did the same with the other. After she lifted her cheek, she carefully removed her mask and pushed it into the pocket next to her shoes. She put her hand back on the wall.

She loved Venice. The buildings were so close together here, and in her line of work, that was a big plus.

CHAPTER TWO

"Everything good on your end?" The voice of Jake, his second in command, filled his ear.

Mitch tapped his ear again. "Fine. All clear."

"He wants to leave now. Is the boat ready?" Jake asked.

"The boat is at the slip waiting. Let me deal with one thing up here and then I'll be down."

"You know he hates to be kept waiting. I don't want to spend the next hour being lectured at, so hustle your ass down here."

Mitch ground his jaw and frowned. "Give me two minutes." He turned away from the scene below to deal with the mystery woman. "Now. You have—" She was gone. He glanced around, but he was alone on the balcony.

"What the hell?" He walked down to the other end, but there was no sign of her. He knew she couldn't have gone in through any of the doors because they were all alarmed. Taking the remote out of his pocket, he checked that the alarm was still on. Yes. Red.

His hands curled into fists. He'd made a mistake. A rookie mistake. He'd turned his back on the woman. Stupid didn't even cover it. *Fuck*.

He started to walk over to the far balcony doors when something registered out of the corner of his eye. He reached down and picked up a feather. From her mask. She was up to something. He had felt it in his bones as soon as he saw her. He had felt something else too, but he was working tonight, and work was the most important thing. It was the only thing. He'd laid everything on the line, and if it didn't work, he'd be finished and he'd be taking his family down with him.

No distractions. No matter how attractive they were. That's what he'd told the guys at the beginning of the night, and here he was the one who screwed up.

He tried to recall what she looked like, but with the costume on, there was no way to know. What he did know was she was sexy, and she smelled like...like orange blossoms, sunshine, and spice. Not helpful. Not at all. He cursed.

He glanced over the side of the balcony. Nothing, not that he'd expected her to be there. This was Venice. If she had been hanging off a balcony over a canal, someone would have noticed. A voice went off in his ear again.

"Callahan. Are we good to go?"

He reached up and tapped his earpiece. "On my way." He keyed the alarm fob in his pocket and walked through the doors to the interior of the building. He pressed it again and locked the doors behind him. The feeling that something wasn't right dogged him as he made his way down the stairs. He ordered a check of all his people, but everyone responded that all was fine.

It wasn't his party, nor was he responsible for the security of the guests. He was private security for one client, and that client wanted to leave. He briefly toyed with the idea of telling Santini's head of security about the woman, but it would hold up his client. At least that's the excuse he was using. The fact he would sound like an idiot describing a disappearing woman wasn't lost on him. Nor the fact that he'd made a massive mistake turning his back on her. No need to share that with anyone.

This was his first client since he and his brothers started the new personal security division of the business they'd taken over from their father. This night had to go well. He'd just screwed up big time. Whatever game the woman was playing, he said a prayer that his client wasn't her target.

He hit the bottom of the stairs and quickly made his way through the ballroom. He tossed the alarm remote to Vincenzo, the security guy at the door, and gave him a wave. Vincenzo gave him a nod in return. When he arrived on the jetty outside of the building, he gave his men the signal to move out.

The client and his date were just settling onto the speedboat they'd hired for the evening when suddenly another guest started shouting. Mitch whirled around, his hand automatically moving toward his gun in the shoulder holster under his jacket.

"*Mio orologio*! My watch!" the man yelled. "It's been stolen!"

Three of the Santini security guards moved over to the guest. "What kind of watch was it, sir? What does it look like?" Mitch heard them ask in Italian. Learning new languages had always come easy to him, so he had picked up a few during his free time, Italian being one of them.

"It's a Rolex Pearlmaster. Gold with the sapphires and

the diamonds on the front." The man's accent was thick. "Someone, they take it!"

Mitch turned back around and stepped onto the boat. Now he knew what she had been after. As they left the dock, a slow smile spread across his face.

CHAPTER THREE

A lex took her time as she turned slowly so that her back was to the building. She took a deep breath. She lifted one leg and braced herself with it against the far wall. She brought up her other leg so that her back was on one building and her feet on the other.

"You can do this," she whispered. "You're a badass." She *was* a badass, but she'd be jailed badass if she wasn't careful. She glanced down at the alley below and shuddered. If she fell, it would be a very hard landing. It would have been fabulous to have water beneath her rather than an alley but then the buildings would have been farther apart, and she wouldn't have been able to escape this way.

She took a deep breath and started moving sideways. She had practiced it several times, so she knew her dress would snag on the stucco a bit, but if she kept up a decent pace, it wouldn't get too caught. First her left foot, then her back, then her right foot. Left, back, right. She repeated the words silently as she shimmied across the length of the building until she was at the back corner. She let out a deep breath.

This was the tricky part. She had gone a bit higher as she worked her way across so that the balcony of the other building was slightly below her now. She took a beat. She thought about the watch and felt the weight of it again in her skirt. Her client was going to be very happy to get it back. Pride swelled in her chest. That she could give someone back some joy, some modicum of happiness, made every job worth it.

Her back throbbed. It was scratched up and stung from the salt of her sweat. Her legs were a bit wobbly, but the end of the job was in sight. She just had to make it to the balcony. The adrenaline that had worn off poured back into her system. She could do this. She was a badass. No. She was *the* badass. She rocked this job.

She said a silent prayer as she reached out with one hand and grabbed the rope she had tied off on the opposite roof. She pulled it closer to her. Then with a deep breath, she pushed off the wall with all her might and swung toward the balcony. It was an odd angle, and if she missed, she would end up splattered all over the cobblestones below.

She lifted her legs and sailed over the railing. Letting go of the rope, she landed with a soft thud, but her momentum caused her to fall backward into the railing, hitting it with her lower back. She reached out and grabbed a drainpipe that was hanging off the side of the building. It gave a bit and then halted her fall. She froze until she was sure it would hold her, and then slowly, she regained her balance.

She took a deep breath. Her hands were shaking. That had been much too close, but she'd made it. *Yes!*

She straightened up and then proceeded to remove her shoes from the dress pockets and put them back on her feet. That done, she removed her wig and then took off the dress to expose a smaller, black cocktail dress underneath. She took off her gloves and tucked those and the wig into the costume dress. Then she folded everything so it resembled a wrap and draped it over her arm. She paused for a minute to straighten her clothes, making sure she was presentable. Then she opened the door from the balcony and stepped into the restaurant.

"Signora, il balcone è chiuso questa sera." The balcony is closed this evening. She whirled around to see a waiter standing there staring at her.

"Mi dispiace. Ho solo bisogno..." I'm sorry. I just needed... And she made the international gesture for a cigarette. *"Non dirlo a mio marito. Gli ho detto che stavo andando in bagno."* Don't tell my husband. I told him I was going to the restroom. She winked at the waiter.

He shook his head slightly and gave her a tight smile. "Of course, Signora." And then he gestured for her to precede him.

She walked casually toward the stairs, and when she noticed in a mirror above the bar that the waiter was no longer behind her, she quickly went down the stairs and out onto the boat landing outside of the restaurant.

She glanced over at the Santini's dock. Polizia had arrived and people were milling about. No one paid her the slightest bit of attention. Tension eased a bit in her shoulders. She hailed a water taxi and climbed onboard.

It had been close. Running into James Bond on the balcony was a huge mistake or massive bad luck. He could have called for Santini's security, but he didn't. Confusion wrinkled her brow. He should have called for security. *I would have called security*, she mused. Her eyes narrowed for a second and then she gave a tiny shrug. The stars were aligned tonight. No point looking a gift horse in the mouth.

She'd done it once again. She had beat the odds and won. Her fingers brushed the watch as her lips curved into a small victory smile.

CHAPTER FOUR

A lex woke with a start, sitting up in bed. She froze, her heart hammering in her ears. Listening intently, she tried to figure out what had pulled her out of a deep sleep. She heard the sound again. "Damn." Below her window, Giuseppe had started to bellow out another song for the tourists in his gondola.

Gondoliers in Venice did not actually sing but every once in a while, Giuseppe would get a group of Americans and they wanted him to sing. He would happily oblige as long as they paid him extra. He would be in big trouble if anyone found out, but the other gondoliers looked the other way. They figured the joke was actually on the Americans because Giuseppe couldn't sing a note.

Alex gritted her teeth in frustration. She'd worked damn hard to pull off last night's job. She deserved a chance to sleep in today. Euphoria zoomed through her blood stream. Success!

She smiled as she rolled out of bed and padded across the hardwood floors to the kitchen. Satisfaction bordering on smugness filled her head. Another job well done. She frowned as the memory of the balcony reared its ugly head. Not so well done really. She had almost gotten caught. Where the hell had sexy James Bond come from?

A hand grabbed her left upper arm. She spun and brought her right fist around to punch her assailant.

"Don't hit me!" Leo yelled, trying to duck out of the way. It was too late for her to pull the punch—the momentum was behind her and she was slightly off balance—so her fist connected with his head.

"Ow!" he moaned as he sat down heavily on the floor. "Are you tryin' to kill me?"

She stared down at him, hands on her hips. "Well, it serves you right for sneaking up on me. What the hell were you thinking? I could have shot you if I had a gun in my hand."

Leo glared at her, still rubbing his head. "You don't own a gun. Besides, you knew I was comin' by this morning."

He was right, she did. Thoughts of Balcony James Bond had thrown her off her game again. She should have known sooner someone was in her place and that it was Leo. She offered him a hand up. He stood for a moment and then wandered over to sit at the little table by the window. "I'm getting' too old to be knocked down by the likes of you, lass. Me old bones can't take it."

"You could have knocked," she grumbled as she turned and grabbed a couple of coffee mugs out of the cabinet. "I expected you to knock." Guilt swamped her. Leo wasn't a young man. She needed to be more careful. She'd die if anything happened to Leo.

"I did knock. You didnae answer, so I let myself in. I wanted to make sure you were OK." Leo's accent, part Scottish, part Italian, part whatever, always got a bit thicker when he was upset. He touched the side of his head again.

Her heart squeezed, but she said nothing. Thankful she'd set the coffee maker on a timer, she filled two cups of steaming black coffee and walked over to the table. She set the mugs on the table and sat before she took a sip of her coffee.

"How did last night go?" Leo asked.

"How do you think?" She couldn't stop the victory smile that curved her lips.

"You got it?"

"Don't I always?" she asked as she slid off the chair. She disappeared into the bedroom and came back with the watch in her hand.

Leo smiled as he took the watch and held it up to inspect it. "It's a beauty. Glad it went okay. My nonna had a bad feeling last night, and she's always right about these things. She had me a wee bit freaked out. Glad it wasn't about you." He tucked the watch in his pocket.

She glanced in his direction, fear and guilt quickly flitting through her. No need to mention how she almost got caught last night. Besides, his nonna had to be a hundred if she was a day. She could have a bad feeling for any number of reasons.

She took a sip of coffee and burned her tongue. "So, what's next? Which city?"

She studied Leo. His blue eyes always sparkled, making his cherubic face seem younger, but his gnarled fingers and his graying hair gave away his advancing years, years that had not always been kind to him. She wasn't sure exactly how old he was but figured he had to be in his sixties. As her handler, he dealt with finding the jobs. He knew her criteria, what she was willing to do, and where she was willing to go. He was the point of contact for her clients.

He gave her an assessing look. "You know, you could take a vacation or even retire. You've made a fortune——"

"Not this again! We've been over this. I don't want to retire, I don't need a vacation, and I had a fortune before I even started this career."

"Alex"—Leo reached out and tweaked her nose—"we've worked together since you were eighteen and I caught you stealing my wallet. That's almost ten years. I love you like a daughter."

She swallowed hard. God knew, she loved Leo far more than her father, wherever he might be. Leo was the only family that counted in her world.

"So, don't take it the wrong way when I say it's high time for us to slow down a wee bit. Europe is getting hot for you right now. A break would do you some good."

Alex reached out and put her hand on Leo's arm. "I know you're just watching out for me, but I'm not ready to stop. Look, the cops aren't really searching for me in any country other than Sweden, and there's no need for me to ever go there again." She shuddered at the memory of the cold night she'd almost been captured.

"What about Croatia and Greece?" he asked archly. "I believe the cops there are asking around for any information about a pretty, young thief."

"Asset Repossession Specialist Extraordinaire, thank you very much."

Leo snorted. "You know the acronym spells ARSE, don't you?"

"Ha, very funny." She shook her head at him. "The cops there don't know it's me. Hell, most of the jobs I do are never reported to the cops. I'm not on a watch list or anything. It's fine. I'd rather continue." She begged him with her eyes to understand. Without her job, she had nothing. This was what she was built for. This was her purpose. Anxiety forced her to move. She hopped up from the table and walked over to the far set of windows. She opened the long white curtains and then did the same to each set in the room. At the last window, she admired the view of the canal below.

She couldn't stop. Stopping was death to her. She needed to be moving, planning, researching. She needed to be busy with something that challenged her, otherwise... she stopped. The past was not going to catch her. Not now. Not ever.

Besides, she wasn't some out-for-profit thief who'd work for the highest bidder. She had principles; she righted wrongs. The last thing a woman who'd had her heart torn out needed was for her ex to take her valued possessions, too. That was where Alex came in. Okay so she wasn't fixing the world, but she got to offer the women who hired her a bit of closure. Give them back some pride. It was a good thing that she was doing, and no one was getting hurt. Well, no one who didn't deserve it.

Turning back around, she went over and sat down on the purple sofa. The whole place had been white when she moved in. She'd painted the walls a soft gray. Usually she didn't decorate, but she'd decided this apartment with its high ceilings and ornate woodwork deserved a bit of attention.

Leo sighed heavily and shook his head. "Okay, have it yer way." He grabbed both coffee cups and joined her on the sofa. "Here," he said as he offered her the mug. "Another offer has come in, but I'm giving you fair warnin'. I'll be hangin' up me hat in the not-too-distant future." He pointed at her. "You should think about doin' the same."

She smiled at him. "So, what do you have for me?" She leaned back into the over-stuffed cushions and sipped her coffee. The fear that had been gnawing at her chest ebbed slowly.

His lips curved into a matching smile. "An American this time, so it's a chance to go home, take a break from Europe for a while."

"Back to California?" she asked, alarm bells ringing in her head. "Who is it?"

"New York. The Hamptons, to be specific, and it's Jameson Drake."

"Drake!" She jerked her hand and spilled her hot coffee down her pajama top and on to the purple sofa. "Shit." She quickly grabbed a bunch of napkins off the coffee table that had been left from yesterday's take-out and mopped up the mess. "Jameson Drake is a ruthless, unforgiving, hard-hearted S.O.B. Who in God's name actually fell for him?"

"Apparently, Diana Sterling."

She threw the napkins back on the table. "Diana Sterling? Isn't she married to Jeffery Sterling? As in the Sterling Bank of New York?"

"Yes, which is what makes it all the more interestin'." When Leo wiggled his eyebrows, Alex smiled. "The client gave him a car that she would like back." He paused. "Seriously, lass, are you sure you want to take on Jameson Drake? He'll destroy you if he catches you. He's the vindictive type."

"You're right, but bullies like him need to be taught a lesson."

Leo grinned. "And the fact that you find him—what was the word you used, despicable?—has nothin' to do with it, right?"

"He is despicable. He ruins family-run hotels so he can buy them for pennies on the dollar.

"Diana Sterling wants her car back, and he should be

gentleman enough to give it to her. He's bringing this on himself. If he wasn't such an asshole, I wouldn't have to steal from him. So, find out all the details you can from your sources and then talk to Diana and get her side of the story. It will be interesting to see what she has to say."

Righteous anger coursed through her. Jameson Drake was exactly the reason she did what she did. Men like him had all the power, and it was time women took theirs back.

Leo downed his coffee in a gulp and got up. "I'll check it all out, but I'll say it again. I'm not big on this one. Jameson Drake has a mean streak a mile wide."

"Noted. Come back once you have the details, and we'll make some decisions from there."

When Leo left, she turned back to the window. Jameson Drake. The surge of energy that always came with the idea of a new job made her fingers tingle. It would be a challenge, but she loved challenges. The chance to put Drake in his place, it was like the Holy Grail.

What if it went wrong somehow? She twisted her long blond hair around her finger. Drake would be out for blood, no doubt. Before last night, she wouldn't have even considered she could make a mistake. A chill ran down her spine as if someone walked over her grave.

CHAPTER FIVE

"Hey, honey, I need a drink. Why don't you bring me another beer and shhpeed it up thisss time," a drunk man snarled at the passing waitress and then grabbed her ass.

Alex seethed as she walked by the slot machines. It was barely six o'clock and this guy was drunk off his ass. It always amazed her how men felt they could do whatever they wanted to women, like women were possessions to be ordered around.

Biting the inside of her cheek, she kept going. The last thing she needed was to call attention to herself. This was a scouting mission. As much as she wanted to turn around, grab the guy by the balls, and squeeze as hard as she could, it was better to let it go. For now. If he was still here when she left, he was in for one hell of a rude surprise.

She rolled her shoulders as she walked up the main staircase of the Long Island Breeze Casino to the mezzanine and searched for a quiet corner where she could stand and overlook the floor below. Usually a month off would relieve all of her stress, but this time, four weeks hadn't been enough. Maybe she was just wired about this new job. Drake was no joke. She rolled her shoulders again and let out a deep sigh.

She hated casinos. Everyone drank too much, gambled too much, and had their egos inflated or deflated depending on the stack of chips in front of them. Thing was, there was no way to tell what was going to happen. It all hinged on the game on the table.

She hated that, the lack of control. Leo was surprised she didn't like to gamble, considering her chosen profession. Being a thief was always a gamble according to him. She begged to differ. Being a good asset repossession specialist was a matter of being prepared for every eventuality. She controlled her environment as much as possible and then created plans to deal with every conceivable circumstance that might occur. It was all coordinated to the *nth* degree.

Except for that not-so-empty balcony in Venice. She dismissed the thought immediately. She walked around another bank of slot machines. She had handled it but was glad to be in Long Island. Always good to have an ocean between her and her last job.

She found a spot at the rail in the corner of the mezzanine. It was a good vantage point to see the whole casino floor, and it was hard for anyone to sneak up on her. She settled in, leaning on the rail. She glanced down at the drunk. The waitress was back, only this time she had a big bruiser of a security guard with her. "Good for her," Alex mumbled.

She missed the apartment in Venice. Standard operating procedure for her had always been to leave the city of her latest job far behind her as quickly as possible. Usually she liked bouncing from place to place, but now she was finding it tedious living in hotels. She wasn't ready to retire like Leo wanted, but maybe buying a place so she had somewhere to go during her downtime wasn't the worst idea.

She noticed a woman working her way across the casino floor. It wasn't her sparkly blue dress that made her stand out—it was the way she moved. A small smile played on the woman's lips. By the time she made it across to the stairs, Alex figured she had lifted two wallets and quite a few chips. From Alex's vantage point, however, she could see casino security closing in. Amateur for sure. This was a Wagner casino, and anything owned by Luke Wagner had top-notch security, cameras everywhere. Whoever the woman was, she was in for it. The security men grabbed her by the arms and ushered her through some unmarked doors off to the right.

Alex glanced at her watch. Drake was usually here by now. According to her research, he and the casino owner had a standing man-date. Unless, of course, business interfered. Drake was a notorious workaholic. She shifted her weight to her other foot and tried to surreptitiously stretch a bit.

Suddenly, there was a yell. A squealing woman in a very skimpy red dress dashed across the floor and launched herself at a dark-haired man dressed in an expensive suit, only to be stopped in mid-air by a security guard. She landed on her butt with a solid thud. Alex winced inwardly. That had to hurt.

Alex squinted slightly to cut the glare from the lighting. "Fuck." She ground her teeth. The target was Drake, and the security guy who'd stopped the woman was none other than the guy from the balcony in Venice. Her hands curled into fists. Well, if that didn't just suck big-time.

What the hell was Drake doing with real security? He usually used the no-neck guys who weren't very bright. She had been excited to learn his head of security had just quit. He'd been the only real security professional of the lot. It hadn't occurred to her that Drake would go out and hire a completely different team, but didn't it just figure? Of course, he'd hired real security *after* she accepted a job stealing from him. An uncomfortable feeling stole over her. Had he somehow known she was coming?

She grabbed the railing, her knuckles turning white, and stood rooted in place. Then she caught herself—this was the behavior that drew unwanted attention to a person. *Get a grip.* She took a calming breath and let go of the railing. What the hell was wrong with her? She never panicked like this. She shook it off.

Drake helped the blond up and gave her a hug. He looked good in his summer suit. The grey pinstripe with the white shirt showed off the tan he'd already acquired. She could understand why women found him attractive. His curly dark hair and deep green eyes had fooled more than one woman into thinking she was in love.

Alex watched the woman in red as she leaned in and planted a big kiss on Drake. She let go and then turned around and started yelling at the security guy. One minute she was wagging a finger in his face, the next she wasn't. Alex hadn't even seen the security guy's hand move, but suddenly the blond became quite pale. It was hard to tell, but it looked like Drake had a smile on his face. What an asshole.

Drake started walking across the floor once again, Blondie following in his wake, and the security guy and his crew moved to form an outer circle around them to keep them protected. Balcony James Bond's head was on a swivel. This must be a bit of a nightmare for him. All casinos had their own security, but still. They were crowded, and anyone could come out of anywhere and then disappear back into the throng.

As the group crossed the floor, the security guy glanced up, and their eyes met. She didn't move. Didn't breathe. She waited a beat, and then two. Finally, he looked away. Had she seen recognition in his eyes? She didn't think so. After all, she was wearing her black long-haired wig tonight to match her dress. Her outfit was blah, strategically chosen so she could fade into the background. She had even worn brown contacts to hide her distinctive green eyes. Besides, it had been dark on that balcony and she'd been wearing a mask.

She willed her heartbeat back to normal. This changed things…a lot. She needed Leo. There was a new player in this game, and before moving forward, she had to know all she could about this security guy. It would mean doing a lot more research. Stealing a watch was one thing. But stealing a car kept under lock and key and—she was guessing—about fifty more layers of security than it had last week? Yeah, that was going to be a bit of an issue.

"Well, shit." This job had disaster written all over it.

CHAPTER SIX

Mitch scanned the crowd again. Back and forth. Nothing seemed out of the ordinary, but it paid to be vigilant. Not that anyone was going to try to kill his client, not tonight at least. Well, maybe *he* would, but that was his personal cross to bear.

The blonde with his client, Honey she called herself, was still shooting dirty looks his way. What did she expect? *You can't launch yourself at someone who's surrounded by bodyguards and expect to get through.* Of course, her landing could have been a bit less harsh. He grimaced. She'd know better next time.

He could feel someone's gaze. All the years he'd spent on foreign soil surrounded by people trying to kill him had given him a great sense of when he was being watched. He scanned the crowd again, holding his hands loosely by his sides. Ready, just in case. He looked up.

There. On the mezzanine. A woman with black hair and a black dress. Their eyes locked. Something tweaked in his brain, as if the gears were trying to come together but couldn't. Was she familiar somehow? She was indisputably attractive, and something else might stir if he'd allow it, but that wasn't what bothered him. Whatever was troubling him played at the edge of his thoughts, but wouldn't come into focus.

He shifted his gaze back to the area ahead of him, scanning for threats as they made their way to the exit. Nothing else caught his attention, just the regular casino crowd, dressed to the nines to lose their money. What a gig. He hated casinos and, truth be told, wasn't too fond of the Hamptons either. He found himself looking for the woman, but she was gone.

"Callahan, are you listening?"

"Yes," he immediately responded. He certainly did not need to devote his entire attention to the man's conversation to pick up the thrust of it. Turning to Drake, he said, "There's been a change of plans, and Wagner's going to meet you at a restaurant."

Drake nodded.

"Okay." Mitch signaled to Jake, a former SEAL teammate and now one of his security guys, who spoke into an earpiece and then nodded back. "The car will be around front in..." He glanced at Jake, who held up three fingers. "Three minutes, Mr. Drake. Let's go."

He glanced around one more time, but the woman in black was still gone. A small feeling of uncertainty crept into the pit of his stomach. As they continued toward the doors, he kept up his sweep of the casino. With all the flashing lights and noise, it was easy to get distracted. There was always something moving in his peripheral vision.

He sent Jake ahead, and when he saw the car outside the doors, they moved forward. He made sure Drake was settled in the back before he got in front. He mentally gave a sigh of relief. Not that the car was much safer for his client, but he could control the environment better. He didn't have to worry about random women throwing themselves at his boss.

Turning, he was about to ask Drake which restaurant they were headed to when he saw that Honey had climbed into the back seat as well. He hadn't gotten the impression his client liked this woman or wanted her around. Drake had let her get away with the hug and kiss, but Mitch could tell he was annoyed. Drake wasn't one for public displays of any kind.

"We're going to meet Luke at Jack's Fishhouse, aren't we, baby?" Honey cooed.

Of course, it had to be the most popular restaurant in the Hamptons, and on one of the first warm summer nights, it would be jammed. A security risk. He briefly entertained the idea of suggesting a more secure location, but the expression on Drake's face told him it was a lost cause. Grinding his teeth, he turned back around. "You heard the lady." The driver raised an eyebrow but said nothing.

Mitch grabbed his phone and texted the new destination to the late-shift security crew. His new client was one difficult son of a bitch, no two ways about it. The man was demanding and exacting. He wasn't interested in Mitch's take on why certain places were best avoided. Drake had been crystal clear: Mitch's job was to do whatever it took to make it safe for him to go wherever he wanted to go. No exceptions.

Mitch had no real idea why Drake wanted this much security. He claimed that he'd been receiving death threats, but he'd deleted the emails and he hadn't gotten anymore in the days since Mitch had taken the job. Or so he said. Maybe he was just paranoid. Whatever the real reason

Drake wanted security, he wasn't sharing it with Mitch just yet.

If Callahan Security didn't need this job so badly, Mitch would've quit. It had been a mistake to take the job in the first place. He'd been the one to suggest branching out into the private security sector after taking over their father's home security business. It had seemed like a natural choice. Fact was, he'd pushed his brothers into it. Convinced them there was money to be made, and Callahan Security had the experience to do it and do it well.

Gage and Logan had reluctantly agreed. They'd both wanted to wait a bit, expand the business gradually, but Mitch had argued that he already had clients lined up, and if they waited any longer, they might lose them. It was a lie, but it wasn't far from the truth. All he'd needed to do was make a few phone calls, send out a few emails.

He'd picked the highest profile, toughest job as his second gig. It was a massive gamble, and he shouldn't have taken it. If this went sideways, it could tank the family company. He shrugged off that thought and instead chose to focus on the woman in black.

Had he seen her before? Maybe she just resembled someone he knew. He shook his head slightly. Nothin' doin'. He couldn't place her.

They pulled up in front of the restaurant twenty minutes later. Unfortunately, Drake's opinion of Honey must have improved on the drive over because they were preoccupied in the back of the limo. Mitch got out and stood next to the car. Jake emerged from the support vehicle behind them and moved to the other side. They exchanged a "you've got to be shitting me" look and then simultaneously turned around to sweep the area for trouble.

Since the restaurant was on the main street in town, the cars were bumper to bumper, and the foot traffic on the sidewalk was no better. Everyone wanted to see and be seen. Between the horns and the conversations coming from the sidewalks and surrounding restaurant patios, it reminded Mitch more of Manhattan than a holiday town, and it was giving him a headache.

Mitch rolled his neck to try to relieve the tension. This was a shit-show as far as security was concerned. Any vehicle or person could come right up to the car, and there wasn't a damn thing he could do about it. The only plus was, if the would-be attacker was driving, he wouldn't be able to make a clean exit. A pedestrian on the other hand would have a good shot at escape in this crowd.

"Unbelievable," Jake muttered.

"He's the client," Mitch mumbled. "He wants to screw some babe in the back of the limo, it's his dime."

The car door suddenly opened and out popped Honey, struggling with her dress as she held her shoes to her chest.

"You asshole!" She fought to right herself and put on her shoes at the same time. "I knew you were a big mistake." She clutched the side of the car and worked her feet into her spike heels. Mitch knew the precise moment Honey realized the crowd on the sidewalk had slowed to watch the spectacle. Her cheeks turned flaming red.

Drake climbed out of the car and straightened his suit. "I merely took what you offered," he said. "At no point did I invite you to dinner."

"Bastard!" She spat as she slapped Drake and then whirled on her heel and stormed off, disappearing into the gathered crowd.

The look Drake gave Mitch was one hundred percent pissed off, but Mitch cut the man off before he could say anything. "Sorry, I don't do domestic disputes. It's in the contract." Jake's face was as serious as ever, but Mitch could hear a slight chuckle in his earbud. No doubt they were in agreement. The client had deserved that slap.

Drake's eyes narrowed, but he kept his mouth shut. He finished tucking in his shirt and fixed his tie. Then he started toward the restaurant, completely ignoring the crowd on the sidewalk. The men fell into the usual formation, Mitch ahead to make way through the crowd and assess the surroundings and Jake directly behind to ward off anyone who wanted to get too close. They went down the alleyway to the back door.

Mitch had sent the late-shift guys ahead to the restaurant. Checking in with them now, it was all stations green, so he let Drake go in and his guys break off. The late shift guys would take over. Two inside the restaurant and two outside to watch the car and monitor the street. He and his team would head back to the yacht for some well-deserved rest. They all needed a break so they could be fresh in the morning.

Mitch wasn't sure how Drake did it, but the man never slept for more than a few hours a night. Maybe he was a vampire. That was one explanation for his particular brand of assholery.

Mitch arrived back at the client's yacht with his team. It was his habit to do a run through and make sure everything was locked up tight before he turned in, but tonight the idea of checking every nook and cranny in the five decks seemed extreme.

"Hey, Jake, grab three other guys and let's go over the yacht."

"You're not doing it?"

"I'm too beat to do it all by myself tonight." They were standing on the main deck. "You divide it up how you want, but I'm doing the lower deck."

Jake shook his head. "Figures you'd pick the deck with your bunk on it."

"Give me a hard time, and I'll make you take the tank deck. Nothing like all that machinery to check."

Jake laughed. "Fair enough. I'll give Dan that job. You take the lower deck. I'll do this deck and get Garrett to do the upper deck and the sun deck. How does that sound?"

"Great. Let me know if anything pops up," Mitch said and then yawned.

"Will do. See you in the a.m."

Mitch nodded and waved and then went down the stairs to start his search of the lower deck. Twenty minutes later, he crawled under the covers and closed his eyes. Images of a woman in black danced before him as he fell into a heavy sleep.

"So, lass, how did it go?" Leo's chuckle rolled across the line.

"Not so great."

"What? What happened?" All humor was gone from his voice now.

"Drake hired more security."

"Oh, is that all? Relax. A few more thick-necks won't make much of a difference. You got this."

"No. You don't understand. Drake hired *security*, as in real, honest-to-God security with brains. Thick necks with muscles and guns I can handle. These guys are different."

"Damn. Do you know who he brought on?"

She ground her teeth. "I'm working on it. I didn't recognize the head guy, but I'm texting you a pic. See what you can find out." It was a small lie. She didn't *know* the head security guy, but she sure as shit recognized him. She would have been able to place that face anywhere. The question was, would he know hers?

"If you don't recognize him, then how do you know he's trouble?"

She could hear the puzzlement in Leo's voice, but she wasn't sure how to answer. Maybe a partial truth would be best. "The way he moved…the way they all moved. They were alert and focused. I'd guess military training. Very professional. Call it a gut feeling, but I'm telling you, this new security team is trouble."

"I got the text. I'll run it and see what I can find out." He paused.

She knew what he was about to ask, so she cut him off. "I know what you're going to say, but I'm not ready to pull the plug just yet. Let's find out who we're dealing with before we make any decisions, okay?"

"S'okay with me, lass. You call the shots. You know I'm ready to get out whenever you want." He paused again, giving her the chance to say something, but she let the silence linger. Finally, he said, "I'll get on this and get back to you. Play it safe." And then he was gone.

She put down the phone and walked over to her hotel room balcony. She had a killer view of Block Island Sound. The sun danced off the water where mega yachts bobbed gently on the waves. The ultra-rich were probably sleeping off the revelry of the previous evening since very few were visible on their floating palaces. She glanced at the picture Leo had sent her of Drake's yacht and hunted down the rows of expensive toys.

There. The last one in the far row. She had booked a room with a balcony on this side of the hotel for this very reason. She'd talked to the kid at the marina office the other day and after greasing the wheels with a fifty, he mentioned there'd been some sort of last-minute fight about the yacht's positioning, though nothing had come of it. She wondered if his new security guy had demanded the yacht be moved to make it harder for outsiders to access Drake. Not that it was likely his boss had cooperated. Drake was not one to keep a low profile.

Case in point. There were three bikini-clad babes already lying in the sun on Drake's yacht, each clutching a drink. The faint strains of dance music carried on the breeze. She was willing to bet it was coming from his yacht.

As if to confirm her thoughts, a fourth bikini-clad babe emerged from below and danced her way over to the others. Drink in one hand, cigarette in the other. European then. Not too many Americans smoked these days. She nodded to herself. She never knew what details might come in handy when planning the perfect heist.

While it wasn't surprising to see the babes on Drake's yacht, it was interesting that the man himself wasn't with them. She'd heard a rumor that he occasionally threw parties full of beautiful people that he himself did not attend. He'd walk through now and again, say "hello" to all the right people, and then disappear.

She had paid his former employees generously for information. She couldn't get much out of any of them, but the general consensus was that he hated parties but understood they were necessary. Was that how he saw the posse of pretty girls on his yacht? A necessity? She'd have to do some more digging. He was big on privacy, and the ex-employees were all worried he would find out they violated the confidentiality contract, so she'd have to find another way.

She turned around and went back into the room. After pouring herself another cup of black tea and adding a hint of sugar, she grabbed the client file and returned to the balcony. The tea and the file went onto the small cafe table next to the lounge chair, and she took off her robe to reveal her own teal bikini.

Releasing a satisfied sigh, she made herself comfortable

on the chair. She studied the yacht again as she leaned back and sipped her tea. This was one of the better ways to do recon. God knew, she had done her share of crappy ones.

She watched as the babe in the purple bikini got up to greet someone under the canopy of the yacht. The rest of the bikini bunch followed. "Drake," she mumbled. Had to be. Sure enough, Drake's familiar figure emerged from underneath the canopy a few seconds later.

His shape was similar to that of his bodyguards, tall and well-built, but he carried himself differently. A tiger came to mind. He was wearing dress pants and a white button-down. His rolled sleeves were his only concession to the early heat wave. He greeted each of the girls with a peck on the cheek and chatted with them.

The purple bikini girl rubbed herself against Drake's arm and then a babe in a black bikini followed suit. Alex gritted her teeth. It always bothered her when she saw women throw themselves at wealthy men, or any men for that matter. The men weren't worth it. An image of her father came to mind. He certainly hadn't been worth all the agony her mother went through. She took a deep breath and let it out slowly. *No need to think about the past.*

It was interesting that she had never heard any complaints about Drake before. In most cases, she had heard multiple stories about her marks before she took the job. They tended to be repeat offenders in the treat-people-like-shit category.

The majority of women who got involved with a man like Drake understood the game they were playing. The young girls liked rich, famous men because they got into the hottest clubs and were treated as part of the "in crowd." Being the flavor of the month or week, as the case might be, they hoped they would either land the whale permanently or meet another, slightly smaller, fish. But most of them knew the rules going in.

The older women, the ones who had their own money, did it for the profile bump. They got to be wined and dined and had a date for all the best social events. Those affairs usually ended by mutual decision, or at least that's what she had been told in the past by some previous clients. No one wanted to admit to being dumped if they were over a certain age.

Hell, most people weren't willing to admit it regardless of their age or position.

Alex had received requests from many scorned women over the years. In the beginning, it had taken her a while to realize which ones were truly crushed and which ones just wanted to use her to exact revenge. She wasn't into that. Now she could sort the legitimately distraught from the wounded-ego crowd in a heartbeat. Usually. Something about this client was different.

She reached out and grabbed the file. Flipping it open, she reviewed Leo's notes. Diana Sterling was a well-known socialite with power and connections of her own. She was part of the over-forty crowd, and her husband, Jeffery, had a good ten years on her. Apparently, Jeffery had gone through some sort of mid-life crisis and left Diana for some young thing or other, maybe even several young things. The breakup had been crushing for Diana, and her normal good sense had abandoned her. Hence the affair with Jameson Drake.

The surprising thing was that Drake, by all accounts, had treated her well. Diana had ended the relationship to return to the ex who'd treated her like dirt.

Comparing the pictures of Jameson Drake and Jeffery Sterling, Alex couldn't understand Diana's choice. Whereas Drake was handsome, fit, and tall, Sterling was short with no neck. He had the profile of a stubby beer bottle. He wasn't aging well either. He had a fringe of hair left on top of his head and a gut to rival Santa Claus.

Well, to each her own.

She turned the page to take another peek at the picture of the car Diana wanted her to retrieve. Not only was the car rare, but it was stunningly beautiful. She studied the picture for a minute before returning her attention to Leo's notes again, searching for any details she might have missed on the first run through.

Diana had purchased it for her husband's birthday as a surprise, but Jeffery had already left her by the time it arrived. Diana had been pissed enough to give it to Drake.

Then Jeffery had come crawling back. Leo had found out from Diana's housekeeper that Diana had made him pay dearly for the humiliation he had put her through. A huge new house in Aspen and an apartment in Paris with an Eiffel Tower view, but she'd ultimately let him back into their Central Park apartment and their huge estate just down the road in the Hamptons.

Now Diana had a major issue on her hands. She needed the birthday gift back, and pronto. According to her, she'd never officially signed anything over to Drake, but he was refusing to give it back. Leo had suggested to Diana to go to the cops for a resolution, and it amused Alex to no end to picture Diana Sterling's reaction to that. No, the matter had to be handled discreetly. So here she was on a balcony in the Hamptons staking out Jameson Drake.

It wasn't the most moving story, and Alex typically preferred to work with women who were legitimately heartbroken over the breakup and whatever they'd lost to it. Still, Diana's story was just a different spin on the usual one, and her embarrassment and shame was just as genuine. Her separation from her husband hadn't just shattered her heart—it had stripped her of her social position.

Alex understood. Being shunned and laughed at by members of society could drive people to do horrible, illogical things. Her mother had been proof enough of that. She shook her head and dropped the file back onto the table. This wasn't the time to think about her mother.

She would get the car back so Diana Sterling could put this whole episode behind her and move on with her life. That was what Alex did.

She checked on the yacht. Another shadow moved under the canopy, and she strained her eyes to see who or what it was. She grabbed her binoculars and sat back in her chair, making sure they were fully in the shade so the sun wouldn't reflect off the lenses. Then she slouched a little to make sure she was hidden behind the wrought iron bars of the balcony railing.

After putting the binoculars to her face, she focused them so she could see beyond the bars and down into the yacht below. As her field of vision passed over the covered area, she saw the shadow move again. It was a man with dark hair, but he had his back to her.

A security guard? She didn't think so from the way he was standing. He seemed to be arguing with Drake. There were two other men flanking him who did look a lot like security. Lightweight shirts that were untucked. Heads on a swivel. They gave off the vibe of good security. And they weren't Drake's guys. At least they weren't the ones she'd seen last night.

She grabbed her camera and zoomed in. The guy had his back to her, so she still couldn't see much. She took a couple of shots anyway. He became more animated. Yes, this man and Drake were definitely arguing.

The stranger turned his head to the side, and she

snapped off a half-dozen shots. She glanced through them, but none of them gave more than a slight glimpse of the man's face. He appeared to be clean shaven and his hair was neat. His skin tone appeared to be a bit olive, which meant little. He could be of Hispanic origin, from any Mediterranean country, or just have a great tan. The shots weren't close enough to pick out details.

She was mystified. She'd thought she knew all the major players in Drake's world. And this guy was someone important. He was dressed impeccably and gave off the vibe of money and position. She scanned the rest of the boat using her binoculars, catching a glimpse of Drake's security team before returning to the mystery man and Drake. She had a good view of Drake's face, and his expression was stone cold. He was livid. Whoever this was, whatever was going on, it wasn't good news.

Balcony James Bond stepped into view, a cell phone in one hand. *Well, wasn't this interesting?* He leaned in close to Drake's ear and presumably said something meaningful since Drake immediately shifted his focus away from his guest and took the proffered cell phone. He moved out of view, leaving his security guy to deal with the powerful stranger, which he did quickly. The next moment, the man in the suit and his security people were on their way off the yacht.

Intriguing. She studied the sexy security guy who'd handled that high-powered guest as if he were a grade-school kid. The aviator glasses he had on covered his eyes, but the rest of him was now visible. Dressed in cargos and a loose T-shirt, he was imposing. And hot. Her fingers tingled with the memory of how his chest had felt beneath them, a mass of solid muscle. A familiar warmth started to spread through her. A night with this guy could be great fun. What was the name she'd heard him use on the balcony? Callahan. She must remember to tell Leo when she went back inside. Too bad he was Drake's guy.

She paused. Maybe this Mr. Callahan could be her way in? It was risky, trying to seduce Drake's bodyguard. What if it didn't work? What if he didn't go for her?

She chortled to herself. That hadn't happened since high school. Not that she was so amazingly beautiful, she just understood how to stroke a man's ego…and other things should it become necessary. She grinned.

But it would make it that much harder to hide once the job was over. If she pulled off the gig—when she pulled it off—his rep would be ruined. That was big in security circles. He'd try to hunt her down and turn her in. She could tell by looking at him. Still, it was an idea. One to keep on the back burner just in case.

After a few more uninspiring minutes of surveillance, she put the binoculars back down on the table and picked up a pen and pad of paper that had been lying there next to an ashtray and some matches.

What had she learned? Drake's taste in women had changed from the classy Diana to a bevy of young co-eds. That could be useful. Go in as a bikini babe? Nah. She was too old at twenty-eight to get away with it quite so much anymore.

Drake had hired a more legit security team. Why? What was he worried about? Not Diana or her husband, surely. If the mystery man had put Jameson Drake on alert, the guy was a dangerous player. A cloud went over the sun, and she shivered.

Her mind returned to Callahan. If she could get him to trust her, maybe he could fill her in. Well, shit, if she could get Callahan to trust her that much, the mystery man wouldn't matter. She could just use him to get the car back.

She took a sip of tea and glanced back toward the yacht. Drake had gone off somewhere, but two security guards hid in the shadows. Her mark wasn't taking chances. Her eyes narrowed. Maybe she shouldn't either.

Callahan wouldn't be the only guy who knew things. There would be other people who had almost the same access, but perhaps not as much to lose. A small smile played on her lips as she turned her face to the sun. Yes. That was the key. Find the weak link and exploit it.

CHAPTER EIGHT

M itch ground his teeth in frustration and then made an effort to release his jaw. The last thing he needed now was a big dental bill. "You should have been honest with me from the beginning. If this guy is a serious threat, then I needed to know about him."

Drake shrugged. "It's your job to determine who or what is a serious threat, not mine." He went back to staring at the computer screens arrayed on his desk.

"I understand that. However, a heads-up might have been helpful. I wouldn't have let him near you had I been made aware of the situation." Mitch's hands were closed into fists. He was trying hard not to lose his temper, but it was a tough fight. He'd been with Drake for about six weeks now and still hadn't earned his trust. It made things very difficult.

His brother, Logan, was so much better at dealing with people's crap with a poker face. Mitch just didn't have a high tolerance for bullshit.

Drake's sigh cut through the room like a knife. "Jason

was aware that this might become an issue. Didn't you speak to him before he took off to whatever godforsaken place he went?"

Mitch did his best to maintain an even tone. "I did speak with Jason. He neglected to mention it." The guy had neglected to say a lot of things, come to think of it, like Drake's capacity to be an asshole and his business connections with seriously scary people.

"Not my problem," Drake stated as he continued to stare at his screens.

"It will be your problem if he or his goons make a run at you. Death tends to be an issue for everyone, no matter how rich or important," Mitch snarled back.

Drake's head snapped up from staring at the screen to meet Mitch's glare. "I would be careful of your tone if I were you. You work for me, not the other way around. I will not have you lecture me."

"Drake, you can be a ruthless son of a bitch in business all you want, but when it comes to security, you don't know dick. So let's not play games here." Mitch was pushing his luck, but he couldn't help himself. This asshole was risking all their lives by not filling him in on important details. "John Tolliver is an underhanded piece of garbage. He's dangerous. He and his last business partner had a major falling out, and the partner ended up in a wheelchair. He wouldn't implicate Tolliver publicly, but privately, it's a different story."

"Yes, I've heard that rumor as well. It's your job to see to my security. Are you saying you can't do your job?"

Mitch wanted very much to break his boss's nose. "It doesn't matter how much recon or how many preparations I take, if someone wants you dead that badly, sooner or later they will make it happen. That's just a fact. But I can make it a lot harder and it can take a hell of a lot longer if I know what's going on." He glared at Drake. "I have half a mind to quit right now and take my guys with me."

"We both know you took this job to make your company's reputation, and I would assume, to help the bottom line. So let's not kid ourselves about you leaving."

Mitch jammed his hands in his pockets because the temptation to punch Drake was too intense. "I don't need any job badly enough to risk my men. Besides, it would be worse if we're working for you when you get capped. So why don't you tell me what the hell is going on, and maybe we can figure this out."

Mitch had spent his entire military career following orders without asking questions. He was done with that life. If he was going to do security work, it was going to happen on his terms. He had told both of his brothers that upfront, and they'd agreed. He certainly wasn't going to change that for the likes of Jameson Drake.

Drake must have seen that Mitch was serious because he stood abruptly and walked over to the bar area. He pulled out a mug. "Tolliver wants something I have. I don't want to sell it to him. It's as simple as that."

"Sure. That's why his security has been checking us out for the past twenty-four hours. They've been practically casing the yacht."

Drake picked up the coffee pot and filled the mug. "John Tolliver is a middle man. He has buyers lined up to purchase something I have." He glanced at Mitch, and whatever he saw made him narrow his eyes and then shrug. "I hired someone to build software for a project of mine. This software has many different possible applications. Somehow, Tolliver got wind of it, probably from his buyer, and he's been after me for months to sell him the software.

He claims his buyer doesn't care if I still use my copy as long as I don't sell it to anyone else. I have repeatedly refused."

"And now Tolliver has resorted to veiled threats?"

"Somehow, he knows the software is close to being finished. He wants to close the deal before it's complete so I don't get the chance to sell it elsewhere." He took a sip of black coffee. "But as I told him, I have no intention of selling the software to the likes of him or his clients. It's for a personal project. Once that project is finished, I will consider selling the software to the US government. Homeland Security and the military would love to have it." Drake walked back over to his desk and sat down. "Satisfied?"

Not even close. There was so much more going on here —that much was obvious from the antagonism that wafted off Tolliver like bad cologne—but he knew better than to push at the moment. There was time yet to figure this out. Now, at least, he knew that Drake was in serious danger, and Mitch was going to have to step up his game. A lot more research and planning were required to keep Drake safe. He had to call in his brothers and a few other people to help him on this one.

"Now that I know the level of risk you're facing, we need to make some changes. We've got to move to the house. I know the wine cellar isn't complete, but this yacht is a safety nightmare. And those girls gotta go. They attract too much attention, and I always have to have one of my people nearby to make sure they don't get drunk and fall into the water. There's a much better security system at the house, and I can make it even tighter."

Drake cocked his head and studied Mitch. "Fine. We'll move to the house." He took a sip of his coffee and then sent a quick text. "Janice will be up momentarily to help you coordinate the move."

Almost before Drake had finished speaking, Mitch felt movement behind him. Glancing over his shoulder, he saw Janice in the doorway.

"Yes, Mr. Drake?" She crossed the room, passing Mitch, to stand in front of Drake's desk. She didn't appear out of breath, but Mitch wondered how someone her age had made it to the upper deck so quickly. Her office was two levels down on the lower deck next to the kitchen. Janice had to be sixty if she was a day. She must have been a beauty in her youth, and she was still a striking woman— tall and trim with a great sense of style. She was also thoroughly competent and intelligent, which made her Mitch's favorite person in Drake's entourage.

"Janice, we're moving to the house today. Please coordinate with the house staff. We're going to stop construction for now. Make sure everything is cleaned up and ready for my arrival after lunch."

Janice nodded. It would be a herculean job, but she didn't seem put out or stressed. "Yes, Mr. Drake." She turned toward the doorway.

"Oh," Drake said casually, "and Janice? Get rid of the girls out front. Mr. Callahan doesn't like them."

With a quick wink at Mitch, Janice said, "Yes, sir," and continued out the door.

Drake regarded Mitch. "There. Are you happy now, Callahan? We're going to the house and the girls are gone."

Mitch just nodded. He headed for the stairs.

"And Callahan? Just because I let you get away with questioning my authority once, doesn't mean you can do it again. Don't forget who's boss."

Mitch didn't bother to acknowledge the comment. He

just turned and went down the stairs. He couldn't decide who he hated more at that moment—Drake for being an asshole or himself for staying and continuing to work for said asshole. The things he did for his brothers. Making a go of the family business just might get him killed.

CHAPTER NINE

Alex saw a flurry of movement on the deck. The bikini babes were being rounded up and, by the look of things, kicked off the yacht. They were clutching bags and random items in their arms as they were hustled down the pier. Was Drake pulling up anchor? That would be disastrous for her. She'd have to find a boat to rent and try to follow them. No, that wouldn't work at all. As it was, she'd only managed to get this room by tipping the guy at the front desk an obscene amount of money.

She bit her lip as she watched the movement on the yacht. No one seemed to be getting it ready to go out. There was no captain that she could see onboard. Of course, someone from the security detail might pilot it.

Then a group of security guys left the yacht carrying a lot of luggage. They went up to a couple of SUVs that were backed up to the end of the wharf and deposited the bags in the trunk. Two guys stayed with the vehicles, and the others went back down to the yacht.

They appeared again moments later and closed ranks around Drake. They walked with him off the boat. They were moving out, but were they coming back? No time soon by the look of all that luggage.

"Damn!" Was he going back to his estate a few miles away? Leo had said Drake was having a new wine cellar built, which is why he was on the yacht. He didn't want to be around while it was under construction. It wasn't finished yet, but maybe scary guy's visit this morning had changed things.

She followed their movements with her binoculars until they disappeared around the corner, then hopped up off the lounger and ran inside her room. Maybe she could find out where they were going if she got down to the marina fast enough. She put on her flip-flops, threw on her cover-up, plonked a large floppy hat on her head, and grabbed her sunglasses. The second she was ready, she dashed for the stairs.

Exiting the lobby, trying not to breathe heavily after her sprint, she made her way out to the pool. She tried to blend in and not move too quickly, but she really needed to get an eye on the situation. Drake heading out for the weekend was one thing, but if her theory was right and he was moving, well, she needed to know where he was going.

She made it to the marina just as their SUVs pulled out. Shit! She stood there for a second undecided. Should she go back upstairs and start making phone calls, or should she check out the yacht? It was risky to hit the yacht during broad daylight. On the other hand, it would be pretty easy to fudge a cover story. She could say one of the bikini babes had invited her and then ask where everyone had disappeared to. That was if anyone was still around. It seemed unlikely.

She strolled along the docks toward Drake's rental, trying to make it seem like she belonged. People didn't notice bystanders who "belonged." She walked right up to the yacht and peered over the side. There was no easy way to get on, The gangplank leading to the deck had a chain across it. She'd have to step over the edge of the dock and duck under the chain.

"Hello?" she called. She wasn't sure if she was hoping for a response or not. "Hello," she called again, louder this time. Still nothing. She studied her surroundings. As the last yacht in the row, Drake had few neighbors. There was one boat behind her as she stood next to Drake's, but it appeared to be empty. She hadn't seen anyone on it all morning.

She gave it one last shot just in case. "Hellllooooo!"

When no one appeared, she took a last glance around and then climbed onto the yacht. She ducked under the chain and went up the gangplank. The deck was very swank. It had leather sofas with mountains of overstuffed cushions on them. There was a hot tub in the corner. She headed toward the door to the salon and gave it a crank. Locked. She took one of the pins from her hair and quickly picked it. The door gave with a satisfying slide, and she headed inside, closing it after her.

She took off her sunglasses and put them in the pocket of her cover up as she stepped onto the thick beige carpet. There was a long gleaming wood bar at the far end with bottles of every liquor imaginable behind it, all top-shelf stuff. The sofas were a warm brown leather, and the coffee and end tables were made of the same wood as the bar— oak would be her guess. There were a few local magazines on the coffee table but nothing else. The whole room spoke of money but *impersonal* money. There was nothing here that spoke of who owned the yacht. No family photos nor knick-knacks. Not a thing to tell her where Drake had gone or if he was coming back. She started walking toward the bar.

"Can I help you?"

Alex whirled around, instinctively bringing her hands up in a boxer's stance to defend herself and came face-to-face with Callahan himself. He'd come silently into the room behind her. "Oh, you startled me." She belatedly moved a hand to her chest, as if he had scared her, which of course he had, but the last time someone had scared her, she'd knocked him flat on his ass. But no need to let Mr. Security know she could do that.

He cocked an eyebrow at her. "What are you doing here?"

She widened her eyes and tried to appear innocent. "Oh, I was looking for Brandi?"

"There's no Brandi here." His eyes narrowed. "Have we met?" He moved slightly closer to her.

"Um, I don't think so. I, um, that is Brandi said there was a party here and I should come join her. I've never been on a sailboat like this before," she simpered. She looked around and tried to appear impressed.

"Yacht."

"What?" She gave him the big-eyed look again. She had to tilt her head up to do it. He was bigger than she remembered, but those eyes were just as intense. Gray, and they were studying her.

He took his time answering her. "Yacht. It's a yacht, not a sailboat."

"Oh, uh, thanks, I guess. So, um, is Brandi here?" All she needed to do now was twirl her hair and chew gum and she would be the spitting image of every too-stupid-to-live college co-ed in the movies.

"Like I said, there's no Brandi here."

"Um, right."

He ran his eyes over her from head to toe and back up again. It was an assessing gaze, not a sexual one. It was refreshing, she had to admit, but it was also a bad sign. She didn't have on her colored contacts, nor did she have the wig. She was glad she hadn't taken off her hat because her blond hair was tucked up in a loose bun underneath it, but now he knew her eyes were green.

"So, do you know where Suzi might have gone then?"

The corners of his lips turned up ever so slightly. "I thought you said her name was Brandi?"

"I—uh—" The stammering was real this time. She had slipped up. Damn! This guy was good, really, really good. Didn't help that his hotness distracted her.

"You just said Brandi wasn't here so I thought you might know about Suzi. She's always with Brandi. They said they'd be here, so I just assumed, but I guess I was wrong." She brought out her sunglasses and put them on. "I'll just get out of your hair." She tried to walk by him to the door, but his hand whipped out and caught her arm. She yelped in surprise.

"Sorry," he said but didn't remove his hand. "Just a couple of questions. How did you get onto the yacht? The chain is across the gangplank."

Deciding honesty was best, she said, "I ducked under it. Brandi mumbled something about security being a pain in the ass. I thought that was what she meant," Alex said and then shrugged.

"I see." That hint of a smile was back. "I didn't catch your name."

"Ah, it's..."

His phone made a piercing sound, or at least she guessed it was his phone. He let go of her arm and brought the cellphone out of his pocket. She moved slightly away from him and whispered a prayer of thanks. The less information she had to give him the better. She had a list of fake identities, but it was better if she didn't have to use one.

The phone sounded again. It had to be the text indicator he'd chosen, but she couldn't fathom why someone would willingly choose such a harsh sound. She would be traumatized by it within the first hour. The phone went off again, another text, and then it rang with an old-school telephone sound. He hit the screen and said, "Callahan."

"We've got a problem," Jake said, casting aside any preliminaries.

Mitch demanded, "What kind of problem?"

"Drake's lunch meeting got cancelled, and he wants to go directly to the estate. The construction guys aren't out yet, and we haven't had a chance to properly secure it."

Mitch closed his eyes and cursed loudly. "Tell Drake to eat lunch. We aren't ready for him at the house yet."

Jake hesitated. "Dan told him that we couldn't go to the estate yet, and he inevitably got pissed. Then Dan suggested he should get a massage or something, which only made things worse."

"I'm sure. Dan needs to keep his big mouth shut." Mitch ran his free hand through his hair, leaving it standing up in tufts. "Where is Drake now?"

"Restroom. Riggs and Hayes are with him."

"Okay. Are Caterina or Jessica or any of the ladies he likes to chat with around? Find someone for him to have lunch with."

"What am I, his social secretary?" Jake complained.

"We aren't ready for him at the estate. The way this day's going, we're likely to get fired, so if you want to get paid, find a distraction. A safe distraction."

"Fine," Jake snapped. "Un-fucking-believable."

There was silence, but the line was still open. Mitch was grinding his teeth again. This client had truly become his biggest nightmare. He could hear Jake walking around, then the sound of murmured conversation.

"Okay, Caterina is here. I told her we needed a favor. She said she'd keep Drake busy by asking him his opinion about some of her business decisions, but in return she wants a favor from me to be determined in the future."

"Deal."

"Easy for you to say. The way she smiled at me, I think I just sold my soul to the devil." There was a short pause. "They're going to the back garden for lunch. We're good."

Mitch cursed again as he blew out the breath he had been holding. "Tell Dan I want to see him as soon as you get back to the estate. I'm headed over there now to take care of everything."

"Will do."

"And Jake, make sure to let Caterina know it has to be a long lunch, Okay? We need time to get everything set up."

"Roger that."

Mitch took a deep breath and turned to deal with the intruder, but she was gone. She'd left, or at least she wasn't in the room. Now he was going to have to search the entire yacht just in case. "Fuck!" He was dropping the ball again and again today.

He took a step toward the doorway, but her scent hit him in the solar plexus, and he stopped dead. He knew that smell. Sunshine and spice. From where? At the office? In his neighborhood? Paris? No. The thief from Venice! He knew it in his bones.

Different look, but it was her. Last time, he'd gotten lucky. His other client hadn't been her mark, and he'd gotten away with his mistake, but this time she was on his client's yacht. Huh. Was she after the software? Did she work for Tolliver? He let that thought roll around in his mind as he did a cursory search of the yacht. She had left, he was sure of it, and since they were moving to the estate, it really didn't matter what she did on the yacht. Even so, he would love to know what she was up to.

He was pulling the salon door closed when he realized she must have picked the lock to get in. He smiled faintly. She was bold, no doubt about that. Picking a lock in broad daylight took guts and skills. He turned and went down the stairs. Making sure everything was locked up and tied down, he gave the place one last visual pass and then hopped over onto the dock.

The hot early summer sun beat down on his back through his T-shirt. The black cargos he had on weren't doing him any favors either. He greatly missed the Jersey shore and the summers he had spent there when he was a kid. Right now, he wanted to be at the beach, going for a swim or maybe catching a wave. Not driving over to a client's estate to yell at one of his guys. And now a thief was sniffing around. Life was not going the way he'd planned.

CHAPTER TEN

S he congratulated herself on her good fortune. That phone call had saved her ass. She knew better than to count on that happening again. She was really blowing it with this guy. She needed to take a step back and reassess her strategy.

She had taken the stairs back up to the room at a run, and now that the adrenaline rush had left her system, she was exhausted and slightly out of sorts. She flopped back onto her bed and closed her eyes. Maybe Leo was right about retiring from the gig. She had enough money, and if she left now, she could still move around the world without a problem. Well, except for Sweden, and she had no desire to go back there. Maybe it was time for her to find something legit to do with her life.

Alex found herself thinking of her best friend, Lacy Carmichael. They had met at boarding school in California. Lacy lived in New York City as a lawyer, which was surprising since her father's business wasn't always, or ever actually, on the right side of the law. Maybe after this job was finished, she would go meet Lacy in the city and hang out. They hadn't seen each other in a while, and she missed Lacy's friendship a lot.

She rubbed her face with her hands. She could hear Diana's voice in her head. It wasn't so much the words her client said but the tone. The desperation in it. Diana was going to do everything possible to get her life back because, whether Alex understood it or not, she loved Jeffery and the status he afforded her.

No getting around it. Diana reminded her of her mother.

As a child, Alex had known her father wasn't like other fathers. He didn't love her or her mother. It was obvious to Alex in everything he said and did. But not to her mother. Her mother had thought the sun shone out of his ass, and when he finally up and left, when her money just wasn't enough to keep him anymore, she couldn't handle it.

Alex had mistakenly believed that her mother would get over it and they could move on and be like other mothers and daughters. Only it never happened. Her mother would spend a whole day ranting about what a horrible person he was and how much she regretted not only giving him her heart, but her father's pocket watch. Alex's father had taken it with him on his way out. Just to make her mother miserable. That was the kind of guy he was.

The next day, everything would shift with no explanation, and her mother would defend the man to anyone who dared mention him, blaming everyone but him for his decisions. One time she'd even shifted the blame onto Alex, accusing her of driving her father away. Alex's Uncle Michael had comforted her and told her that her mother was sick. He had begged her not to take any of the behavior to heart. That was when the family had arranged to send her to boarding school.

She had felt so happy to escape her mother...and so horribly guilty because of it. Slowly, she'd made friends and created a life. Rather than tell them the truth, she created a fantasy about her family so that the other girls wouldn't know anything about her nightmare.

But everything had changed the day the letter arrived. She could still smell her mother's perfume. The envelope was pink with her mother's familiar scrawl on the front. Her hands had trembled as she opened it. Maybe her mother was over her father's departure. Maybe, just maybe, she had noticed Alex wasn't there and actually missed her.

Even now Alex's heart started to pound in her chest just as it did when she was opening the envelope. The letter had been only two pages. Her mother apologized for blaming her for her father's abandonment.

Her mother had finally tracked down her father. After the divorce, he'd taken great pains to avoid her. She'd asked him point-blank why he'd left. He'd told her it was *her* fault. She just wasn't enough for him. It didn't matter that she was fabulously wealthy. Money couldn't make up for *her*. She had driven him away and she, in turn, had driven Alex away. She just wasn't good at being a wife or a mother. She wished Alex better luck in life and love...and that was it. Everything had changed after that.

Alex couldn't bear to think about what happened next. She shot off the bed so fast her head spun. She grabbed the wall to steady herself. Her palms were slick with sweat. Still, even after all this time, her mother and father could torture her.

She took a few deep breaths and pushed away from the wall. She needed a distraction. She texted Leo and gave him Callahan's name. Then, still upset, she opened her laptop.

She assumed security had taken Drake to his estate, but she knew for a fact the wine cellar rehab wasn't supposed to be finished until after Memorial Day. She'd spoken with the general contractor by posing as a decorator trying to break into the scene in the Hamptons. He'd been more than happy to complain about Drake and his nitpicking.

She logged into the camera that was at the end of Drake's neighbor's driveway. It was across and down a bit from Drake's entry gate but it gave her a great view of all the comings and goings of the estate.

She'd realized the camera was there during one of her scouting trips after noticing the sign of a local security company. She was able to hack into the system remotely, but the camera needed to be adjusted slightly to give her a better angle.

The homeowners only spent summer in the Hamptons so they weren't around yet but Alex wanted to play it safe and not call any attention to herself. So, she'd dressed up as a technician from the security company, complete with full uniform and her hair tucked up under the company hat. She'd even rented a maintenance van and had magnets made with the company logo that she'd slapped on the doors.

Making sure she wasn't seen on camera, she climbed up a ladder and adjusted the camera. It still showed the neighbor's driveway but now it gave her a wider view of Drake's gated entry as well. These security companies really weren't as impregnable as they liked to think.

The video showed a lot of comings and goings of the construction crew. No way were they finished. She also noted the uptick in security guards by the gate. They seemed to have added another guy. That all but confirmed that Drake was moving in.

She leaned back in her chair. Whoever the guy was that

came to the yacht, he'd made either Drake or Callahan sufficiently nervous to move in early. She wished for the umpteenth time she'd gotten a better picture of the visitor. Her shot just wasn't enough to identify him.

She logged out of the camera and started searching for information on Callahan. She'd given his name to Leo, who usually did this type of thing, but she might as well look herself. She had nothing else she could do at the moment. Plus, she was curious.

Two minutes into her search, her phone rang. She glanced at the screen and then answered, "Hey Leo. Did you get my text?"

"Well hello to you, too. And yes I got the text. You're a bit late, though. I already know his name. You were half right on him, by the way. He's real security, but new at it. Only been in the business about six months. I just emailed you the file. I'll check on the estate and see what's up. Gotta go. My nonna needs her tea."

"Say 'hi' for me. Talk soon." Alex rang off. She could picture Leo making tea for his nonna back home in Italy. They'd be sitting on their balcony overlooking the sea.

She clicked on her screen and opened her email. There was the one from Leo. A couple more clicks, and she had it on screen in front of her.

Mitch Callahan. Recently retired Navy SEAL. *Great.* Single. Two brothers. Mother deceased. Father recently retired from the family home security business and living in Florida with a girlfriend, possibly fiancée. Mitch and his brothers, Gage and Logan, had just taken over their father's security business based in New York City and were in the throes of expansion. Logan was acting CEO, Gage was in charge of managing the expansion into cyber security, and Mitch was taking on personal security. Drake was their first major client in the new personal security division, but they had a good reputation, and all the men had experience in their respective fields.

Well, Mitch's background certainly upped the ante in this game of poker. Navy SEAL. A professional. What was the term the Israelis used? Security Warrior. So, she was going into battle with one of the best. She squared her shoulders. *Bring it on.* She never backed down from a challenge.

CHAPTER ELEVEN

P ain radiated from Mitch's jaw through his neck. He
unclenched his teeth, and let his mouth go slack for a
ten count. It was one way to postpone a trip to the dentist.
"No, you can't have the night off, Dan. To be honest, after
you mouthed off to the boss earlier and let that guy
Tolliver and his goons on the boat without doing a thor-
ough pat down, you're damn lucky to still have a job."

"Drake was being unreasonable. I was just offering him
suggestions," Dan Montero said in a defensive tone.

"Did you offer Drake suggestions when Jason was here?
I'm guessing not. Otherwise you'd have been fired a long
time ago."

"Drake didn't act all unreasonable like when Jason was
here."

Mitch snarled, "He doesn't have to be reasonable. Get
used to it. He's your boss. Your job is not to tell him when
he's being a dick." *That's my job.* "Your job is to protect him
whether he's a dick or not, understand?"

Montero nodded, his white-blond hair falling in his
eyes. He stood about four inches shorter than Mitch's six

feet, but what he lacked in height, he made up for in neck size. He had the shortest, thickest neck Mitch had ever seen. The man was built like a brick shithouse but was sadly lacking in brain power. He wasn't sure where Drake's previous head of security had found this guy—maybe he'd dug him up from under a rock—but Jason made him promise to keep Dan on. Mitch had agreed, but time was running out on that promise. The guy was a dud. He needed tier-one operators, not bruisers from the gym.

"And if you ever let anyone on any premises again without fully frisking them, I'll fire your ass. Are we clear?"

"Yeah," Dan muttered, "we're clear." He turned and walked out of the small security office, bumping shoulders with Jake who was on the way in. Mitch was pretty sure Dan had also mumbled that he was an asshole, but he didn't give a fuck. If the guy couldn't do the job, he didn't get to stay. And the sooner he understood that, the better.

"Yo, boss man," Jake said as he slid into the chair across from Mitch's desk.

"Report. What's going on?"

"So much for small talk." Jake grinned. "Been a day, huh?"

Mitch took a swig of water from the bottle on his desk. "You have no idea."

"Actually, I do. I spent it with Drake and Dan."

Mitch laughed. "Okay, you got me. What's going on? Any new catastrophes?"

"The construction guys were pretty good about clean-ing, but Drake's house staff still went in with scrub brushes to the wine cellar area and the stairway to the back door. Oh, and the downstairs bath. I guess the construction crew didn't like the Porta Potty as much as Mr. Drake's half bath."

"Oh, fuck." Mitch ran his hand through his hair.

"Yeah. They broke a towel rack and some vase thing, but the housekeeper, Mrs. Glen, had the yard guy fix it. It all looks as good as new. Drake doesn't use it anyway, but it was done just in case."

"I put Jasper in charge of keeping an eye on the construction workers. He's usually on the ball. What happened?"

"Don't know, man." Jake shook his head. "You'd have to ask him."

"Tell him I want to talk to him when you see him, okay?" Mitch took a swig of his water. He should really text Jasper right now, but it had been a hell of a day, and he just needed it to be over. "Anything else?"

Jake frowned. "The new cameras are being installed in the morning, but I think we're still going to have a blind spot in that back corner of the house. There's just no way to get a hardwired camera back there. I can get a wireless one up."

"No. No wireless. Too easily hacked. It's got to be wired to a closed-circuit system."

"Okay, well there's no way to get anything wired out there without making the wires too obvious. Any guys who are good would spot them a mile away and cut 'em." Jake shrugged. "To be honest, that's a possibility with all the wires."

"It's a possibility, but we've done a damn good job of hiding the wires and making the cameras hard for anyone to access without turning up on film. Make sure the guys know that even the slightest disturbance needs to be checked out thoroughly. I won't allow this team to fail because someone thought there was a camera malfunction. There are no malfunctions."

"Yes, sir." Jake nodded. "So, what do we do about the blind spot?"

Mitch took another swig of water. "Put a man there. It will help to have another physical body on the grounds." He tilted his head for a second. "As a matter of fact, take the guys out in small groups and walk the whole grounds with them. Go over the whole setup, but make sure they know where to stand when it's their turn to cover the blind spot. I want everyone on the same page. Make sure Dan goes with the first group and tell him he's first up for blind spot duty tomorrow. Maybe that'll teach him some manners," Mitch mumbled.

Jake laughed outright. "Yeah, sure. That'll fix his attitude problem."

"I have no idea why Jason wanted me to keep him around. He's shit at this kind of work." Mitch shook his head. "Do me a favor and call Jason. Maybe he'll tell you the real story."

Jake stood up. "Will do, boss."

"Check on everyone and make sure they're on point. This transition must go smoothly. For all of our sakes."

Jake nodded and left the room.

Mitch leaned back in his chair and propped his feet up on the edge of his desk. He hated to admit it, but Logan had been right. They weren't ready for a client like Drake, but Mitch had insisted he could handle it. He'd been adamant he could run the personal security arm of the company and that Drake was the perfect client to build their reputation.

Logan and Gage had been reluctant. Gage thought cyber security would be a better place to put their energies and Logan, well, Logan just disagreed with anything Mitch said. Eventually they came around and decided Mitch would run the personal security branch while Gage would develop a cyber security department. Logan would oversee the whole damn thing. Take care of the day-to-day running of the business and be the face when it came to meeting new clients.

Mitch had to stick it out now. Had no choice. His stomach churned with regret. Money was tight, and this job was going to cost way more than anticipated because of the extra security measures he would need to put in place to deal with the whole Tolliver situation. He'd need more boots on the ground as well as equipment. Fuck. He'd screwed up, and he knew it. Maybe he wasn't cut out for this type of job. What would he do if he didn't do security work? What else was he good at? Nothing apparently. He shook his head. He really needed to get his head on straight. This line of thinking wasn't getting him anywhere.

The only thing to do was keep going. Maybe he'd get Logan to argue with Drake over money. As a lawyer, he was much better at that sort of thing, but then Logan would lecture *Mitch*. Yeah, no way in hell was he doing that.

He finished his water and threw the bottle across the room to the recycling can where it hit the rim and bounced off. He shook his head. His ego had driven him to sign on with Drake. He'd let his need to prove himself to his brothers get in the way of making smart business choices. If he'd made decisions like this in the SEALs, it would have gotten him thrown off the team. Hell, it might have gotten him killed. This could still be a life or death situation if Drake was to be believed. It sounded like Tolliver was a real threat.

He cursed and ran both hands through his hair. He had a lot riding on this job, and it was turning to shit before his eyes. He needed to double, no triple check, everything. Cursing, he popped open his laptop and went through the security routine to access his email. He wrote a quick email to Gage, requesting any and all information they could find on Tolliver and his unnamed client.

Mitch paused, his hands hovering over the keyboard. Though he knew he should tell his brothers this detail was getting more serious than anticipated, he couldn't bring himself to do it. He could practically hear Logan complaining that Mitch had leapt without looking again, leaving them to clean up his mess.

Instead, he finished up the email with a quick request for information about a young female thief who might be working in the area. He gave brief details, told Gage to check Europe as well, and then sent the email. Hopefully, his brother could dig up some solid intel. He needed all the help he could get.

CHAPTER TWELVE

Alex checked her reflection in the window of the pastry shop. Her wide-brimmed sun hat blocked out most of her face, and with the addition of her oversize sunglasses, it was difficult to make out any of her features. She wore an emerald green maxi sundress covered in large flowers. It fell to the tops of her feet where it met her strappy sandals. Her designer bag, slung carelessly over her shoulder, helped her blend in. She looked like any other Hampton socialite on her way to the shops.

She tracked her quarry. Drake was sitting in an outdoor café, having lunch with a friend. She had no doubt that Mitch Callahan would have had a coronary over Drake's choice of outdoor seating. It made her smile. They were a match made in heaven, those two. She imagined neither one of them liked to be told "no."

She'd spent the last week getting reorganized after Drake left the yacht. She'd had to move and dig a little deeper into Drake's background. The more research she did on Jameson Drake, the more she'd come to respect him. Yes, he was a cold fish, ruthless as hell, but it served him well. His mother had abandoned him, left him to be raised by his grandparents. No one seemed to have an ID on his father.

Drake's grandparents didn't have much, just a few acres in the mountains in upstate New York, but he'd managed to get a scholarship to one of those exclusive private schools in Massachusetts. He'd made friends with all the high society types. His contacts had invested in his first company after university, and friends in Washington had since helped him out whenever he needed a contract or a tax break.

He'd become famous, or maybe infamous was the word, after dating a reality star for six months. Being handsome had just been the icing on the cake. Now the world wanted to know all about Jameson Drake. Rumor had it, Drake was now on the billionaires list, which is what made this job so confusing. He could buy himself whatever he wanted, so why was he refusing to let Diana's gift go?

She moved farther down the street, checking the reflections in store windows to make sure Drake was still in place. Her plan was simple. Drake was having a Memorial Day weekend party to celebrate the unofficial kick-off to summer, and she needed to find a way on to the guest list. She had briefly contemplated getting Drake himself to invite her, but her weak-link plan seemed like a better call. Besides, she was pretty sure she'd already figured out a way in.

Her phone buzzed. Pulling it out of her pocket, she saw Leo's name on the screen and hit the green button. "What's up?" She sat down on the nearest bench.

"Hey, lass. How's it going?"

"Not too bad. Thanks for the info. I found what I'm looking for."

"That's great. When do you think you'll get it?" Leo sneezed.

"Bless you."

"Thanks."

"I'm thinking over the long weekend. His party's going to provide the perfect window of opportunity." She turned slightly on the bench and glanced over her shoulder. Drake was still eating lunch. The waiter gave the empty plates to another server but poured more wine. Good sign. He was staying longer. She turned back.

"Have you been invited to the party yet?" Leo asked.

"No, but I will be."

Leo made a tsking sound. "You aren't going to go directly to the source, are you? Not sure that would be the best course of action in this case."

"Relax, Leo. I agree with you. I don't have a death wish." She glanced around again. Drake was not at the table. Her heart thumped in her chest. Where the hell had he gone? There. One of his security guys was standing next to the men's room door. "Sorry, what was that?" she asked.

"You're watching him, aren't you? I can tell 'cause you're distracted."

"Yup."

"I said, so how are you planning to get on the guest list? I'm betting it will be pretty tight."

"I was thinking of going through the security team, but I rejected that idea. No need to put myself on their radar."

Leo coughed. "Glad to hear you're using your head, lass. That would be an unnecessary risk. You really don't want Drake to know you exist."

"Yeah. So I think I've identified a friend of Drake's. He's having lunch with her as we speak, but it doesn't look romantic. I've seen them lunching together a few times this week. I think she's my way in."

"Huh. What's your approach?"

Alex shifted on the bench to see the reflection of the café in the store window across from her. She didn't want to keep turning around. It wasn't working, so she got up off the bench and walked down the street to the corner.

"I figured I would use the whole 'I'm new in town, just coming off a rough break-up or divorce, and I need a friend' shtick. I've done my research, and Caterina Sinclair is the sympathetic type. She's on her own after a bad breakup a couple of years ago. The café she owns is finally a success after years of struggling on her part. I'm thinking I'll approach her as someone who's in the same spot she was once in. Chances are good she'll respond." She crossed the street with the light and moved over to sit down on another bench. The restaurant was only a few doors down. She could see a couple of Drake's security guys from here, so she would know if he moved.

"And if she doesn't? Not that I'm doubting your acting skills, kid, but..."

"There are a couple of others I can approach if this doesn't work. I found an article in one of the local magazines about last year's party. Apparently, Drake always invites a group of his school cronies to this event. I can always hook up with one of them to get an invitation, but most of them are incredibly repugnant. Quite frankly, I would rather strike up a friendship with Caterina."

"Well, sounds like you got it under control. Let me know if you need anything." Leo coughed again. "In the meantime, I'm working on the delivery angle. Ms. Sterling is getting antsy. She has decided to throw her husband a late birthday party/barbeque on the Monday of the long weekend. She says she wants to give him the gift at the party. I told her that wasn't the deal. She tried to push back on the timeline, but I told her that we would walk. This type of thing can't be rushed. She apologized and begged for us to stay on the job. If at all possible, she would like to get it back for the party, but if not, she'll live with whenever we can get it."

"Well, if all goes well, she'll have it in time for her barbeque. Drake's party is Saturday night."

"Still"—Leo hesitated—"you could wait until Drake leaves town. I can't imagine he'll be hanging in the Hamptons for too much longer, and it's unlikely he'll bring it with him. You could steal it back once he's gone. Security would be laxer. It would be a much easier job."

"You just told me Diana wants it ASAP."

"She can wait," Leo growled.

Alex frowned. "What's this about? Are you getting cold feet?"

"Lass, I have a bad feeling about this. Have from the beginning." Leo sneezed again.

"Bless you. Leo, are you getting a cold?"

"I think so," he said, his voice muffled. The next thing she heard was the sound of him blowing his nose. She grimaced as she pulled the phone away from her ear.

When he was back, she said, "I think the cold is interfering with your mojo. We are going to be fine. The party will give me the perfect opportunity to repossess the item in question. By next Monday, Diana will be giving her husband his birthday gift and we will be on our way out of here. Stop worrying so much. Let your nonna make you some soup and then have a nap. You'll feel much better. I'll call you later." She clicked the red button and put her phone back in her pocket.

Leo knew better than to say anything negative once they were past the planning stages of a job. She didn't need any negative vibes floating around her. No, she had to believe the job would go smoothly. That Caterina would get her on the guest list. That she would reclaim the gift, deliver it, and get out of town. And she'd already decided she would get a friend at one of the big culinary magazines to write a glowing review of Caterina's restaurant. This friend owed her big time, and it would ease her conscience to do Caterina a good turn. It was the least she could do. She hated using people, especially women, but sometimes it was a necessity in her business. She always tried her best to make it up to them.

With that decided, she stood up and turned away from the cafe. She really didn't need to watch Drake right at this moment. He didn't have the item with him, so it wasn't going anywhere. Still, she liked to get to know her target's habits. The more she watched, the more she learned—and she could certainly learn more about his security team. Mitch Callahan was going to be a thorn in her side. She walked back across the street and turned back in the direction she had come. There was a boutique she'd noticed on the walk up—Giselle's.

She entered the narrow space. It was deceiving from the outside. It went back further than she'd imagined. It was tastefully decorated in lovely shades of blues, browns, and greens, very much like a summer day on the beach in the Hamptons.

"Hello," a voice purred from behind the counter. Alex looked up into the smooth face of who she guessed had to be the shop owner. The woman's neck and hands indicated she was in her late sixties, but the work she'd had done on her face put her at forty-five. "Can I help you?"

Alex gave the owner her *I'm friendly but not overly so because I have more money than God* smile. "Yes, I would like to try on the dress you have in the window, the green one."

"Of course," the woman behind the counter responded immediately. Smug satisfaction had Alex smiling. Yup, she could read a person at fifty paces. She had to play this friendly but aloof. That was the way women with money acted, or at least the classy ones. And she would know since she'd grown up around them. She could pull off this act with her eyes closed.

The woman brought over the dress in Alex's size. "There are a few other items in the shop that are similar if you would like to see them. Why don't I put them in a dressing room for you while you have a look around? That way you can try them on at your leisure."

Alex smiled. "That would be perfect, thank you."

The shop owner walked over to the first dressing room at the back of the store and hung up the green dress. "I'm Giselle. Please let me know if you have any questions."

"Of course." Alex smiled. She took a quick look around the shop before heading into the dressing room. Giselle had put two more dresses in there for her to try on. She started stripping off her disguise—the bag, the sunglasses, and the hat. The brown wig stayed on. She hadn't bothered with contact lenses today. The sunglasses offered plenty of protection, and she found the contacts made her eyes dry out and turn red.

The first thing she tried on was the little white cotton sundress Giselle had brought over. It had little cap sleeves with a deep scoop neck in the front that showed off some of her curves nicely. It was fitted to the waist and then had an A-line full skirt that stopped at the knee. She put it on and started adjusting.

"How are you doing?" Giselle called from somewhere close by.

"Fine." Alex pushed the curtain aside and stepped out. "Do you have a three-way mirror?"

"Yes, of course. Right over here." Giselle led her back to the front of the store. "That looks beautiful on you."

"Thank you," Alex murmured as she stood in front of the mirror and gave herself a once-over. The white didn't do much for her pale skin, but it was only the beginning of summer. In a few months, her skin would be a sun-kissed golden brown, and the white would pop then.

The style was not something she would usually wear. The capped sleeves and the A-line bottom were a bit 1950s for her taste, but it would be a great camouflage dress. That's how she thought of certain outfits in her closet. Even if she retired, which was a big "if," she would always have camouflage outfits in her closet. She didn't think it was necessary to always show the "real" Alex to the world.

She'd been in the spotlight so much as a child. She wasn't interested in having the world know that she preferred jeans to yoga pants or speculate on if she was pregnant or not. She hated the very idea of people following her every move on social media. It made her ill to even contemplate that.

She glanced in the mirror one last time and nodded. It would do nicely. It was bland and hid her real figure, like a suit of armor or a uniform. She headed back to the changing room.

The bell jingled, indicating that someone had entered the store, and Alex heard a couple of new female voices. They greeted Giselle warmly, old friends by the sounds of things, and moved toward the back of the store.

Alex tried on the next dress. The jade-green jersey fabric was super soft to the touch and had a halter neck-line, which was extremely flattering on her. It ended with a slight flare just above the knee. She was sure the dress fit her perfectly. Alex once again pulled the curtain aside and walked over to the mirror. Giselle was caught up discussing some health issue with her friend at the back of the store, so she didn't come over this time.

Alex had been right—the dress clung to her curves, accented her long legs, and brought out the green of her eyes. It would look even better with her real blond hair than it did with the brown bobbed wig she had chosen for this job or the black one she'd worn to the casino. She did a little twirl so she could see the back. The halter top left most of her back bare so she hadn't bothered putting on a bra.

"This one looks much better than the other one."

The voice sent shivers down her back, and she whirled around to find herself face-to-face with Mitch Callahan. "Uh, sorry?"

"The other dress, the white one, doesn't suit you nearly as well as this one does. This one accentuates your…" His voice trailed off as he ran his eyes over her entire body. The corners of his mouth turned up slightly. "Eyes."

He was leaning casually on the wall just inside the doorway, a spot that gave him a view of the whole store and out the store window. His muscular tanned arms were crossed over his chest, making his navy T-shirt pull at the shoulder seams. He was also wearing her favorite pair of faded jeans. She knew they would hug his gorgeous butt even if she couldn't see it at the moment. She had spent enough time looking at him through binoculars over the last week to know exactly what his ass looked like in those jeans. He wore them whenever he was off duty. He wore black cargos when he was working and they looked mighty fine as well.

"Thanks for your unsolicited opinion. I'll make a note of it." She rolled her eyes. Great. Now she was getting clothes advice from the enemy.

"You're welcome." The smile grew, and his gray eyes

seemed to sparkle at her. "This is the perfect color on you. You're too pale to wear white. Maybe later in the summer after you've spent some time in the sun. Even then, the cut is wrong for you."

She arched an eyebrow at him. Where did he get off telling her what to wear? "I see. You're a fashion expert, are you? Spend a lot of time studying women's clothing?"

She knew she should be hightailing it back to the dressing room and getting out of there, but she couldn't help herself. She loved sparring with her opponent. Nothing like a little game of cat and mouse to get the blood rushing though her veins.

"You'd be surprised."

"I'm sure. Well, Mr. Whoever You Are"—she turned around and looked in the mirror—"it just so happens I agree with you. This dress is better than the white one, but the white one also has its uses." She turned back around and gave him a smile. "If you'll excuse me." She walked back toward the dressing room.

"Callahan."

She stopped and turned back to him. "Pardon me?" It was official. She had lost her mind. Rather than ignore him, which she knew she should do, she'd stopped to talk to him, engage with him. It was like her body had a will of its own. Leo was going to flip his lid when he found out about this.

"My name is Mitch Callahan." He pushed off the wall and walked toward her. He moved like a panther, all pent-up energy just waiting to pounce. Stopping just in front of her, he offered his hand. She looked down at it, her nerve endings tingling in anticipation of his touch… and yet something told her it would be the most dangerous thing she'd done yet. If she indulged in skin-to-skin contact, she wouldn't be able to escape. Panic gripped her throat and for an instant she was compelled to run.

She bit her tongue, and the pain cleared her mind. She was being stupid. She shot out her hand and grabbed his, pumping it once before trying to let go, but his large hand held on to her much smaller one. A gentle hold, but she could feel the calluses on his fingers. She looked up into his gray eyes. His smile grew and turned sexy.

He flipped her hand over as if he was going to kiss it, and her breath hitched. No man had ever kissed her hand before. She'd always laughed at the weak-minded ninnies in books who swooned over courtly hand kisses, but now she was not so sure. She looked at his lips. They were quite full, and suddenly she found herself imagining what it would feel like for those lips to kiss more than her hand.

"I-I'm sorry?" He had been speaking, and she had no idea what he'd said. His eyes sparkled with mirth. Great, now he was laughing at her. She needed to focus. This man was beyond dangerous to her.

"Do you have any more to try on? I'm happy to help out, provide you with sound sartorial advice."

She gave him a tight smile. "I'll keep that in mind." She yanked her hand away and turned back around, making a bee line for her dressing room. Once inside with the curtain pulled, she leaned back against the wall and pressed her hands to her cheeks. She could feel the heat in them.

She had been studying this man for the past week. She knew to the tips of her toes that trying to get through his security would be one of her toughest jobs yet, so engaging with him on a personal level was just plain stupid.

She took off the green dress and reached for her own, but her eye caught on the last outfit Giselle had pulled out for her. It was a little black number, more of a cocktail dress. She shouldn't. She needed to be smart about this. On the other hand, maybe she could use this development to her advantage. If she did use him to get an in with Drake, at least she wouldn't have to play Caterina. She pursed her lips and then reached for the dress.

He wanted to play?

Well, now it was game on. May the best player win.

CHAPTER THIRTEEN

Mitch was being a dumb ass. He never should have entered the store. The right move would have been to keep following her to figure out from afar what she was planning. She was a thief, after all, and she wanted something from his client.

It had been dumb luck when she'd walked past the window of the dry cleaners. He'd recognized her immediately. There was just something about the fluid, graceful way she moved that had stuck with him. It was his afternoon off, but he'd been trying to track her for days, so he followed her.

Now he was in a clothing store giving out fashion advice like he knew what he was talking about. He wouldn't have done this for any of his former girlfriends, so what the fuck was he thinking?

He ran a hand through his hair and rolled his shoulders. After his thief's visit to the yacht, he'd done some research, figured out where she'd been staying. It was a matter of logic, really. She'd happened by the yacht just after Drake had left. He reasoned it wasn't dumb luck but that she was watching it. Where was the best place to scout out the yacht? The hotel next door.

He'd started at the front desk asking questions, but it wasn't until the bell hop approached him that he learned she had stayed there up until a few days ago as Carrie Bradshaw, which had made him smile. She obviously had a sense of humor. The information had cost him fifty bucks, and the bell hop had no idea where she was staying now. Neither did he. Wherever it was, it wasn't under the same name.

He surveyed the store and the street as he leaned against the wall, keeping an eye out for anything unusual, as was his habit. He heard the changing room curtain slide across the rod and looked up. Their eyes locked. Her eyes were the color of emeralds. He guessed she was likely wearing a wig, but there was no way those eyes were anything but real.

He gave her a once-over as she walked to the mirror. The dress was killer. Whereas the green one was perfect for day wear, this black one was for the night. A night of incredibly hot sex. The blackness of the dress accentuated the creaminess of her skin. It was like a second skin, moving with her, and it made every motion seem like an invitation to touch her. That dress was made for one thing and one thing only, getting laid.

Catching his eyes in the mirror, she asked, "So, what do you think of this one?" She cocked an eyebrow at him.

It was the sexiest thing ever. Not just the dress, but the sight of her standing there, arching an eyebrow at him, waiting for him to comment. He couldn't help but picture her in his bed, wearing nothing but her strappy sandals and that look. He cleared his throat. "I think it looks...sexy as hell." He ran his eyes over her again.

She smiled and then turned back toward the mirror.

The plunging V-neck showed off her high, round breasts, and the form-fitting material made her waist look tiny. The dress clung all the way down, so it hugged her ass in a way the last two hadn't.

"Hmmm. I don't really have anywhere to wear it, though. Seems like a waste to buy a dress like this and not wear it."

Was he crazy, or was she flirting with him? Man, she had balls. Their gazes locked again, and there was no mistaking the taunting look in her green eyes. What was the saying? *Keep your friends close but your enemies closer.* If that was the way she wanted to play it, game on.

"I'd be happy to take you out so you can wear that dress."

"And where would we go?" she asked.

He smiled. "I can think of a few places." His bed, for one. "What do you say? Are you up for a night out?"

"I don't know. I don't know anything about you."

"That's not true."

Her brow furrowed. "What do you mean?"

"Well, you know my name, which is more than I can say." She opened her mouth to respond, but he cut her off. "You know I work for Jameson Drake. You were looking for your friend Nikki on his yacht the other day. Did you ever find her by the way?" He watched her very closely. A ripple of emotion passed over her features. Fear maybe? It had happened too quickly for him to be sure. She hadn't expected him to bring up their last meeting. Her eyes changed. Damn. Now he'd put her guard up. *Better keep quiet about Venice.* For now.

"I never found *Brandi*."

Score one for her. She was sharp.

"I think I had the wrong yacht. She seems to have disappeared. I didn't know her all that well anyway. I'm new to the area. I just met her, and she suggested it would be a fun way to pass the day."

When she bit her lip, his body responded with instant awareness. She looked so lovely, so decadent. He put his hands in his pockets to keep from reaching out and pulling her hard against him. "So, what do you say? Let me take you out?" He moved off the wall again and came toward her. He was stalking his prey and from the way she shifted her weight away from him, as if trying not to back up, she knew it. When he reached toward her, her green eyes went wide, turning a deeper emerald color. Her hands clenched into fists as he picked a piece of fluff off the strap of her dress.

He had never been so aware of another person.

Color washed up her cheeks. Her chest rose as she took a breath, her lips parted. Finally, she tilted her head, signaling, consciously or not, that she had reached a decision.

"Come out with me," he coaxed, his voice coming out rougher than he would have liked. She nodded just once. The start of a smile formed on her lips. He couldn't tear his gaze away from them. They were luscious and red like ripe strawberries. He leaned forward just slightly, and to his delight, she mirrored his movement.

"So how did you make out?" a voice chirped. He swung around to see the shop owner bearing down on them. His frown must have been fierce because her steps immediately faltered. "Is everything Okay?" she asked, hesitation clear in her voice.

"Fine," his beautiful thief managed to croak. She cleared her throat. "Just fine. Thank you, Giselle."

A feeling of smug satisfaction filled his chest as he watched her struggle to get herself under control. At least he wasn't the only one who felt this strange energy between them. He shifted, trying to get more comfortable in his jeans.

She turned back to the mirror. "I think I'll take all three of them." She met his eyes in the mirror again. "It seems I'll have a place to wear the black one after all." She walked back into the dressing room and pulled the curtain closed behind her.

Mitch waited for her outside. He took a deep breath and blew it out as soon as the shop door closed behind him. He needed to be very careful with this one. It was a very risky game he was playing. She was dangerous as hell, and he needed to win this war no matter what. His future was riding on it.

The door opened a few moments later, and she walked out. "Thanks for the advice on the dresses." She gave him a teasing smile. Her hat and sunglasses were back on, so her mouth was her only visible feature. No doubt she'd done that on purpose.

"No problem. It was my pleasure. Truly." He shot her a grin. "So, let me know where you're staying, and I'll pick you up at eight. We can have dinner, and then I'll take you somewhere you can show off your dress."

"Make it ten. I have a few things to do first. I'm staying at the Marina Hotel." She wasn't...not anymore, but he wasn't going to let her know he knew that. She smiled and waggled her fingers in a small wave as she turned to go.

"Can I have your cell number so I can call you when I arrive?"

She chuckled and said over her shoulder, "Don't worry, I'll find you. The lobby isn't that big."

"By the way, my name is Carrie." The words floated back to him as he watched her hit the end of the sidewalk and cross the street. When she was out of sight, he left the opposite way. He grimaced. He hadn't asked her name on purpose. He didn't want her to lie to him. It was stupid, but he wanted to keep things pure between them.

She was a thief, but somewhere along the way, he'd started seeing her as *his* thief. Reality hit him in the gut. He'd do well to remember she was the enemy.

Day off or not, he drove back to the estate and texted Jake, asking him to drop by the office, and then he made the rounds. He checked the security daily, sometimes more than once, making sure that everything was as it should be. He drilled his people on protocols and actions, checked and rechecked equipment. He was becoming obsessive. But the party was this coming weekend, and he was worried about it. Drake was heading to Europe immediately afterward—and the businessman already had a team in place over there. Although it would be great for business if Mitch earned permanent placement on Drake's security team, he would be relieved to escape this mess.

Sitting at his desk, Mitch took out the thin file he had on "Carrie." From the looks of things, she was a fairly busy woman. His hunch that she'd stolen the watch at the Santini's party—more specifically, from Hans Gabriel—had helped him link her to other crimes in Europe.

He'd asked an Interpol contact he'd served with overseas, and she'd filled in a few of the blanks. They knew she existed, but they didn't know who she was. She popped up on their radar because of the odd nature of the items she stole. She didn't always go after expensive jewelry or artwork. Sometimes she took what amounted to only keepsakes. Strange.

Apparently, she'd almost been caught in Sweden, but they'd ended up with nothing more than a wig and a cape of some sort. They had DNA evidence but nothing to match it against. Besides, when really pushed, the victim,

Sven Svenson, had refused to press charges, so there was no case.

As far as Mitch could tell, "Carrie" had hit most of the countries in Europe.

A wave of guilt hit him in the chest. Interpol had no idea what she looked like. The only picture they had was a blurry profile shot where she was wearing huge sunglasses and a long, dark wig. With her complexion and the light dusting of freckles over her nose, he was willing to bet her real hair color was light, like a light brown or dark blond. He should call up his contact and tell them what he knew. Hell, he should take a picture for them, but he couldn't bring himself to make the call. He didn't want to think too much about his reasons.

"Hey." Jake walked in the door and sprawled in the seat across from him. "You wanted to see me?"

"I need a favor. I know I'm supposed to cover the night shift tonight, but I need you to work for me."

"Why? Got a hot date?"

Mitch hesitated slightly before opening his mouth to answer.

"You do!" Jake clapped his hands together. "It's about damn time. You haven't had a dry spell like this since....well, since never. You had more action when we were overseas in the desert than you do now."

Grinding his teeth, Mitch shook his head. "It's not a hot date, exactly. It's business, and besides, I'm not in a dry spell. I'm putting work first. There's a difference."

"Dude, you're in a dry spell. Own it." Jake grinned. "Where are you taking her?"

"NY East."

"The hottest dance bar in the Hamptons? Damn straight, it's a date. Ain't no business being done in that place that's above board. So, who's the lucky lady?"

Mitch shook his head as he closed the file. "It's business." He didn't want to tell anyone else about his thief just yet. He wanted to feel her out more. *Feel her up, more like it.* He came down hard on the voice in his head.

"I'll cover for you, but you owe me big time." Jake hopped out of the chair. "I'm going to grab a late lunch/early dinner. You're free after that."

"I won't leave here 'til shortly before ten, so take your time."

"That late? I'm concerned you don't recognize this is a date, my brother. You need to get out more." After Mitch gave him the finger, Jake laughed all the way out the door and down the hallway.

"It's business," he called out. Tonight was going to be all business.

Yeah, sure. Who was he kidding?

CHAPTER FOURTEEN

Alex paced back and forth along the wall of windows in her rented guest house. Her stomach clenched with guilt. She was seriously considering lying to Leo, and she'd never *ever* lied to Leo. She came to a stop at the island in the kitchen and picked up her water bottle. She downed half of it, wishing wholeheartedly it was vodka.

Looking out at the sand dunes, she thanked her lucky stars and Mrs. Olsen her temporary landlord for her safe haven. It had a direct line of sight to Drake's compound and the beach front. She'd been able to watch Mitch's team as they worked on the security system over the last week. She'd also watched Mitch when he went for his daily early morning swim. The sun glistening off his well-muscled body was her favorite part of this gig so far.

She played with the bottle's label as she walked across the room before stopping at the fireplace on the far wall. She and Leo had come to an agreement that she would not use Mitch as a way in, that it was too dangerous, and here she was going out on a date with him. What the hell had she been thinking?

The issue was she hadn't been thinking with her brain. That man was sex on a stick, and he was a challenge. It was a deadly combination for her. Like catnip.

She loved a good challenge, physically craved it. And here it was wrapped in the sexiest man she had ever come across. Emerging from the dressing room in that black dress had been akin to making a declaration of war—a war that promised to be as pleasurable as it was dangerous. She wasn't backing down so she either had to tell Leo the plan had changed or lie to him.

She frowned as she paced back toward the kitchen. She was seriously leaning toward lying to him. He was sick and cranky already. No need to make it worse by telling him the truth.

She slammed her water bottle down on the island. No, she could justify anything. She just had to put on her big girl panties and tell Leo the truth.

The truth. She turned and looked out at the dunes. The truth was she was still searching for something after all these years. She ran headlong into job after job, each one more challenging than the next, always looking for that one job that could help her feel true joy. The one that would make her feel like she'd accomplished something, helped someone, changed the world, even if only a little. Leo's talk of retirement or taking a rest, which he was sure to repeat once he heard just how badly she'd messed up, was anathema to her.

No matter how much she tried to humor Leo and entertain the idea, she knew she would never be able to remain still. If she stopped now, if she gave up, what would come next? Everything would catch up to her, that was what. Her breath hitched in her throat. She wasn't going there. The past was a void better left unexplored.

She shook her head and took a couple of deep breaths.

She caught movement out of the corner of her eye. Her temporary landlord, Mrs. Olsen, was coming over the dunes and along the path from the beach. Her pure white hair was held back in a loose bun at the nape of her neck. She was wearing an old pair of jeans and sneakers. Her blue and white striped blouse hung loose. She had her hands full of what looked like shells and a bucket that was obviously heavy.

Alex threw open the door to her deck and headed down the stairs to the path. "Can I help you with that, Mrs. O?" she asked.

"Bless you, dear. I could use the help. These old bones are getting pretty tired." She handed the bucket to Alex.

"How far did you walk?"

"Three miles, but it was slow going. I can feel all of my eighty-eight years today. It must be going to rain later. You can smell the salt in the air."

Alex took a deep breath and nodded. Yes, they were mere feet from the Atlantic Ocean, but Mrs. Olsen was right, the air was saltier somehow. "Is that what it means when the air smells like this? Rain?"

"Yes. It always smells different when the rain is coming. And my bones are aching, so there'll be rain tonight. I hope you don't have any big plans."

"Um…"

"Well, then take an umbrella."

They walked along the path past the guest house and on to the main lawn. The grass was lush and green already, even though there hadn't been a lot of rain yet this spring. The pool sparkled in the setting sun as they passed.

Mrs. Olsen pointed toward the pool. "Have you gone swimming yet, dear? John keeps it at a decadent eighty-five degrees for me. You should enjoy it."

"I haven't had the chance, but I plan to this weekend."

She smiled at the older woman. "Thanks again for renting me your guest house. I..." What could she say? *I needed to hide out?*

Mrs. Olsen reached out and patted her arm. "No need for any thanks or to explain. I have been around long enough to recognize a woman in trouble when I see one." They took the stairs to the terrace. "You know what else I see?" Mrs. Olsen looked over at Alex, her brown eyes full of warmth. "I see a woman who is lost."

Alex opened her mouth to say something, but nothing came to mind. She couldn't bring herself to tell the woman she was mistaken when she wasn't. After knowing Alex for a matter of days, she'd pinpointed exactly what was wrong with her.

"My advice? Figure out what it is you really want and then figure out what you need. Many times, they are part and parcel of the same thing." She gave Alex's arm a squeeze and then took the bucket back from her.

"Mrs. Olsen?"

"Yes, dear?"

Alex wanted to say so many things at that moment. She opened her mouth again, but everything got caught up in a tangle in her throat. She swallowed hard and then blurted out, "Why do you carry a bucket of water with you on your walks?" It was a stupid question, but it was the only one that didn't wrench at her gut. Besides, it had been bothering her for the last few days and she really needed to know.

"Why, for the dogs. Everyone brings their dogs to the beach, and they forget to bring fresh water for them."

"Oh." She smiled. "Of course." It made sense. Mrs. Olsen was perfection. Plain and simple and helpful and good. She was a reminder of everything Alex felt compelled to protect.

"Have fun tonight, dear." Mrs. Olsen turned and went into the house.

Alex walked back across the yard to her guest house. It was funny. She had met Mrs. Olsen in town when she was feeling desperate and, yes, lost. Staying at the hotel was out, but where could she go next? She had sat on a bench to think it all through, and Mrs. Olsen had joined her. They started talking and, before she knew it, she had a place to stay with no strings attached.

She was half convinced Mrs. Olsen, with her insightful, warm eyes and generosity, was some kind of good witch. The woman had never even asked for her name—she'd immediately taken to calling her "dear." And the guest house was now her safe haven in a stormy world. Best of all, its location was phenomenal.

Alex opened the door to the guest house to find Leo poking around in her fridge. "Don't you ever eat?" he mumbled as he came out of the fridge with a yoghurt in his hand.

"Don't you ever wait to be let in?" she countered.

"Not necessary. We're family," he said and then promptly sneezed.

"If you get me sick, our family will be down a member," she threatened as she walked over to the coffee table and grabbed a box of tissues. Coming back, she placed it on the island in front of Leo. "When did you get into town?"

"Last night, and I'm fine. Thanks for asking," Leo mumbled through the tissue. "Threats. I get threats instead of concern over my state of well-being."

"You've got a cold, Leo. You're not dying." She rolled her eyes. She walked back to the living room and crashed onto the white comfy chair with the big, cushy pillows. She put her feet up on the matching ottoman and laid her head back on the cushions.

"Well, it feels like I'm dying." Leo wandered over and sat down on the matching sofa, sinking into its depths. "Oh, this is nice," he said as he snuggled deeper.

"Don't get too comfortable over there, you." She pointed an accusatory finger at him. "We have work to do."

Leo just grunted in reply and closed his eyes.

"Seriously, Leo, we have to go over a few things so don't fall asleep."

She watched him as his breathing became even. He'd always had the enviable ability to fall asleep anywhere at the drop of a hat. She picked up a pillow to throw at him to wake him up, but then she noticed how pale he looked. Dark circles bagged under his eyes, and his cheeks were gaunt.

Leo had never talked about his past. She wasn't even really sure if his nonna was any real relation to him. They were strays together, she and Leo. What if this was more than a cold? The thought was like a sucker punch to the solar plexus. She suddenly couldn't breathe. Leo was the person she was closest to on this earth, and if she lost him... Her throat got tight with tears.

"Relax, doll, it's just a cold." His breath wheezed out of his chest, but he cracked one eye open and then winked at her.

She threw the pillow at him. He deserved it. He'd given her a good scare. Somehow, he always seemed to know what she was thinking.

He sat up straighter and put the pillow down on the sofa beside him. "How are the plans going? Did you make contact with Caterina yet?"

She bit her lip. "Um, about that..."

Leo's eyes narrowed. Not a great start.

"See, I bumped into Callahan, and he asked me out." The words came out in a rush. "It wasn't a setup, I swear. It just kind of happened. It seemed too good of an opportunity to pass up, and you know I hate to manipulate other women unless there's no other choice…and this kind of just worked out." Her voice petered out on the last word.

Leo assessed her and then gave the barest shrug. "Okay, then I guess we have to go with it."

All the air rushed out of her lungs. She hadn't needed to lie to Leo after all, and he'd given her the green light anyway. Sure, she hadn't told him everything, but she didn't want Leo to worry that Mitch was already on to her. She was worried about that enough for the both of them.

"I'm going out with him tonight. Hopefully, it will be enough to get an invite to the barbeque this weekend. Do you have the things I'm going to need?"

Leo got up and went over to the kitchen counter, grabbed a bag, and came back to the sofa. He sat down and upended the bag. "This is everything. I still have no clue what any of it is."

She got off the chair and joined him on the sofa. "So" —she picked up a square plug-looking thing—"this is an ODB2. It's a car diagnostic scanner."

"You're telling me that thing-a-ma-bob will scan the car? But I bought it on Amazon for seven-fifty."

Alex nodded. "Yes. They aren't expensive."

"So why do people spend all that money going to the garage to find out what's wrong with their cars?" Leo asked.

"Because it needs software to work, and that's harder to get. And, besides, even if they knew what was wrong with their car, would they know how to fix it?"

Leo scratched his chin. "Huh. Ya got me there, I guess.

So, do you think there's something wrong with the car then?"

"No. Diana gave all of the keys to Drake. I need this to reprogram the blank car key you got me so I can start the car. It's Bluetooth enabled, by the way. Cool, huh?"

Leo shook his head. "It's beyond me lass, but if you say so."

She grinned. "If people only knew what can be done with these things. I already downloaded the app to my phone, so I am set to go. All I need is access."

Alex grabbed the bag, put the key back in it, and then added the ODB2.

"Can you walk me through it? Maybe I can learn something." Leo said as he leaned back on the cushions.

"Assuming the car is unlocked, I plug the ODB2 into the car underneath the dash. The Bluetooth will connect automatically to my phone. I'll use the app to pair the blank key to the car, and voila! I'll be able to start it and drive away." She leaned back on the sofa next to Leo. "I gotta say, the hardest part of this job is getting invited to the party and getting into the garage. Leaving with the car should be a breeze once I have access to it."

"What happens if the car is locked?"

"That's harder but not impossible. I have several options. None will take very long, though, so it shouldn't add too much time to the job."

Leo asked, "You good on the rest of the plan?"

"Yup. This one is relatively simple, all things considered. He's storing it in the very last bay of the farthest garage. It's a straight shot down the driveway, and the gates will be open because of the party. They take about thirty seconds longer to close than I'll need. There's no way they'll get them secured in time, even if someone hits the panic button the moment I pull out of the garage. Zero to sixty in three point two seconds, baby." Her grin was so wide her cheeks hurt.

Leo smiled back. "You aren't looking forward to this at all, are you?"

"Do you know how rare it is to be able to drive a car of this caliber? I'm gonna love every second of it."

"Are you sure you can handle it?"

She hit him on his arm. "Seriously, is that even a question? I was born to drive cars like this."

He shook his head. "All right. After you leave the grounds, hightail it over to the Sterling place. She's agreed to be out for the night and leave word with her people. Her gate will be open until you pull through, and then they'll close it behind you. She'll have guards on duty to stop anyone who may be chasing you, but it shouldn't be an issue since she has the title for the vehicle. Once you're through her gate, you're home free." Leo looked over at her. "I know I've said it before, but I'm not feeling great about this one. I still think we should take a step back. Maybe wait until he leaves the country."

"We just went over the plan. I've pulled off jobs that are a lot more difficult. Bottom line—the car doesn't belong to Drake. I'm bringing it back to its rightful owner." She paused. "Although, I have to say, Drake seems more like the sports car type than Jeffery Sterling." She frowned.

Leo glanced at his watch. "If you're sure, lass"—he continued when she nodded—"then I'll be going." He paused. "Please be careful on this one. I just have a gut feeling it's not going to go as planned. Make sure you have your disguise in place. Sterling's people shouldn't be able to identify you." He walked toward the door. "Just don't let Callahan get too close. He's good. He'll remember every-thing about you, which is going to make it hard to hide from him once this job is over. Make sure you wear your contacts and your wig and anything else that can change your look."

She walked to the door with him. Guilt reared its ugly head. This was something else she'd kept from Leo. Purposefully. Mitch had already seen her real eye color. "Leo, relax, it's going to be fine. Maybe we can take a break after this one. I have a friend close by. Maybe I'll go visit her after this one." It would be good to visit Lacy, if only for a little while.

It was Leo's turn to nod. He paused and then leaned over and kissed her on her forehead. "See you Saturday night. Call me if there's any change in plans." He opened the door and went out into the dusk.

Alex glanced at the clock in the kitchen. She had just enough time to fix something to eat, get ready, and drive over to the hotel for the meet. Grabbing the brown paper bag off the coffee table, she then stowed it in her little hidey hole, a hollowed-out version of her favorite book, *To Catch a Thief*.

CHAPTER FIFTEEN

M itch fixed the cuff of his snowy-white shirt and then slid his arms into his navy blazer. Taking a quick glance in the mirror to confirm his hair wasn't standing up in tufts, he lit out of his temporary quarters at Drake's estate and walked toward the study. The on-duty bodyguard had texted him to say Drake had been on the phone with Tolliver, and Mitch wanted to hear how everything had gone down. He didn't need any more surprises.

He knocked on the study door and entered. Drake looked up, slightly startled that someone had entered before being told to do so. Oh, well. Too late for any empty politeness now. "I heard you spoke with Tolliver. What did he say?"

Drake's eyes narrowed. Mitch was prepared to be yelled at for barging in and demanding to know what was, essentially, Drake's private business. He wasn't good at playing the political game, but he *was* damn good at his job, and he needed every bit of intel to keep his client safe. Drake must have come to the same conclusion because he stood up from his desk and walked over to the bar area.

"Going out?" he asked.

Mitch nodded. "You'll be in good hands. Jake is lead this shift, and I'm a phone call away. I've already checked all the systems twice and spoken to each team member. We're good to go for the evening."

Drake poured himself two fingers of Scotch. "I'm sure it's all fine. I wasn't commenting on your security. Just observing."

Mitch remained silent. He knew Drake had heard his original question, and the man would answer it or not in his own time. Mitch was finally starting to understand his boss's rhythms. He was certainly better at reading Drake after these last weeks.

"Yes, Tolliver called. He said he wanted to make one last-ditch effort to get me to sell the software. I refused. He said he was sorry we couldn't do business."

Drake took a sip of his drink. "To answer your next question, no, I don't think that's the end of it. He has a plan up his sleeve, and I'm sure I won't like it." He took another sip and walked out from behind the bar.

"In case he plans to try something with the markets, I have people checking and rechecking things at the office and with all of my holdings. I'm not in any kind of vulnerable position, but I'm also not sure what kind of run he's going to take at me, so I'm covering all my bases."

Mitch gritted his teeth. He had a feeling he knew what Tolliver's plan was, and it stood about 5'5" in bare feet and had a hell of a smile. He grimaced as he contemplated telling Drake about her. But it didn't seem right when he didn't know for certain what she was after. Hell, that wasn't true. He knew in his bones she planned on lifting something of Drake's. Why else would she have snuck onto his yacht? Hung out on the same street where he was having lunch?

"I...may have a lead on something."

Drake's eyes narrowed. "Were you planning to keep it a secret?"

"I'm doing my due diligence. I have no proof at this point, just a whole lot of suspicion, but it makes sense. I should know more after tonight." He sincerely hoped that last bit wasn't a lie.

"Care to share details?" Drake asked before he took another sip of his Scotch.

"Not yet. I want to make sure I've got it right first. What I can tell you is that there's a known thief in town. I'm taking all the necessary precautions with your security."

Drake sat down at his desk. "You can't get more specific than that?"

Mitch sat down abruptly in the seat in front of Drake's desk. "This is the Hamptons at the start of the summer season. The playground of the rich. How many celebrities and billionaires do you think will be here this weekend? How many are here now?"

Drake opened his mouth to speak, but Mitch cut him off by raising his hands. "I know, and yes, as my employer, you are the only one who matters, but I can't say with absolute certainty that you're this thief's target. I'm working on it, but I don't have definitive proof at this time. I will tell you as soon as I know for sure either way. My staff is on top of things, and the system is working perfectly. You are secure."

Drake eyed him for a moment. "Believe it or not, I do trust you and I'm listening to what you're saying. I know the system is top-notch and you're doing your utmost to keep it that way. I just hope for both our sakes it's enough."

Mitch stood up. "So do I. We haven't found out who the real buyer is yet, but through our sources, we've eliminated a few groups. With any luck, we'll be able to track down who's behind this before anything happens. Have a good night." He gave a single nod to Drake and left the room.

In the hallway, he let out the breath he'd been holding. He was a little uneasy about the information he'd shared about his thief, but he wanted to be upfront with the client as much as possible. Communication worked both ways. Drake was the type of guy to appreciate that.

Mitch pulled up in front of the hotel about twenty minutes later. He was slightly early by design. His cell rang. He hit the green button to answer. "Callahan."

"No sign of her yet, boss," Jasper said.

"Okay. I'm going into the hotel. Text me when you see her."

"Roger that," he said and hung up.

Mitch got out of his car and put his cell in his jeans pocket. He'd asked Jasper to stand watch so he could find out how "Carrie" arrived. With any luck, he could tail her once the night was over and find out where she was staying. He walked into the hotel lobby and crossed over to the bar area, which had a great view overlooking the marina.

The bar was part of the main lobby with a few hidden corners for intimate conversation. He glanced around as he grabbed a stool that was as far from the main doors as possible. It gave him the best vantage point of the area with his back to a wall, albeit one made out of glass. The place was moderately full, but there were still seats at the bar. It would probably be super loud in about an hour.

The bartender came around, and Mitch ordered a beer. He let his eyes roam over the crowd. These were the first of the city people, here a few days early to enjoy the kick-off to the summer season. The bartender arrived with his beer, and he took a sip. He glanced at his watch, figuring his thief had decided on fashionably late.

A few moments later, a commotion by the door drew his attention. Men who had obviously been drinking for a while were making a big show of watching something or someone.

Two seconds later, he saw her head through the crowd. Of course, it was her. Her stride full of confidence and liveliness, she walked the length of the bar before coming to a stop next to him.

She was the sexiest woman he had ever laid eyes on. He trailed his eyes from the top of her head down to her shoes and back again. Was she wearing a wig? This afternoon he'd have bet on it, but now he wasn't so sure. Her hair was the same color as earlier, but now it gleamed in the overhead lights. The bob just emphasized the curve of her jaw.

Her emerald-green eyes sparkled, and she was wearing earrings that matched their unique shade. The dress emphasized and enhanced every curve. She'd worn sleek black stilettos that laced up her leg somehow. Fuck-me shoes, if he'd ever seen a pair. They made her legs look like they went on for miles.

"Are you finished with the once-over? Do I pass inspection? And think carefully before you answer that question." She smiled as she sat on the stool next to his.

"You look incredible." His voice was huskier than he would have liked. Damn. He had to hold it together tonight. This was work. "Would you like a drink?"

She nodded and turned toward the bartender, who had just appeared at their end of the bar. "I'll have a vodka. Grey Goose. Neat." The bartender nodded.

"That's an interesting choice. I would have thought white wine or Scotch. Vodka never entered my mind."

Mitch twisted his stool to face hers and leaned forward a bit so he could hear her better.

She shrugged. "I like vodka, always have. None of that flavored crap either. Just vodka, straight up."

When she smiled at him, his resolve to keep this solely a business venture died right then and there. If he wasn't careful, he'd be telling her Drake's security codes in no time flat. He took a sip of his beer and tried to muster some restraint.

"So, where are we going tonight?" Her voice was deep and sexy.

He wanted to bring her somewhere private so he could spend the rest of the night exploring every inch of her. He cleared his throat. "I promised you we'd go somewhere you could wear that dress. You'll just have to wait and see."

He saw something like worry flicker in her eyes. He reached out and took her hand. " I promise I will be a complete gentleman. Even if it kills me. You can leave any time you want."

He held her hand lightly, rubbing small circles on the back. Though he meant every word, it would be the struggle of his life. Sitting this close, he could smell her scent, sunshine and spice. He wondered if she would taste that way, too. If she was game, he sure as hell wanted to find out.

"I— Thanks for the reassurance, but I'm okay. I trust you." She pulled her hand back as her drink arrived, but he heard her clear her throat before she took a quick sip of her drink.

So, he wasn't the only one feeling it. Good to know.

The bar was starting to get louder. He took a long swallow of his beer and then leaned in and spoke directly in her ear. "Do you like to dance?"

She looked up at him and nodded. He noticed how

long her eyelashes were. They were dark against her skin. He was wondering about her hair color—could she really be a brunette?—when she leaned forward and said, "How about you? Do you like to dance?"

Her breath tickled his ear and lit his skin on fire. He stifled a groan. If he didn't put some space between them, they weren't going to make it out of the hotel.

"Yes." At her surprised look, he said, "My mother made me take ballroom dancing classes as a kid. After that, I just liked to move on the dance floor."

"We're going dancing?"

He nodded. "As soon as you finish your drink."

She picked up the glass and downed it in one swallow. He burst out laughing and signaled the bartender. After paying the bill, Mitch helped her up off the stool. Her hip brushed against his for a brief moment before she turned to walk out, but it was enough to make his heart beat double-time in his chest and his blood start running south of his belt buckle. This was going to be one long, tortuous night. The sway of her hips teased him as he followed her out of the bar.

They left the hotel and came to a stop by the passenger door of his BMW.

"Are you any good?" she asked with a slight smile on her lips.

He cocked an eyebrow at her as he leaned past her to touch the handle, unlocking the door. The alarm chirped. "I'm very good. Some have even said exceptional." He opened the door and helped her slide into his car.

She released a sultry laugh. "Modest, too."

He walked around and got into the driver's side. "Of course. I didn't say I was the best you'll ever have. As a dance partner, that is." He winked at her as he started the car, then pulled out of the parking lot. Before they got very far, it occurred to him that Jasper had never texted him. Had something happened to him? He pulled over to the side of the road. "Sorry, got to send a quick text."

"No problem," she said as she leaned back into the seat.

He pulled out his phone and checked the screen. Nothing. He texted, *Are u okay? She came about 45 mins ago.*

Fine. Didn't see her at all. Sorry boss. Do you want me to tail you? I can follow her afterwards.

He paused, considering the idea. If she had gotten past Jasper on the way in, chances were excellent she'd get past him on the way out. He'd need more people, and he didn't want to pull anyone off the estate for this. He glanced over at her. This woman was scary good. He needed to bring his A-game for sure.

No. It's okay. Go back to the estate. We'll catch up in the am.

Roger that.

"Sorry about that," he said as he put the car in gear. "Ready to go dancing?"

She responded with a slow, sexy smile. "I'm ready to see what moves you've got on the dance floor."

If she kept looking at him like that, he was going to have a hard time on the dance floor, for damn sure. "You want to put your money where your mouth is?"

"What do you mean?"

He deepened his voice. "Well, if I perform beyond your expectations, I get something." He wanted her to play. He might be able to get her to admit something if he posed it as a game. Something told him she wouldn't be interested if it wasn't a challenge.

She narrowed her eyes at him. "Something like what?"

"I don't know yet, but nothing you won't want to give."

"There's that modesty again." She laughed. "What if you disappoint me?"

He chuckled. "That would never happen. But if, for the sake of argument, you're less than impressed, then you get something." He glanced at her and flashed her his megawatt smile. "What do you say? Want to live dangerously?"

She reached over and put her hand on his thigh. "It's a bet."

The simple contact of her warm hand on his pant leg sent shock waves through his system. If she moved it any higher, they were going to have a serious problem. A moment later, she took it back, and he felt an immediate sense of loss.

He passed the valet stand and pulled into the parking lot. He hated anyone else driving his vehicle. It meant they had access, and access led to trouble. He came around to her side and held the door for her, offering her a hand out.

"You are such a gentleman. Your mother would be so proud," she said as she let him help her out of the car

"She would be if she were alive."

She turned to him and put her hand on his chest. "Oh, my God, I'm so sorry. I wasn't thinking."

He put his hand over hers. "It's okay. You didn't know." He smiled at her, then took her hand in his and walked toward the club. The long line was filled with beautiful, young people standing behind a red velvet rope, waiting to get into the hottest club in the Hamptons.

They bypassed the line, walked right to the door, and stopped in front of a colossus of a man. The bouncer took one look at Mitch, and his stone-cold face broke into a radiant smile. "My man. It's good to see you. Where you been keeping yourself?"

"Been busy, Tank. How are things with you? How's Tanya and the baby?"

"Tanya's doing great, and my little angel is growing by

the day. Unbelievable, man. You need to get yourself one. Kids change everything," Tank said as he shook his head.

Mitch laughed. "Someday maybe. Tank, this is Carrie. Carrie, Tank."

"Nice to meet you, Tank," she said and offered her hand.

Tank's hand completely engulfed hers. "The pleasure is mine, beautiful lady. You two have a wonderful time tonight." He let go of her hand and moved the velvet rope aside. Tank ushered Carrie in and then bumped Mitch with his shoulder to keep him outside for a minute. "She's one hot babe. You take good care of her in there. It's the beginning of summer, and all the crazies are out tonight. Be on your toes."

He glanced up at Tank and saw the man was serious. After serving together, they implicitly trusted each other. "Roger that, Tank. Thanks for the heads up."

Tank nodded and let him go. Mitch put his arm around Carrie's waist, whose real name he still didn't know, and walked into the club. Apparently, he would need to be on his guard tonight in more ways than one.

CHAPTER SIXTEEN

A lex loved the fact that she had just walked into the hottest club in the Hamptons with the sexiest man around without having to rely on her family name. As an underage teen, she just had to show up at a club, and they'd let her in. She was after all a Buchanan of the California Buchanans, great, great, granddaughter of Andrew Buchanan, who had made a fortune in oil and railroads along with Rockefeller and Carnegie. She'd taken great pains to step away from that life, and now no one even recognized her. She was thankful that social media hadn't been as prevalent when she was in her obnoxious teen years.

Mitch hadn't noticed, but he'd garnered a lot of attention from the line outside. More than one female head had swiveled in his direction. And she didn't blame them one bit. He looked amazing in his dark jeans and a crisp white shirt that showed off his tan. He'd left his blazer in the car and had rolled up the sleeves of his shirt to reveal his well-muscled forearms. Tonight, she had the hottest arm candy in the club, and she planned to enjoy every minute of it.

Mitch took her hand and led the way through the crowd to the bar. The bass vibrated in her ribs. Strobe lights went off for a few seconds, and then colored lights came back, swirling over the crowd. The smell of alcohol, sweat, and she would swear, raging hormones, had her wound up already. Just thinking about those strong arms touching her, holding her, made her lady parts clench. She remembered what he looked like after his swim the other day, all wet muscles rippling in the sunlight.

There was no denying she wanted him, but the job had to come first. If she let things go too far, he would find out some of her secrets. Too bad she couldn't just tell him what she was after, but from everything she'd managed to dig up about him with Leo's help, he didn't strike her as the type to throw away his reputation for a bit of fun. It was too bad—the sex would have been amazing. She was sure of it.

They reached the bar, and he pulled her up beside him. "Vodka?" he asked. When his breath grazed her ear, an involuntary shiver shot down her back. She nodded. He turned, waved the bartender over, and ordered two shots. When she looked up at him questioningly, he shrugged. "I figured you wouldn't want to stand here and yell at each other over the music. We'll have a drink and hit the dance floor. You can show me your moves…and I can show you mine."

"I like the sound of that." She was aware that somehow in the last minute he had run his hand up her back. It was now resting behind her neck. When he spoke to her, she could feel his breath on her ear. It was very sexy. She was finding it hard to concentrate. *Down girl. This is work*, she reminded herself, but a grin lit up her face for a second, nonetheless. God, some days she just loved her job.

She let out a deep breath and bit her lip. *Focus. Get in the game*. She ran through her plan again. Flirt a little, dance a little, and then take him to a quiet corner and chat a little. Ask questions to see what he was willing to reveal. Most importantly, get an invite to the party.

Their shots arrived, and he handed her one. She immediately felt the absence of his hand on her neck.

"Bottom's up," he said with a wink and then tossed back the shot.

She did the same and gave herself a moment to enjoy the exquisite burn that always accompanied a shot of vodka. It immediately pooled in her stomach, sending rays of warmth through her body. She grabbed his hand and led him to the dance floor. Once they reached the middle, she turned to face him. "Let's see whatcha got," she said and gave him her best sexy smile.

It might have been the vodka or the pounding beat or even a trick of the lights, but she could have sworn she saw a look of raw lust cross his face. More animal than human if that was possible. It was gone in an instant, but she had felt it in her core, as surely as she was standing there. And then he started to move.

She realized in an instant that he was right. He was much better than she had expected. As she started to move to the driving beat, he matched her motion for motion. It was almost obscene the way his body found hers at every turn. Even though the dance floor was full, he managed to move her around, making sure their bodies met exactly as he wanted them to, but never once touching her to do it. There was no doubt he was in charge and leading the dance. She was just along for the ride, and she was enjoying every minute of it.

One song led to the next, and she lost track of how long they were out there. She didn't notice the crowd or the noise, just the beat and Mitch and his body moving with hers.

After a while, the music changed and slowed, and Mitch immediately brought her in close. She was going to protest, tell him that she was sweaty and out of breath, but the words died on her lips when he put his hand behind her neck and brought his lips down to hover just over hers. She could feel his breath on her lips. She looked into his eyes. Neither of them said anything, but he silently communicated that he was waiting for her to close the distance, to say it was okay.

She wanted to kiss him. She wanted to do a whole lot more than that, but for the first time in a long while, fear spiked through her, making her heart crash against her ribs. She'd kissed marks in the past when it was necessary, but this was different. She'd never actually wanted to kiss one. Maybe she was in over her head.

Never.

She immediately shut that thought down and closed the gap.

The instant their lips touched, someone slammed into her back and sent her staggering off to the side. Mitch grabbed her by the arm to steady her. "Are you okay?"

She nodded, too startled to speak. Mitch turned to see who had hit her. These were the same guys from the end of the bar at the hotel, the ones who'd catcalled at her on the way in. They were totally trashed now and belligerent by the look of things. There was no telling which of them had shoved her.

She tugged on Mitch's hand. "Let's just go," she said above the noise. "It's not worth getting into a thing."

He looked at the men who were flailing around, too drunk to dance, and then nodded. They'd just turned to leave, hand in hand, when a voice roared, "Look, it's the hot babe from the hotel." A guy stumbled past Mitch, weaving as he moved.

Alex tugged at Mitch, but the guy lurched in her direction. He started making lewd gestures and trying to rub his body against hers.

"Get off me," she snarled. She grabbed Mitch's arm. "Go before I hurt this asshole." "

Mitch immediately grabbed the guy's arm. "You don't want to do that, buddy."

"Why the fuck not?" the guy yelled. "Have you seen her? She's smokin', and that dress…" His words came out in a slur. "Man, she's beggin' for it in that dress."

Mitch acted before she did. Grabbing the guy's arm, he twisted him around so he fell down to his knees on the dance floor. His mouth started opening and closing like a fish. His eyes were bulging out of his face.

The crowd moved back. His friends were all standing there, mouths open in shock. Alex glanced around, noticing several bouncers were on the way. "Mitch, let him go. It's over." As much as she wanted to pound the guy into next week, she didn't need any trouble. She touched Mitch's shoulder.

Mitch leaned down and said something into the guy's ear that was impossible for her to hear. The guy's face twisted in pain and then his body heaved. Great. The last thing she wanted was this guy's puke on her shoes. The bouncers were fighting their way through the crowd. Damn. This could get ugly enough for the police to get involved. She wasn't sticking around for that. "Mitch, we have to leave. Now."

Mitch straightened up and then let the drunk guy's arm go. The man instantly face-planted on the floor.

She grabbed Mitch's arm, and he led her farther into the club, away from the drunk guy and the bouncers. Why weren't they leaving? She tugged on her arm to get Mitch's attention, but he held it firmly. He led them down a hallway and past the restrooms to a fire door. Before she could tell him to not, under any circumstances, open the door, he pressed the bar to do just that. No alarm sounded. The cool night air hit her face, and she took a deep, relieved breath.

Mitch brought her down the alley. There was a light above the door behind them but none at the end of the alleyway. The clouds were blocking the moon. He looked around and then leaned her against the wall of the building. He asked, "Are you all right?"

She nodded. "Yes, fine."

He ran his thumb gently over her lips, his eyes following the movement. "Are you sure he didn't hurt you? It was a pretty hard knock."

She found it hard to breathe, and her lips tingled where he touched them. "Yes." Her voice was breathy to her own ears. She cleared her throat. "Thanks for taking care of that, but I could have handled it myself."

He nodded. "I don't doubt it, but what kind of gentleman would I be if I made you do that on our first date? The second or third date, all bets are off. You can even take care of me." He offered her a sexy smile, and she smiled in return.

"I'll remember that…assuming we have a second or third date."

His eyes turned a smoky gray in the ambient light. "We will."

"You're awfully sure of yourself."

The smiled stayed on his lips. "I know you were having fun in there. Your body responded to every move I made. Are you telling me you don't want to go out with me again?" He moved his hands to bracket either side of her head and then leaned in. His lips were so close to hers she could feel his breath on her cheek again.

"I was dancing. I like to dance. Don't confuse that with liking you. The jury's still out on that one."

A laugh rumbled out of his chest. "I see. What can I do to get a favorable verdict?"

Heat was spreading up from her core. She licked her lips, and his eyes darkened as they followed her tongue, melting any resistance she had left. She brought her hands up around his neck as he slanted his mouth over hers.

His lips were demanding. He kissed her and then kissed her again, nipping her bottom lip with his teeth. She parted her lips and his tongue swept in to dance with hers. Heat slammed her in waves. She shifted her weight, bringing her hips against his and then fisted her hands in his hair to hold him closer. She needed to feel the length of him against her.

The dancing had been enough foreplay. She was already wet. She wanted him inside of her, and she wanted it now.

He slid his hands down to her ass and pulled her hips hard against his. He moved her over his hard-on, making her groan as he deepened the kiss. Her breath was starting to come in little pants as he kept up the delicious rhythm with his hands. She was going to explode. She started to lift one leg to hook it around his hip so she could get better access, but he abruptly stopped kissing her and whirled around.

"Wha—?" She fell into his back, but he didn't move a bit. It was like hitting a wall.

"Are we going to have a problem?" Mitch's voice rumbled out of his chest. She peeked over his shoulder and saw the drunk guy from the club and a half-dozen of his friends. Shit. She'd been so wrapped up in Mitch, she hadn't even heard them come through the fire door.

"You owe my man here an apology. You hurt his arm and his shoulder." The largest guy on Mitch's right came forward a step. "You need to make it right."

"I think you must be mistaken. If anything, your friend here owes my friend an apology, but she's willing to let it slide, so why don't you all just fuck off?" Mitch said in a calm voice, but Alex could feel the shift in his body. He was getting ready to fight, and these guys were at the stage where they were mean drunks. This could go bad, and fast. She needed to figure a way out of this mess. The odds weren't so good, no matter how drunk these men were, and she didn't want to end up in the hospital or jail.

"Gentleman, why don't we just call it a night, huh? No harm done," Alex said as calmly as she could.

"No can do. Your boy here insulted my friend. All he was doin' was admiring your smokin' hot body. If you didn't want the attention, you shouldn't have dressed that way. That dress and those shoes just scream that you want some of this." He gestured to his dick.

Alex bristled and started to move out from behind Mitch. She wasn't about to put up with this type of shit from any man. "Listen here, asshole," she started, but that was as far as she got. Mitch stepped forward and punched the guy in the face. It was a hard hit. The man just stood there stunned, and then he slowly crumpled to the ground. He was out cold.

"Anyone else want to try your luck?" Mitch snarled.

"Please give it a go. I haven't had a good fight in ages." Tank spoke up from the corner of the building. Alex hadn't seen him until then, and neither had any of the drunk guys, but it was clear from Mitch's stance that he must have known. Jesus, did this guy have some kind of super hearing? How else had he sensed Tank's presence?

"Uh, we'll just go." The guy that was farthest away put his hands up in a no-harm, no-foul gesture and started walking carefully back down the alley. Two of his friends reached for their fallen friend who had started to groan.

Mitch gave them all a hard look and then grabbed Alex's arm and started around the corner. He and Tank exchanged a nod, but Mitch kept going with her in tow.

"Thanks, Tank," she called over her shoulder.

"My pleasure, ma'am," came the reply.

They were moving quickly across the parking lot to Mitch's car. "Hey, slow down. I can't move that fast in these heels. No need to run. Tank has everything under control back there." She tried to tug free, but he wasn't letting go. "Mitch, let go of my arm."

"No."

She frowned. "What? Did you just refuse to let go of my arm?"

"Yes."

Alex twisted her body in toward Mitch's arm, and after raising her other arm high, slammed into Mitch's elbow. His hand immediately dropped from her arm, and she moved out of reach. "What the hell is your problem?" she demanded.

"My problem?" he barked as he rubbed his arm, "I could ask you the same question. What possessed you to open your mouth and engage with those assholes?"

"Excuse me? Engage with those...? Listen, I've been taking care of myself for a long time. I don't need you to tell me what I can or can't do. That guy was a total asshat, and I wasn't going to put up with it."

"I had the situation under control until you opened your mouth."

"Are you for real? Until I opened my mouth?" She was practically screaming at him now, but she couldn't bring herself to care.

Mitch grabbed her by the shoulders.

"What the fuck?" She moved to break his hold, but he let go and held up his hands.

Speaking through clenched teeth, he said, "You could have been seriously hurt back there. Those men weren't just out to get me, they were there for you, too. You almost stepped out where they could reach you. I had no choice but to hit the guy. If any of those guys had balls, we'd be in one hell of a fight right now. You're lucky that guy dropped like a stone and Tank showed up. It could have easily gone the other way."

"Are you finished?" She moved closer, so they were practically nose-to-nose. "I have been fighting my own battles since long before you hit the scene. I don't need you to do it for me. So back. The. Fuck. Off." With that, she turned on her heel and started back toward the club.

Mitch cursed. "Where are you going?"

"I'm calling a cab. No way in hell am I going anywhere with you!" She walked back to the ropes and arrived at the same time as Tank. "Tank, what's the number for a cab company?"

He looked over her head and then back at her but said nothing.

"What?" she demanded. She whirled around to find Mitch was two steps behind her. The sight of him made her want to scream in frustration. "Fine. I'll look it up myself." She whipped out her cell phone and started typing frantically.

"A cab at this time of night will take forever." Mitch's voice was calm, but she could feel the anger coming off him in waves.

She ignored him and kept looking at her phone. "I'll use Uber."

Tank sighed. "Ma'am, listen to your man. He's right. It will take too long to get out of here that way. Just let him drive you home. I won't be able to relax if I don't know you got home safe."

She whipped her head up, ready to snarl at Tank— what the fuck did he care?—but she stopped when she saw the look on his face. He was serious. His worry took all the fight out of her. The fact that the heavens opened just then didn't hurt either. She did not want to wait in the pouring rain for an Uber.

"Fine." She stalked back to Mitch's car. He easily kept up with her and had the door open by the time she arrived. The drive back to the hotel was an uncomfortably silent one. As soon as Mitch pulled up to the door of the hotel, she hopped out without a backward glance. She walked in the doors, through the lobby, and over to the waiting elevator. She got in and hit the button for her floor hard enough to break it.

She got off on the sixth floor and took out the key for the room she'd booked for the night. She'd told herself it was so Mitch couldn't have one of his cronies follow her, and that was partially true…but if she were being honest, there was another reason. This was her "just in case" room, i.e. just in case she and Mitch decided to sleep together.

She opened the door to her room and immediately went over and flopped onto her bed. Exhaustion overwhelmed her. She'd just blown it. Big time. Now how was she going to get into the party? "Shit." She sat up, took off her shoes, and then stalked over and got a T-shirt out of her bag.

Time to regroup and come up with another plan.

Maybe Leo was right. Maybe she should wait until Drake left for Europe or wherever and get the car then. She caught a glimpse of herself in the mirror. She looked like a drowned rat, sad and deflated. No one had ever beaten her at this game. No one. Not even the Swedish police. She straightened her spine. The hell with Mitch Callahan. She would figure out another way into the party, and she'd kill this job. She was Alexandra Buchanan, and she did *not* fail.

CHAPTER SEVENTEEN

M itch swore as he rolled over for the thousandth time. Damn that woman. She had him all tied up in knots, and not in a good way. He needed to purge her from his brain if he was ever going to get any sleep. He could still feel her ass in his hands, her body nestled perfectly against his. If those men had come out a couple of minutes later, they would have found Mitch screwing his thief against the wall in that alley, because there wasn't a doubt in his mind that's where they'd been heading.

Instead, he was here by himself, tossing and turning with the worst case of blue balls he'd ever had the poor luck to experience. How was he ever going to find out what she was up to now? What the hell was he going to tell Drake?

If only he'd reined in his temper, but the thought of that guy touching her, even getting near her, had him seeing red. He'd damn near had a heart attack when she stepped out from behind him. Didn't she know those men had intended to rape her? His stomach lurched at the thought. She could have been seriously injured or killed.

He mulled over her reaction to the situation. Obviously, she was used to taking care of herself, but she was extreme about it. Most women could take care of themselves to some degree. Lord knew, they pretty much had to with all the entitled assholes out there, but no one had ever rejected his help so forcefully. Did she really think she could have taken out six men? He grimaced as he flexed his arm. The move she'd done on him was good, but still, it was just one move. Six men was a whole other ballgame.

It didn't make sense. None of what happened made sense. He'd completely lost control of the situation way before those men had confronted them in the alley. Somehow, he had to fix things. To decipher her plan, foil it, and protect Drake. No way could he fuck this up any more than he already had. He wasn't going to let everyone down. He had to get it together. Focus.

HE WOKE WITH A START. His phone was vibrating on the bedside table. He glanced at his watch—6:05—and let out a groan as he reached for his phone. "Callahan."

His brother Gage's voice came down the phone line. "Hey, bro. You sound like you're still in bed. Did you miss your alarm?"

He rolled over onto his back and groaned. "I didn't get much shut-eye last night. What's up?"

Gage laughed. "I hope it was for a good reason."

"Not so much," Mitch mumbled.

"What? Are you losing your mojo with the ladies? Women everywhere will weep."

"What do you want, Gage?"

"Breakfast," was the prompt reply.

"What?" Mitch went still.

"I'm in town at something called The Sunshine Diner.

You got twenty minutes before I start without you."

Mitch hopped up off his bed and strode toward his bathroom. "Order me coffee. I'll be there in ten," he growled and then hung up the phone. He dropped it on the counter and turned on the shower. Stepping right into the icy spray, he swore. His body recoiled, but he forced himself to stay under. During his SEAL days, it was always cold water and three-minute showers. Maybe this would help him get his head back in the game. After last night's mess, he needed all the help he could get.

He got out, toweled himself dry, and then got dressed in his work uniform of a black T-shirt and black cargo pants. He sat down on the bed, pulled on his boots, and then went back to the bathroom to finish getting ready. On his way out of the house, he sent a text to Jake to make sure he was up and on it. Then he headed to his car.

Finally, he had an interesting enough mystery to temporarily shift his thoughts from his thief. If his brother had driven all the way out here from New York, something was up. He frowned. The last thing he needed was more trouble. He had screwed everything up last night, and the whole Tolliver issue was still hanging over his head. He needed a win.

He pulled his car into one of the slanted spaces in front of the diner. Other than the occasional dog walker or jogger, it was way too early for most people to be up in the Hamptons. He strolled into the diner and immediately spotted his brother. Gage stood up, and they clasped hands and bumped shoulders. His brother looked good despite whatever ungodly hour he must have risen to be here this early. He was wearing his hair long again, and it flopped over his forehead.

"Mom would be yelling at you about your hair, you know."

"It's nice to see you too, bro." Gage shook his head as they sat down. Two full coffee mugs were already waiting on the table.

"Thanks for the coffee." Mitch took a sip of the black gold in his cup and immediately felt the jolt his system craved.

Gage smiled. "Feel better?"

Mitch nodded and took a quick scan of the menu.

"Good. And yeah, you're right about the hair. Mom would hate it, but after all those years in the navy, I like wearing it long again."

"I know what you mean." He rubbed his jaw and felt the morning stubble scratch his palm. Even though he'd had a bit of leeway in the SEALs, he'd always been clean-shaven. After leaving the military, Mitch had grown a big, bushy beard. He'd enjoyed the novelty for a while, but the itchiness had compelled him to shave it off.

The waitress came by. "Ready to order?" she asked as she plucked the chewed pencil from behind her ear and licked the tip. At their nods of assent, she asked, "What can I get you?"

Gage said, "I'll have the Iron Man with wheat toast."

"I'll have the same," Mitch said, "and more coffee when you get the chance."

Her brassy blond curls shook as she wrote down their orders. "Be right over," she said as she grabbed their menus and walked off, her white orthotic shoes squeaking the whole way.

"So, what's up? I assume you didn't drive all the way out here just to see my ugly mug."

Gage smiled again. "You're right. Your mug is ugly, but"—his expression turned serious—"it's damn good to see it." He opened his mouth to say more and then stopped.

Mitch nodded. "Same." They were both thinking the same thing. His last mission with the SEALs had been a close call, and he had the scars to prove it. He was beyond thankful to be sitting here with his brother. It had been about two months since they last saw each other, but somehow it felt much longer.

Gage smiled and held his mug out as the waitress came by with the coffee pot. He waited until she left before saying in a quiet voice, "You don't look so good. Everything okay?"

Mitch shrugged. "Things are more complicated than I thought with this job."

Gage nodded. "You're not sleeping."

"Well, I was until last night. Stayed out too late, and then I had a hard time shutting down my head."

"What did you do last night?" Gage asked as he played with the sugar packets in the middle of the table.

"Went dancing."

Gage threw his head back and laughed. "You went dancing last night? I have no sympathy then. Serves you right for showing off for the ladies."

Mitch grinned. "I suppose it does, but it was a work-related matter."

"Sure, it was. Uh huh. I believe you." He shook his head. "Well, was it worth it? Did you at least get somewhere?"

Mitch's brain flicked to the memory of his mouth on hers and her breasts pressed against his chest. His smile was slow. "Yeah, it was worth it." He took another sip of coffee. "So, what brings you out here?"

Just then, the waitress came over with their food. The platters were huge. Mitch looked down at his. "Think we got enough food?"

Gage, who already had a forkful on the way to his

mouth, just grunted out, "I'm hungry," and proceeded to eat at a rapid rate. Mitch wasn't too far behind him. The sausages were fantastic, and he had forgotten what pancakes tasted like. His usual breakfast of coffee and an egg or two paled in comparison to this feast.

Ten minutes later, with his stomach stuffed beyond capacity, Mitch said, "You started to tell me why you're here." He caught the waitress's eye and pointed to his cup. She promptly arrived with hot coffee and took their empty plates.

Gage leaned back and took a swig of his coffee. "That woman you asked about, the thief. I think I might have a name for you."

Mitch froze. A name for his thief. He wanted to know, or at least he thought he did, but now his heart was hammering in his chest.

"Uh how'd you find that out?" he asked, stalling for time. What if his brother told him something he didn't want to hear? Like she was married or had five kids or... she'd actually hurt someone during one of her jobs. He slammed that thought down. It didn't matter. This was business, and he needed to know as much about her as possible.

"I know a guy who knows one of the people from the list of robberies you tied together. There were some prominent names on the list. Anyway, he said that it took some digging, but he was told one of her victims had managed to discover her name is Alex. I don't have a last name.

"When I ran that name up the flag pole, I got a hit with another friend, a guy who deals in...well, let's just say he's a guy who has a lot of interesting friends."

"Does he count you among them?" At Gage's puzzled look, Mitch clarified. "Are you one of his "interesting" friends?"

Gage grinned. "You know it."

Mitch laughed.

Gage continued. "He asked around, and apparently your girl is American and from out west, but beyond that, no one knows. He can't even swear she's the one you're looking for. There's no proof, but there are plenty of rumors, and he's pretty sure there is some truth to them."

He could feel Gage's eyes on him as he raised his coffee mug.

"Do you know anything more about her?" his brother asked.

"No."

Gage's eyes narrowed. "It's her, isn't it?" he pressed.

"What?" Mitch frowned, feigning a lack of under-standing.

"It's her that you went dancing with last night. She's the one you screwed up your sleep over."

"I, uh, it's complicated." Mitch picked up the discarded sugar packets and started fiddling with them.

"What are you not telling me? What exactly is going on out here?" Gage leaned across the table. "And I want the truth. You might be able to bluff your way out of all kinds of crazy shit with other people, but I've known you since birth and know when you're lying."

Mitch grunted. He wanted to tell his brother to fuck off. To go back to New Jersey and leave him alone. Fatigue suddenly hit him like a two-by-four. But he had gotten his brothers into this mess, and it was time to be honest. "I went out dancing with her because I was hoping to find out what she was after or, at the very least, figure out if she was a real threat."

"A threat to who?"

"Drake."

"Why would she be a threat to Drake? I thought you

had his security all set up."

"I do, but Drake wasn't entirely honest about his situation."

Gage sat back. "Why don't you fill me in from the beginning?"

Mitch leaned back, too. He stared at his brother for a moment, shrugged, and then told him the whole thing. He admitted to diving in too deep with this job and then explained to him about Tolliver and the software and finally about his thief, Alex. At least he now knew her name.

"So how do you want to play it?" Gage asked.

"What do you mean?"

Gage shrugged. "This is your show. As far as I can tell, you've done an excellent job so far. You've done everything I would have done and more. You tell me what you need to keep going, and I'll do my best to help."

He studied his brother's face. Gage clearly meant every word. A huge weight lifted off Mitch's chest. He took a deep breath and let it out. None of his problems were solved, but he was a thousand times better off now that he knew his brother had his back. Well, one brother at least. "Logan—"

"Logan may be a tight-ass about business, but he'll be there if you need him." At Mitch's doubtful look, Gage said, "Remind me to tell you about Logan's first time in court when he was in JAG." He smiled. "You're not the only one who leaps before you look on occasion. Anyway, tell me what you want me to do. What comes next?"

"I'm not sure. I guess I need to know more about the software, and I should confirm whether Alex is after that or something else." Her name rolled off his tongue. It felt a little too good to know her real name. He tamped down that thought.

"Once I talk to Drake, I'll need some help tracking down Tolliver's interested buyer. Jake has helped me eliminate some people as possibilities, but we're stuck now. We've got no leads on who it could be."

"On it," his brother said as he stood up. "I'm sticking you with the bill since I drove all the way out here, little brother."

Mitch stood up. "Thanks for the information and for coming out." He offered his hand to his brother. Gage brushed it off and wrapped him up in a real bear hug. "I know we saw each other at the office a couple of months ago, but it's damn good to see you, Mitch."

"Likewise." He knew what his brother meant. They'd spent time together setting up the office and discussing the changes they wanted to make in the business, but not much of it was quality time. It was just nice to sit down and eat together. Made him feel like they were kids again.

Gage stepped back, but there was a serious look on his face that told Mitch he wasn't done. "Don't ever hesitate to tell me everything again. Even if I think you're an idiot, I will always have your six."

Mitch's chest got tight, but he managed to nod. "Same here."

Gage nodded and clapped him on the back on his way out the door. Mitch sat back down to catch his breath. Gage's support meant everything to him. Ever since they were kids, Mitch had always felt like the odd man out because his brothers were closer in age. The two of them had been as tight-knit as twins, and he'd always felt the need to prove himself. Gage's support—and his promise that Logan would support him, too—made him feel like a million bucks. Now all he had to do was not let his brother down.

Easier said than done.

CHAPTER EIGHTEEN

A lex swore as the knife slipped and cut her finger. Served her right for screwing up so royally last night. She dropped the knife on the counter next to the apple she had been slicing.

"Stupid!" she yelled as she grabbed a paper towel and wrapped it around her finger. She sighed heavily. It was impossible to concentrate this morning. She had gotten little to no sleep last night, so she'd left the hotel before sunrise and driven around for a while to make sure she wasn't being tailed. Now she just wanted some breakfast and a cup of hot coffee. "Damn."

She grabbed a mug in her other hand and, trying not to use her bleeding finger, poured herself a cup of coffee. After blowing it with Mitch last night, she needed to review her options. She could try Caterina for an in to the party. She'd paid one of the bus boys at the restaurant to give her the scoop. He'd said his boss was a soft touch and really nice. So maybe her plan would work.

She remembered that it was Thursday, though, and the bus boy had said Caterina was going to be at the farmer's market all day and then at a closed event at the restaurant tonight. She could crash it, but it was for proctologists. She'd seen a proctologist convention before, and it wasn't pretty. So, the event was a no, and that didn't leave her with much time to cultivate a friendship.

She sat down on a stool by the counter. There was always another way in. She just had to find it. Normally, she would have a plan B already lined up, but she'd gotten cocky. Now she was paying the price. She took a sip of her coffee and let the needs of the job roll around in her head.

A few minutes later, an idea came to her, and she texted Leo. She needed a bit more info to make it happen, but she was pretty sure it would work. With that plan in play, she took her apple slices, minus the one with blood on it, and the blackberries she'd cleaned and sat on her deck to finish her breakfast.

It was amazing to her how quickly she had come to love this little cottage on the beach. It was beautiful and peaceful here before the crowds showed up. She popped a berry in her mouth as Mrs. Olsen made her way up from the beach. "You're out early this morning," Alex called.

Mrs. Olsen looked up. "Good morning. May I join you?"

"Please do." Alex gestured to the porch swing beside her chair.

Mrs. Olsen smiled. "Ahh, so nice to sit down."

"Can I get you a cup of coffee or glass of water? Would you like to share my fruit?" Alex offered the bowl of apple slices and blackberries.

"I'm good, dear, thank you." She pulled out a small bottle of water from her pocket and took a sip. "Well, you're not usually up this early. What happened?"

Alex blinked. "What do you mean?"

Mrs. Olsen smiled. "Dear, not to be rude, but you look

like you haven't slept at all and not in a good way," she said with a wink.

Alex burst out laughing. "That obvious, huh?"

"Mmm-hmm. The date didn't go well, I take it?"

"Oh, the date part went fine. Better than fine…until the bottom dropped out."

"I see. Well, that's disappointing."

Alex nodded. "You have no idea."

"Did you like him then?"

"Uh"—she licked her lips—"yes I did. I do. But he… he doesn't get it."

Mrs. Olsen frowned. "Doesn't get what, dear?"

Alex heaved a sigh. "I've been on my own for quite a while. I know how to handle myself. He…he stepped in and took care of a situation last night for me." She stopped speaking. How to explain the rest?

"And you didn't like that he took care of you?" Mrs. Olsen took another sip of water.

"It's not that. I appreciate what he did, but he doesn't seem to get that I *could* have handled it myself. He went on to lecture me on how much danger I'd been in, acting like I couldn't figure that out myself."

"Ahh" Mrs. Olsen nodded.

Alex continued. "I understood the situation perfectly, and I could have handled it—differently than he did, but I would've been fine." A flash of guilt hit her. Maybe not fine, but she would have survived. She'd been through worse.

"I don't need a man to handle shi—things for me. I can take care of myself, and I'm good at it. I don't need to be lectured by a guy who barely knows me." She threw another berry into her mouth.

"You didn't like being told you were weak."

"Exactly. Wait"—she frowned—"he didn't say I was

weak. It was more like he doubted my ability to get out of the situation."

"Mmm-hmm. When did he tell you this? Right after it happened?"

"Yes, on the way back to the car."

"And you were having a great time before that?"

Alex nodded.

"Did it ever occur to you that he was scared?"

"Scared? Him? No." She shook her head. "He's former military. He wasn't scared."

Mrs. Olsen sighed, just a little. "No, dear. Not scared for himself, scared for you. Scared that you might get hurt. Any decent man would feel responsible for his date if they found themselves in a dangerous situation. He wanted you to let him deal with it so you wouldn't be hurt. It sounds like he was worried enough to try and warn you off handling situations like that by yourself in the future. As you say, he doesn't know you well enough to know that you can take care of yourself."

Alex cocked her head. He had been so overbearing last night. It had never occurred to her that he'd acted that way out of fear for her. She'd interpreted it as controlling behavior, something she hated. Her father had forced her mother to be dependent on him, and then he'd left. Lesson learned. Alex had taken control of her life as soon as possible, and she'd never looked back.

"I guess...I guess I can see your point. Still, he could have dealt with the situation better."

"Yes, I'm sure he could have, and I'm sure you probably could have been a touch calmer as well."

She glanced over at Mrs. Olsen to see if she was laughing. Her mouth was still, but there was a twinkle in her eye.

"I suppose I did say a few things I might regret. What would you suggest I do?"

"Well, I would call him and apologize. Perhaps invite him to lunch." She paused. "A picnic would be good. I always liked picnics."

"A picnic. I guess it's a possibility. We'll see."

Mrs. Olsen stood up. "Well, good luck, dear, and enjoy the rest of your day."

"Thanks, Mrs. Olsen. You, too," she called as she watched the woman walk up the path to her house.

A picnic. Maybe. But first she had to get his phone number. She smiled for the first time all morning. She glanced at her watch. She'd give it a couple of hours and then call her source. It would give her time to figure out exactly what she wanted to say. Maybe she could still get an invite to Saturday's party and then she wouldn't have to use her new plan B.

CHAPTER NINETEEN

"I get that you want to keep everything shrouded in secrecy, but time is running out, and I might have a lead. I need some answers to help me track down who's after the software." Mitch did his best not to sigh or grind his teeth, but the conversation kept going in circles, and he was tired of it.

"I fail to see why it's necessary for you to track down who's after the software. Isn't it enough to know that someone's after it? Your job is to protect me from any and all harm regardless of where it comes from," Drake stated in a flat voice.

"Yes, it is, but if the person behind it is an agent of a foreign government, that's slightly different than if it's some start-up geek that wants your code. Foreign government agents tend to carry big guns and shoot to kill. Tech geeks hack your bank account—bit of a different ballgame. I think maybe it's time for you to share a bit more information, because if it's a tier one recon team who are coming, I'm going to need a helluva lot more fire power."

Drake stood still for a solid minute and studied Mitch.

Mitch didn't much care. He'd been through SEAL training —he could stand still and stare with the best of them. If this was the game, he was a master.

"Fine," Drake said between clenched teeth. "I will tell you what you want to know, but I want the room swept for bugs first."

Mitch started to point out they'd just swept yesterday, but why argue? It was easier to just do the damn sweep. He took out his phone and texted one of his guys. They showed up two minutes later, equipment in hand. Ten minutes after that, they left and closed the door after them.

"Now, fill me in."

Drake gestured to the chair in front of his desk, and Mitch sat down. "I have a sister."

Mitch didn't know what he'd expected Drake to say, but it wasn't that. "Okay."

"She disappeared almost fifteen years ago, and I have been looking for her ever since." Mitch started to speak, but Drake waved him off. "A while ago, I found a computer programmer who was interested in helping me build a facial recognition software that actually worked.

"It's not like in the movies where they can identify a person who has only the slightest bit of skin showing. As you probably know from your former profession, unless a person's face is caught looking straight at a camera, it's hard to conclusively identify anyone, let alone a person in a crowd. Things like hats, scarves, and facial hair can make it impossible to identify someone."

Mitch shifted slightly in his chair. He knew the government was working on building Artificial Intelligence software that could be used for facial recognition. China already had one that was supposed to be excellent.

Drake continued, "I needed something that could do facial recognition and project what someone would look like fifteen years later. My programmer has been working on it, and the prototype is almost finished."

Mitch sat stunned for a second. "Are you telling me you're sitting on actual facial recognition software that can accurately age a person and pick them out of crowd? How is that possible?"

"Amazing, isn't it? I don't understand the details of how it works just that it does. The program can calculate and extrapolate how a person's face might be altered and create dozens of different outcomes for that person. Then it can take those dozens of new images and look for every single one of them in a crowd in milliseconds. It's not one hundred percent accurate, but it's damn close. Closer than what anyone else has come up with."

"Son of a bitch," Mitch mumbled. "That's why you wanted more security. If news of the prototype got out, it would bring all kinds of dangerous people to your door."

"Yes. I knew it would make me a target. Now you know what Tolliver wants. To be honest, though, I'm not sure how that's going to help you figure out who's pulling Tolliver's strings."

"Yeah, I see the problem. There's not a group on the planet that wouldn't want it. Every small country that can't afford to build its own, all law enforcement agencies, every security firm, not to mention every terrorist cell in the world. This takes things to a whole new level."

Drake frowned. "Yes, it does."

"How did Tolliver find out about the software? Do you have it here? Is that why he was casing the yacht? Or do you think he's after you?"

Drake lifted one shoulder. "I have no idea how he found out about the software or the fact that I have a prototype here. That's what he's after."

Mitch swore long and loud in his head. It might have

been nice to know all this before he agreed to this job. "What about the programmer? Could he have said something to someone? Could he be selling it on the side?" Mitch asked.

"*She* wouldn't do that. She's paid enormously well, and there's no upside to having me chase her down for the rest of her life if she screwed me over."

He had a point there. "Where is your programmer? Is she safe? Are they going after her, too?"

"She's fine. I spoke with her recently and told her to keep an eye out. She's hidden away and perfectly content to stay that way until the project is finished. There's nothing to indicate that they—whoever they are—have found her or that she's in any danger."

"Okay. One problem at a time, I guess. If you'll permit me, I would like to bring my brothers in on this. I think we need to find out how Tolliver came to know about the software. That might help us identify who's hired him."

Drake studied Mitch again, who tried to remain still, but he very much felt like he was on a microscope slide. "Okay, but I want to speak to them about it, and I want all the necessary security precautions in place. I don't want anyone listening in."

"Of course. I'll set up the call. Is this morning convenient?"

Drake glanced at his calendar. "Eleven a.m."

"Very good. I'll have my brothers call at eleven. You can fill them in, and we'll discuss strategy after that."

Drake nodded and went back to his screen. Mitch was clearly dismissed, but he hesitated. "Can I ask, how are you going to use this software to find your sister? You would have to have access to cameras in very busy public places like airports or use a city's infrastructure to scan the crowds. Are you planning on—"

Drake sighed. "I have no need to hack anything or pay anyone off if that's what you are asking. You forget that my main business is hotels. I not only own boutique hotels, but I have interests in some of the largest hotel chains in the world. Everybody stays in hotels at some point or another."

"That's why you got into hotels, isn't it?" Mitch asked, his voice filled with awe.

"Yes." Drake nodded. Now…" He gestured to his screen, and Mitch took the hint. He left the office and started down the hallway. His phone vibrated in his pocket. He took it out and glanced at the screen. Not a number he recognized. His first instinct was to ignore it, but given the current situation, he wanted to be sure he didn't miss anything.

"Callahan."

"Hey," came the breathy voice on the other end.

Mitch stopped dead in the hallway. It had never occurred to him that she'd be the one to reach out. "Carrie?" He'd almost said Alex since that was how he thought of her now.

"Yes. Hi. Um, how are you doing today? All recovered from last night?"

"Ah, yeah sure. You?"

"Tired actually."

There was a bit of a pause. Mitch thought about what he should say. He needed this woman to trust him enough to answer some questions. "So—"

"I—"

They both stopped again. Mitch said, "Please, ladies first."

"Okay. So, I might have overreacted just a tad last night. Not saying you were right or anything, but I could have been nicer about it."

Mitch bit back a grin. "I see. I guess I could have

handled it better as well." *Not really*. He still wanted to tell her to smarten up—it was always best to avoid a conflict you might not win—but he had an agenda.

"So, I was thinking maybe you'd like to get together again. You were right. You're a much better dancer than I anticipated, so I guess I owe you your victory."

This time he let the grin slip into place. "Glad you admitted it. I'd be happy to collect. What did you have in mind?"

"Your modesty overwhelms me, yet again."

He could imagine her rolling her eyes as she said it and couldn't help but chuckle. "Glad I didn't disappoint."

"I was thinking of a picnic. Are you free today to meet me for lunch?"

Mitch did some rapid calculations. He had some calls to make, including the one he needed to set up with his brothers, and another meeting with his security team. After that, he wanted to walk the grounds one more time and double check the yacht security. Even though Drake wasn't living there at the moment, it didn't mean he could relax about it. "I can do a late lunch, say around three."

"That works," Alex said. "Where do you want to meet? I don't have a parking permit for any of the beaches, but I think there are a couple that don't require them. Do you have a parking permit for any of them?"

"No, but why don't we meet on the yacht? I have to go there anyway. Do you remember it? It's by your hotel."

"OK, how about at three? I'll bring the food. See you lat—"

"Not so fast," Mitch said. "I agreed to the picnic, but that's not the prize. The prize is you have to answer all of my questions. Truthfully."

Silence echoed down the phone line.

"Well? A bet is a bet. Are you welching on the deal?"

"That's too broad. Questions about what? What if it's too personal or it's just simply none of your business? Nope. Picnic is off."

"Ten. You have to answer ten questions, and I won't make them too personal."

"Three," she said, "I'll answer three questions. If they're too personal or none of your business, I can pass and you can ask another one."

"Deal. See you at three." Mitch rang off and started down the hallway again. He couldn't help but smile. He had a few questions for his little thief, and she was going to answer them come hell or high water.

The morning dragged on as he went over the security for the estate again and again. He wanted to make sure all his men had the protocols drilled into their heads. There could be no screwups. They only had to get through the next few days, and then Drake and his software would be someone else's problem.

The call with his brothers had gone surprisingly well. It helped that Logan and Drake had people in common. Drake had texted those mutual contacts to run a background check on Logan during the call. The man did not trust anyone, apparently not even those he'd already hired. No doubt he hadn't meant for Mitch to notice, but Mitch could read upside down and backward—a trick learned in childhood.

The boss had received nothing but glowing reports on Logan and Callahan Security. Good to know their company reputation was growing in a positive direction. At least for now.

When he finally headed out to the yacht, he called Logan and Gage on the way and spent the drive talking strategy. They needed to find the leak about the software. The best, most direct way would be to talk to the programmer and discuss who had physical access to her workspace. Drake said they could email this mystery woman, and he gave them her email address. He would instruct her to answer their questions, but she was not allowed to divulge her location, nor were they allowed to ask questions about the software. It seemed extreme, but now that he knew what the prototype was, he could see Drake's point.

Gage wanted to review the security at the lab or wherever the programmer worked. It could be that Tolliver, or whoever, had discovered the existence of the prototype because of some kind of hack.

Drake wouldn't give Mitch or his brother's access to the security for the mystery lab just yet, but at least he'd opened the door by providing the email address. Again, this could be huge for them or it could blow up in their faces. Mitch rolled his shoulders. It felt great to no longer carry the full burden alone.

He pulled into the marina and made his way to the yacht. The captain and the first mate lived on the yacht full-time, and Mitch had installed a state-of-the-art security system on board, but he also had one of his guys buzz by at different times each day.

He still wasn't happy with the setup. He really needed a security detail living here full-time, but it just didn't make sense on the budget Drake had given him. Drake didn't think it was necessary, so it wasn't going to happen. Something told him Drake would change his mind on security after all this Tolliver business. He was just starting to realize he was vulnerable.

Mitch climbed on board the yacht. He didn't immediately see anyone, so he worked his way around the yacht until he hit the top deck where he found the captain and the first mate chatting away with his thief.

"Captain Fletcher," Mitch said in clipped tones, "how are things?"

The captain got up off the couch and offered Mitch his hand. They shook. "Things are good. This lovely lady let us keep her company until you arrived." He smiled at Alex. Mitch had the irrational urge to punch him even though the man was sixty, if he was a day. Still, he'd obviously enjoyed his conversation with Alex. He even had a glass of what looked like champagne on the table in front of him.

"Well, now that I'm here, perhaps you can pull up the logs and let me know if anything has been going on. Also, you need to start planning for a long trip."

He and his thief were playing a little game, and it was time for some diversionary tactics. Why not let her think he was accompanying Drake out of town? That they were taking the yacht rather than flying?

The captain frowned. "Where are we going?"

"We'll discuss that later. Right now, I need you to make a list of what's needed for a month-long voyage. Any repairs, replacement of equipment, that kind of thing. I need to know. We'll be leaving soon, so I need everything to happen quick-time."

Fletcher nodded. "Well, Carrie, it looks like I have to go to work. It was an honor to have met you." He bowed over her hand, gave a nod to Mitch, and disappeared below deck with the first mate following at his heels.

Mitch turned to look at Alex. She was wearing a transparent black coverup over a dark green bikini. Her pebbled nipples poked the tiny fabric triangles covering her breasts. *Oh boy*. He still couldn't tell if the hair was real or a wig.

Sleeping with her had to be off the table, but the memory of her body pressed against his from the other night haunted him. She had been turned on, too. He remembered the sound of her breath coming in little pants and how she'd ground her hips into his.

"Where's my champagne?" he asked, his voice a bit rough. Their eyes met, and he knew she could see her effect on him. He cleared his throat.

She smiled slowly as she reached into the old-fashioned picnic basket on the table and brought out the champagne. She filled a glass and handed it over, then stood and raised her own flute. "To second chances."

They clinked glasses and then took a sip. It was cool running down his throat, but it was the only thing that wasn't sky-rocketing in temperature. He couldn't resist. He wrapped his free arm around her waist, bringing her against him. He dipped his head and claimed her mouth for what should have been a quick kiss but ended up being much longer. Finally, a distinct cough brought them up for air.

The first mate stood there, trying very hard to keep a smirk off his face. Mitch scowled at him.

"Mr. Callahan, the captain wanted me to tell you that he is making some calls but, because of the long weekend, it looks like it will be Tuesday before certain things can be done."

"All right, Patrick. Tell the captain to determine what is essential for us to do before heading out and what can wait until we hit the next port."

"Yes, sir." Patrick turned on his heel and disappeared down the stairs.

Mitch took the opportunity to step back from Alex and take a breath. He had lost his head again. He needed to focus on the mission at hand and not be so distracted by how much he wanted her. And he did want her—badly.

She sat back down and appeared greatly unaffected by their encounter. He, on the other hand, was having binding issues with his black cargo pants. He plunked down on the couch beside her but made sure there was a cushion in between. "So, what have you been up to?" he asked as he put his glass down on the side table.

"Research," she said with a smile.

I'll bet. "What are you researching? What exactly do you do? I don't think we've discussed it before." It was ridiculous, but he couldn't keep his hands still. He ached to touch her. He reached for his champagne and took a sip, keeping the glass in his hands this time.

"I'm in asset management."

He choked, trying not to snort the drink out of his nose.

Asset management. She was slick. He coughed again. "Yes. It went down the wrong pipe. So, asset management requires a lot of research, does it?"

"Tons," she responded. "Success is in the details." She smiled.

He tried not to laugh again. She was so damn clever. Too bad she wasn't on his team. He could use her fresh perspective on things.

"So, what did you bring for lunch? I'm starving."

She stood, pulled a blanket out of the basket, and proceeded to spread it out on the deck. "It's not a picnic unless you have a blanket." She knelt down and started unloading the rest of the hamper. "I have cheese and crackers, carrots and hummus, egg salad, a baguette, and some berries and grapes with whipped cream for dessert."

"Looks great," he said as he set his champagne glass down next to the blanket. He grabbed a couple of pillows off the couches and threw them down on the blanket.

After he sat down beside her, she handed him a plate and started opening containers.

He put some of everything on his plate. "Is this the part where you fan me and feed me grapes?"

"Ha! No, that's your job," she said as she handed him a bunch of grapes.

"Hmmm. You mean like this?" He pulled a grape from the bunch and put it in front of her lips. She opened her mouth just enough to let the grape slide in. He got hard thinking about what she could do with those lips. Before he could shake the image of her lips closing around his length, she grabbed his hand and gently licked his fingers. He groaned, and she gave a throaty laugh.

"You're killing me." He sat back, admitting defeat.

"So, how's your work going?"

The question brought him back down to earth with a thump. "Fine. The usual."

"Really? It sounded like you were getting out of town in a hurry. Is that always the way things work?" She looked like the picture of innocence.

He shrugged. "Just a precautionary measure." In truth, no one was going anywhere on the yacht, and the captain knew it. He'd called earlier and told the man to just go along with whatever he said. The captain agreed. He was doing a nice job of playing along though, and it looked like his little thief was buying the ruse. He planned to make her job damn near impossible by providing her with as many conflicting clues as possible.

"Is your boss in some kind of trouble?" she asked as she took a cracker from the spread.

"No more than usual. Rich people are always on the move." He reached for his champagne glass. "What about you? Are you getting things all worked out? With your research, I mean?"

"Uh, it's coming along. I think I have a good handle on it, but it's hard to be completely sure."

Don't bet on it. "Yes, most of life is a bit of a gamble."

"I'll drink to that." She clicked glasses with him and then took a sip.

"So, where are you from? I don't think we ever covered the basics." He took another bite of egg salad.

She took a gulp of champagne, and he thought he saw a flare of panic in her eyes. "No, I guess we didn't. Is this one of your three questions?"

"No. Just a general 'get to know you' type question."

She lifted one shoulder. "All over really. I grew up on the west coast, but I went to several different boarding schools, so I moved around a lot."

"Do you have any brothers or sisters?"

"Only child."

"Aunts and uncles, cousins?"

"A few, but only one or two I'm close to."

Mitch stopped eating. "You're not very good at this 'getting to know you' thing. You're supposed to give longer answers. You know, share a bit about yourself."

"Not much to share, really."

He frowned. "I doubt that." This wasn't going so well. He was the one who was supposed to get information, not give it, but maybe if he threw her something, she'd do the same. "So how did you come up with the idea for a picnic? I haven't been on a picnic in years." He smiled. "My mom liked them. I grew up in Brooklyn, but we had a place on the Jersey shore. My mom grew up there. My family would spend a lot of the summer at the beach. My brothers and I would go out and run around like crazy in the morning and then my mom would show up with a blanket and a basket of food in the afternoon. She'd whistle, and we'd all come running.

It's one of my fondest memories of my mom. What about you?"

She popped another grape in her mouth. "A friend suggested the picnic."

He got the distinct impression she did not want to talk about her childhood. "Well, tell her or him thank you for me."

She gave him a quick smile.

He decided to press his luck. "Tell me about your family." When she hesitated, he said, "I told you a story. Now you're supposed to tell me one. That's how this works."

She ate some baguette, probably to buy herself some time, following it up with a gulp of champagne.

Looking out at the water sparkling in the sunshine, she said, "My parents were usually busy with friends and doing charity work. I spent most days with a nanny or a tutor and my uncle. He's the one who taught me about asset management."

"That sounds lonely," Mitch said, picking up on the sadness in her voice. Something told him she was telling him the unvarnished truth.

"It was sometimes. I learned a lot and it's come in handy." She tore off another chunk of baguette.

"I'm sure it does." Did she learn to steal from her uncle? Was it a family affair?

She paused, her eyes flickering with some emotion he couldn't identify. "I was sent off to boarding school. Anyway, my childhood wasn't filled with great memories. I'm glad yours was, though. Those picnics on the beach with your family sound wonderful."

Mitch put his plate down on the blanket and finally gave in to the urge to touch her. He reached over and stroked her face with his thumb. "I'm so sorry you were lonely and sad." He leaned in and kissed her forehead while he continued to run his thumb along her jaw. "We'll just have to make up for it now. More picnics and days at the beach."

She smiled at him. "I'd like that."

He slowly lowered his mouth over hers. She immediately opened her lips and let his tongue slide into her mouth. He tried to deepen the kiss, but she pulled back.

"I don't have any great stories of my youth, but I'd love to hear more of yours."

He smiled. "Why is it I don't believe you? I am sure you have lots of interesting stories to tell."

She laughed. "No, not really." At his disbelieving look, she said, "What can I tell you? I'm boring."

"I highly doubt that." He watched her eat a grape, and his thoughts instantly went back to sex.

"I think you'd be surprised."

"Maybe."

She looked up at him and must have seen the desire in his eyes. She stopped chewing suddenly. Then she swallowed, hard.

"I thought you were hungry," she said, pointing to his plate.

"I am, but not necessarily for food." A small smile played at the corner of his lips. He reached over and swiped a finger through the whipped cream. Then he brought it to her lips, but when she opened her mouth, he pulled it back. The second she closed her mouth again, he brushed his finger against her lips. She stuck her tongue out and licked it off. He did it again, but this time he used his own tongue to clean them off. Then he dipped his finger in the cream again, ran it along her jaw and down her neck, and started kissing her along the trail he'd created. Little kisses, nipping, licking here and there. When he kissed the hollow of her neck, she let out a small groan.

He stopped and pulled back. "I—" Whatever he'd been about to say completely left his head when she grabbed his hand and licked the last trace of whipped cream off his finger. He watched her, fascinated by the way her tongue moved.

"I thought you might need some help getting rid of the stickiness," she said. Her voice was deep and throaty. It was the sexiest thing he had ever heard.

"There are a few other things I might need help with as well…"

She chuckled. "Really, like what?"

He opened his mouth and shut it again. He was all for flirting, but this was getting hotter than he had anticipated.

"I don't know about you, but I think I need to work on my tan a bit." She shifted her position and then untied her coverup. It fell to her waist. She watched him as he ran his eyes over the length of her.

The dark green string bikini barely covered her breasts. He saw the twinkle in her eye. Oh, game on. "You know, that sounds like a good idea." He pulled off his shirt and lay back on the pillow.

"You've got something on your chest."

"Really?" He sat up. "Where?"

"There," she said as she hit him in the chest with a blackberry.

He caught it on the rebound and popped it in his mouth. "Be careful, I'm a crack shot."

"Yeah? Me, too." She grinned.

"Really? Who taught you?"

Her answer was to throw another blackberry grenade. His eyes narrowed. "I'm warning you. Keep going, and it's not going to be pretty."

"Oh, yeah? What are you going to do about it?" she

taunted as she raised her hand to throw a grape. He grabbed her hand, and she squealed when he pulled her across the blanket to him. Holding the back of her neck with his other hand, he slanted his mouth across hers and kissed her deeply. He felt her hands explore the ridges of his torso, run across his chest, and then link behind his head.

He deepened the kiss as he tried to pull her even closer. It was an awkward angle, but he needed to feel her body against his. She pulled back from the kiss and then, without warning, straddled his lap.

"Are you sure?" he managed to croak out.

She smiled. "I got in your lap, remember?" She fisted her hands in his hair and kissed him fiercely as she lowered herself directly on top of his crotch.

He groaned. He could feel her heat through his pants. She started to move her hips, but he stilled them. Jake was right about one thing—the past few months had indisputably been a dry spell. If she kept moving against him like that, he was going to come in seconds. "Here's the deal. You can't move unless I tell you to, and if you do, I'll stop what I'm doing." Her eyes narrowed. Her weight shifted off him. He was losing her. He blurted out, "Unless you don't think you can control yourself..."

"Challenge accepted," she murmured as she sat back down, pressing her hot center into his hard-on.

Her eyes were brilliant green, and he watched them darken as he rubbed his thumb across her breasts. Her nipples puckered through the material of the bikini top. So he rubbed them again and again, not stopping until she moaned. He finally moved the piece of material aside and sucked on her nipple. Her moan was louder this time. With his other hand, he pushed the other triangle of material out of the way and cupped her breast. He went back and forth between the two, sucking and fondling each nipple until she started to move again.

"No moving," he growled.

"I want to touch you," she whispered.

"You can touch my chest or my back but nothing else." She frowned at him, but when he ran his fingers over her breast again, her eyes closed and her head arched back, her hands gripping his shoulders.

He moved his hands up and down her thighs while he continued to suck her nipple. He could feel her breathing getting faster. He pulled her up slightly, just enough to give his fingers access to her clit though her bikini bottoms. Her body jerked in response, and she bit her lip. As he continued his torment, she fisted her fingers in his hair and thrust her nipple deeper into his mouth.

He pushed the material of her bikini bottoms aside and put one finger inside her. She moaned. He moved it in and out in a slow rhythm while he started rubbing small circles on her clit. The sight of her reacting to him—head thrown back, teeth biting her lip, hips moving—made him hard as a rock.

He put another finger inside her and started to speed up the rhythm. Her hips moved faster in response. She was riding his hand now, grinding her hips into him with total abandon. He marveled at the fact she was naked where anyone could see her and still she didn't stop, didn't care. It was the hottest thing he had ever seen.

He caught one of her nipples in his mouth again and sucked hard, increasing the tempo of his fingers and his thumb at the same time. Her breath came in little pants and her hips were bucking wildly against him. She cried out when she came. Her core squeezed his fingers, her fingers dug into his shoulders, and then she slumped forward over him.

She opened her eyes and saw Mitch's smoky gray gaze staring back at her. His lips were curled up at the corners. She could feel his hard-on beneath her.

For a moment, everything was pure bliss…and then she suddenly came to her senses. She'd just had the most amazing orgasm of her life while she was half naked on top of a yacht, out where anyone could see her. "Oh, my God." Heat flooded her face. "I'm sorry. I—"

"I'm not. That was the sexiest thing I have ever seen. You're amazing." Mitch tipped his head up to kiss her, but she turned her head away.

"I've never done that before."

He cocked an eyebrow, but his mouth still had that maddening curve to it.

"I meant out in the open like this," she said as she adjusted her bikini top. When she shifted her weight to move off him, she rubbed against his hard-on again. "Oh." Her cheeks got hot. "I didn't realize. I mean I should have…"

"You're fine. I didn't have a condom." He smiled, and his eyes got that smoky look again. "It just means that I'm going to enjoy next time all the more."

"Next time," she breathed out. There couldn't be a next time. What the hell had she been thinking? That was easy—she hadn't been thinking. At least not with her head. This man was sex walking. She couldn't be around him without wanting to screw his brains out. She could still feel his fingers inside her. Bloody hell.

She tried to hop off his lap, but he grabbed her hips. "Hey, why are you in such a hurry all of a sudden? Relax."

"I think it's time I got moving." She tugged, and he let go. She hopped up and adjusted her bikini bottoms. Then she grabbed her cover up and pulled it on.

He frowned at her. "Are you embarrassed?"

"Seriously? Is that even a question?" The heat was back in her face. *Mortified* was a better word. She quickly started gathering up the food and dirty plates. The sooner she got out off the yacht, the better.

"Hey," he called softly. She ignored him and kept cleaning up. "Hey," he said again and grabbed her arm. "Stop." She kept moving, trying to shake off his hand.

"Enough," he insisted. "I have no idea what's going on, but a few minutes ago we were having a great time. You—"

"Stop, please." She put up her hand. The last thing she needed was to hear what he thought of her. She was all about having sex when she wanted it, but she had never done it with such abandon, such disregard for her own safety. She was on a job and she, she…let herself relax. She let herself be normal because he had listened when she spoke. He actually seemed to care what happened to her. It was all so…enticing. Hell, she'd even told him the truth about her childhood. But she wasn't normal. He was the mark, and she was on a job. She had screwed up big-time.

"Listen to me," he said, his voice sharp. "We're consenting adults. There's no shame in us enjoying each other. Maybe you made yourself a little vulnerable, but that's what's supposed to happen during sex."

"Not to me," she said through clenched teeth. "Look, I've got to go." She finally escaped his grip and stood up, turning toward the stairs.

"Alex—"

She froze. She couldn't breathe. Had he said her name? Her real name? She whirled around to face him, and she saw the truth of it written all over his face. He knew who she was. All the conversations they'd had ran through her brain. All the layered meanings. "How long?" she whispered. "How long have you known?"

"I...I knew you were the woman from the balcony in Venice when you came on the yacht the first time. But Alex, I didn't—"

"From the beginning then. You were setting me up from the very beginning." Horror raced through her body as she realized how badly she'd been played. She was an even bigger fool than she could have ever imagined. "Congratulations, well done," she said in a strangled voice and then whirled around and ran down the steps.

She could hear him coming down behind her, calling her name, but she didn't want to hear it. Didn't want to see him. She needed an out and fast. Instead of going down the next set of steps to the wharf, she went to the stern of the yacht and dove into the water. Down, down, down she went. She knew the water was murky so Mitch could no longer see her. She only prayed he didn't jump in after her. She swam for all she was worth across the U shaped berth, saying a silent prayer of thanks to her best friend Lacy for making her join the swim team all those years ago at boarding school.

She surfaced cautiously on the far side of the dock, across the water from Drake's yacht, and watched as Mitch walked along the side of the vessel, scanning the water. She dipped below the surface again, swam under the jetty and came out on the other side. The water was cold, and she was shivering, but the humiliation that burned in her cheeks and her stomach kept her plenty warm.

All this time she'd thought she was the smart one, she was the master manipulator, but no. She was the puppet. Well, no more. She made a solemn vow. She was going to get that car tomorrow and she was going to do it in grand style. Mitch Callahan's reputation would be in tatters by the time she was through with him.

CHAPTER TWENTY

M itch cursed for the hundredth time. "Can someone please go check and see what the hell Dan is doing? I can't reach him on his earbud. He keeps wandering in and out of camera range. He's supposed to stand still and monitor the one blind spot. Why am I seeing him where he isn't supposed to be? We've got an hour 'til the party starts, and he's moving around."

"On it," Jake called to him and walked out of the dining room.

Mitch, finding his office too small to manage the new security monitoring equipment he had installed for the party, had converted the dining room into his command center. It gave him more space to set up extra monitors and more room for his men to congregate while discussing last-minute changes to the security for the day. He'd also brought in a mini fridge full of water and soda as well as a coffee maker and snacks. It was going to be a long day.

He knew deep in his bones that Alex was going to try to steal the prototype at the party. He'd spent a sleepless night trying to figure out how she was going to do it. The look she'd given him when he'd slipped and said her real name would haunt him forever. Horror and then hatred. She thought he had seduced and then humiliated her on purpose. He knew it, and it made him sick to his stomach. He hadn't been able to eat for the last twenty-four hours.

He'd wanted to explain that he'd never met anyone like her before. He was so taken with her he couldn't help himself. He never should have touched her. He hadn't planned on it. It just happened. He couldn't blame her for running. She probably thought he was going to turn her in. Deep in his heart of hearts, though, he wasn't sure if it was panic that had made her run. Or fear? Resentment? Whatever it was, she'd been so desperate to get away from him that she'd risked her own life to do it. He shook his head, as if that would clear the memory of her face from his mind.

"You don't?" one of his team, Gunnar, said.

"Sorry, what Gunnar?"

"I asked if you wanted me to do a final door and window check yet?"

"No. Not yet. I have to talk to Drake, and then we'll do it together."

Gunnar nodded. "Roger that."

Mitch left the makeshift war room and walked down the hall to Drake's office. The door was open, but when Mitch stepped in, his boss wasn't there. Before Mitch could go off in search of his employer, Drake walked into the room.

"Are we set to go?" he asked as he crossed over to his desk.

"Almost."

Drake sat down and pointed to the chair behind Mitch. Mitch sat down and said, "We've arranged everything, so it should go like clockwork. I don't imagine anything will happen until after nightfall."

Drake leaned back in his chair. His hand adjusted the collar of his navy polo shirt. "You're sure it's going to happen today?"

"Yes, she's here. She's moving forward with her plan." Mitch ground his teeth. He wished he could have caught her yesterday. They could have talked. He could have made her see reason. Now she was going to get caught. By him. And there was nothing he could do to mitigate the damage. Drake was out for blood. Mitch's gut churned. He didn't want to hurt her any more than he already had.

Drake narrowed his eyes. "You don't seem pleased by this."

"I just want this to end. Allowing someone to breach my security doesn't make me comfortable."

"I understand your objections, but I think it's the easiest way for me to find out who Tolliver is working for. We catch her in the act and use her to get more information. She's bound to know something. You've assured me time and again that your security setup is second to none, so there shouldn't be a problem."

Mitch bristled. "My security setup *is* second to none when I'm allowed to put all of it online, but you're tying one hand behind my back by allowing her to break in. The system works best when it's keeping people out, not when it's catching people on the inside."

"I'm sure you will make it work." There was no doubt that Drake was threatening him.

"It will work. You can count on it." Mitch stood up. "I'll let you know when we're all set."

Drake nodded, and Mitch turned and walked out of the room. This plan of Drake's was killing him. He'd called his brothers, and they both agreed it was asinine, but the three of them had also concluded there was no way to change Drake's mind.

Gage and Logan were working on tracking down Tolliver's movements. They had boots on the ground trying to find him as well as people trying to find any kind of electronic trail, like credit cards, cell phones, but so far nothing. Mitch was left here working the Alex end. "Shit," he mumbled as he rolled into the war room. Just a couple more days, and Drake would be out of his hair. Tuesday could not come soon enough.

ALEX SCRATCHED HER HEAD. Her curly red-haired wig was the itchiest by far, but it was also the most distracting. People never remembered her face after seeing the mass of curly, orangey red hair.

"Here you go." Tony handed her a set of keys. "Park this one on the side of the drive, in front of the Porsche."

"Sure," she said with a smile. She walked around the Mercedes and slid into the driver's seat. She moved the seat up slightly and then set off to park the vehicle as directed. A yawn escaped her. Her brown contacts were sticking to her eyes a bit, and she was flat-out exhausted. It had taken her all night to work out a new plan and put it into action. She'd been paranoid that if Mitch knew who she was, he also must know her game plans, all of them, so she'd come up with a new one. Luck had more to do with it than she wanted to admit.

She heard Mitch's voice on the walkie-talkie of a security guy walking by. Her cheeks flamed with humiliation at the thought of what happened. She had been so sure, positive in fact, that she'd had everything under control, but her cover had been blown the whole time. Her stomach rolled when an image of Mitch finger fucking her surfaced in her mind. *Focus.* Today was the day, and then she could put this sorry town and that asshole completely behind her.

She jogged back to the valet stand at the front steps of Drake's estate. One of the other valets, Pete, was already driving away in an Audi. Tony stood waiting for the next person to arrive. The quick glance he gave her seemed nervous. "Don't worry," she said with a seductive smile, "you're not going to get in trouble. You just need to help me keep Pete from blocking the garages, and you'll get all of the tips."

He gave her another quick glance and shrugged his shoulders. "Whatever."

Pete came jogging up. "We're running out of space down there. Should we start parking some in front of the garages?"

"Uh, no." Tony shook his head. "What if Drake wants to show off one of his cars or something? Then we'd have to move everything. Better keep them clear."

"Oh, right. That happened at the Mason place last weekend. The jerk son decided he needed to take his Lamborghini to the store even though their Mercedes was clear. It took us ten minutes to move everything. He was screaming at us by the end. I don't want to go through that again."

Alex allowed herself a small smile and silently thanked the jerk son, whoever he was, for making her job easier. More cars pulled up in rapid succession over the next hour and a half. Finally, the slowdown occurred. Guests were inside and having fun. She'd overheard the security guard who was working the door say there were only a couple of guests who hadn't arrived. It would soon be time for her to act.

She would wait until dark since it would be easier to get away in the cover of night. There would be very little moonlight as well. Another plus. She stood and chatted with Tony and Pete for another forty-five minutes until the last two guests arrived. After the second person was checked in, the security guard moved inside. It was just after eleven. Later than she had thought it would be but she gave it a few more minutes before making her move. "Why don't you guys take a break? I'll stay in case anyone else shows up."

Tony looked reluctant. "I don't know."

Pete, on the other hand, seemed desperate. "I gotta take a piss, man. Let's go."

Alex said, "Look, even the security guy went inside. I'll radio you if anyone shows up."

"Come on, man." Pete was practically dancing.

"All right, but call us on the radio if anyone comes." Pete was already moving toward the side door that led to the downstairs kitchen with Tony following more slowly behind him.

Showtime.

"ANYTHING YET?" Mitch asked for the thousandth time.

"We have liftoff." Jake's voice came through Mitch's earbud loud and clear. Mitch's heart started to pound. This was it. The moment of truth. He needed to catch Alex to save his boss, but his gut churned at the thought of doing his job. Catching her would mean jail time in her future. And if he knew her at all, she was not going to go quietly.

He looked over at Drake and gave him a nod. He insisted on being in the room to watch the whole thing unfold, and as much as Mitch hated the idea, he didn't have a choice. "She's changing her position." Drake stood up and came closer to the screens.

"The prototype is in the safe, correct?" Mitch asked.

Drake nodded but didn't take his eyes off the monitors.

"Eyes open, everyone. She's on the move," Mitch said as he watched Alex on the security monitor. He had to hand it to her. If he hadn't been looking for any sign of her, he might have missed it. A last-minute valet substitution. It was smooth.

TONY AND PETE would take a twenty-minute break. Alex knew it would give her more than enough time for her to get the car and get out. She waited until the boys were out of sight and then gave it an extra minute before moving to the side of the stairs and grabbing her backpack. The backpack had been a calculated risk, but—as expected—the guards had only given the clothes and beach towel stuffed inside a cursory look.

She glanced at her watch as she walked over to the garage. She was on the clock now. If the security was as tight as she imagined it would be, someone would have already noticed her. She figured she had about five minutes tops before guards showed up.

The guy watching the video monitors would give her sixty seconds to come back into view. He would then ask the people around him what they thought. Another sixty seconds or so. Then he would call down to the guard in the kitchen and tell him to go check.

The guard in the kitchen would come out and look around. And then he'd head to the garage. Two minutes. He'd move around back and not be able to see anything so there would be another sixty seconds of conversation. Then he would move around front and they would either open a bay door or more likely come around and unlock the side door. Five minutes.

It could be less, but she was counting on everyone

being so hyper that no one wanted to sound the alarm until they were absolutely sure since they'd be drawing security away from other spots if it was a false alarm.

Hugging the side wall of the garage, she made her way quickly toward the back of the garage, which faced the forested part of the yard and not the pool area.

It was a two-story garage with an apartment on top, and there was a small balcony with sliding doors around the back. Leo's research said that the grounds guy lived up there, but he was off that evening and had gone to Queens to visit family like he did every Saturday night.

She waited until her eyes adjusted to the darkness. She combed the area, making sure that she was alone and no one was around to see her. There were security cameras everywhere, but if she stayed against the side wall, they wouldn't pick her up. They were more concerned with people attempting to break in than with lurkers.

When she reached the back corner of the garage, she peeked one eye around the corner. The AC units were against the back of the garage, and rather than expose people to such an unsightly mess, the groundskeeper had planted a hedge of arborvitae around them. The security camera in the back would only see the hedge, not her. Biting her lip, she pulled on her gloves and then slipped around the corner. There was no going back now. Jumping up, she grabbed hold of one of the balcony supports and then wrapped her legs around it, shifting so she was on top of the slanted wooden beam.

Then she jammed her foot into the crevice between the support and the building, reached over her head and grabbed the balcony railing. After pulling herself upward, she flattened her body against the wall and waited a beat. No lights turned on. No alarms went off. All good so far.

She slowly eased across the balcony and then turned so

her stomach was against the glass slider. A quick tug confirmed it was locked. She slid down the door and flattened herself against the floor, taking cover behind the gardener's barbeque against the far railing. She opened her backpack and unrolled the towel. She selected a glass cutter before sliding back up the door. After making a strategic cut, she pulled the glass piece toward her and caught it in the towel. Wrapping it up, she put the towel in her backpack and the glass cutter on top of it with the rest of her tools. She put her hand through the opening and unlocked the slider. Again, she gave it a second or two, but no response was evident. She finished opening the door and stepped inside.

"ANYONE GOT EYES ON HER?" Mitch asked. A series of negative responses filled his ears.

"She's inside," Jake said. He was standing beside Mitch in the war room now, watching the security monitors. "She's not just good, she's amazing. There's no way we would have spotted her if we hadn't known where to look."

Mitch acknowledged Jake's comment with a quick nod. She was beyond good, and that fact was making him sweat bullets. When he was told late last night there was a personnel switch on the valet list, he knew that was her way in. It was an easy leap to guess her route—around the garage, through the apartment, and down the stairs. In his mind's eye, he traced her route. Once at the bottom of the stairs, she would turn left and walk through the door into the main hallway. She would move down the hall and take the third left into Drake's office where the prototype was sitting on a thumb drive in the safe.

Or at least she'd try. Mitch's security personnel were dressed in street clothes, so they'd easily blend in with the partygoers. He had all entrances and exits manned, so no one could come in and disturb the op. Once she was in the office, he and Jake, who were both wearing their all-black work uniforms, would follow her in and scoop her up. He also had five guys outside of the office in case she tried going out one of the windows. He watched the feed. Any second now she would open the door to the house.

SHE WAITED a few seconds until her eyes adjusted again and then moved across the apartment. Leo spent some time last night drinking with the groundskeeper. He'd managed to get the man drunk enough to find out all sort of things, like the apartment door wasn't alarmed, but she checked for a security panel anyway. There was none. She opened the door leading to the garage and went down the stairs to the small office area below. There she turned right and walked over to the door leading to the vehicle area. She took a breath. Everything had gone according to plan so far. *Almost there…*

She reached into the backpack and took out the power line finder and ran it along the wall beside the security key pad. It flashed and then went solid when it hit the power line for the security sensor. No need to deal with the key pad when she could disable the sensor.

She took off her black Mary-Jane shoe and gave the wall a mighty whack, then quickly slid the shoe back on. Not the best shoes for a little B&E work but they matched her valet outfit and made a hell of a hammer. She took out her pen light. Flicking it on, she cleared out the hole, giving her a good view of the line. She got out her alligator clip and wire strippers. After stripping the sensor wires, she clipped them together to keep the circuit from breaking. She put all the tools back into her backpack and then reached out and opened the door. The keypad still showed the door as closed.

This was almost too easy.

"WHERE IS SHE?" Mitch asked under his breath. He stared intently at the screen.

Jake leaned over the dining room table and stared at the screens as well. "This is taking too long."

"I agree. Gunnar, what's going on?"

"Not sure, boss. I'm still showing all doors closed. She's got to be either in the apartment or in the office at the bottom of the stairs."

"Do you think she stopped to search that office?" Jake asked.

Mitch's gut rolled. Everything had just turned to shit. He knew it in his bones. "Gunnar, are you sure no door has opened?"

"Yes, sir. All lights showing red."

"She hasn't come out again either," Dan said.

"Copy that, Dan." Mitch frowned. "Something is wrong." He stepped back from the table and started out of the room. "Jake, stay here and give me feedback on what you see." He walked out into the hallway but turned away from Drake's office. Instead, he left the house from the door by the pool and made his way through the crowd toward the garage.

"Maybe she got spooked and went back out the way she came in?" Gunnar's voice in his earbud echoed his thoughts.

"Jake," he asked "anything on the cameras?"

"Nothing. No joy."

. . .

SHE GRINNED as she walked into the garage. Using the penlight, she took a quick look at her watch. Four minutes and twenty-three seconds had passed. She needed to hustle. She jogged to the last bay and flashed the penlight over the car.

She was a beauty, no doubt. Not very many of these in the world. The Ford GT shone in the beam of the penlight. Frozen White. That was the color Diana had picked and Alex had to agree with the choice. The car looked awesome. A boost of adrenalin hit her veins as she ran her hand over the roof in a loving manner.

She approached the door and tried the handle. It clicked, and the door opened. Her breath caught. No way could she be this lucky. She'd thought she was going to have to break in and risk triggering the car alarm. Fear hammered in her chest. She could hear her heartbeat in her ears. Was this some kind of setup? She had visions of the cops waiting for her the moment the garage door went up.

She moved over to take a quick peek out of the window in the garage door. No one was out there, which gave her a modicum of comfort. *Finish this. You're almost there.* She went back and slid into the seat, got out the OBD2 and the key and set about creating a cloned key for the car. It was done within moments.

Next up was the scariest part. The getaway. She took a deep breath and then started the car. It was a huge garage, and she had tons of time before carbon monoxide would fill the massive area, but she still didn't want to be in an enclosed space with a running car for any longer than necessary. She got out of the car and ran to the door. Taking a huge, heartening breath, she hit the button. As the garage door rolled up silently, she sprinted back to the car and threw herself in.

. . .

"WE HAVE MOVEMENT. Garage door going up bay four. She's stealing the Ford!" Dan yelled.

Drake's voice roared in his earbud. "The prototype is in the car! Don't let her get away!"

"What?" Dan bellowed.

"Fuck!" Mitch took off at a dead run, weaving his way through the trees. Who the hell had given Drake an earbud? Not once did it ever cross his mind she was here to steal a car. He'd been so sure she was mixed up with Tolliver. His only hope to cut her off was to reach the driveway before she passed him. He pushed himself to run faster than he ever had before. He had to get to her before she got out. His whole world depended on it.

THE GARAGE DOOR had barely cleared the roof of the car when she shot out from under it. Alex turned right, gave the beast more gas, and the car rocketed ahead.

The driveway curved at the end, so she couldn't yet see the gate. She could only pray Leo had done his part to ensure it was open. But a man came running out of the trees on her left. She swerved and fishtailed on the grass. As she brought the car back onto the drive, the asphalt behind her blew sky-high. The fireball was immense. The car rocked and slid. The boom was deafening. She looked in her rearview mirror but all she saw was smoke and bits of debris.

She caught a flash of black out of the corner of her eye. Mitch. She'd know him anywhere. He was moving to intercept her. Their eyes locked. A piece of debris landed on her left, ripping her gaze from him. She pushed the gas pedal to the floor. The car growled and took off with a jolt.

Mitch was a blur when she blew past him. She came around the curve just as the gates were starting to close. She kept going and squeezed through. She hit the brakes, spun the car, and shot off down the road.

MITCH STOOD there stunned for an instant. Then he took off running toward the explosion, his legs and arms pumping for all he was worth. "Report!" he barked.

"Explosion in the driveway. Can't tell what's going on." Jake's voice boomed through the earbud.

"The guests are all by the pool area. All good here," one of his team responded.

"We have Drake. Repeat—Drake is safe," Gunnar's voice came over the comm.

"Report in!" Mitch demanded as he came up to the hole where the driveway used to be. All his guys registered they were okay except for one. "Anyone have a visual on Dan?" A series of negative retorts came in rapid succession. "Shit." Mitch could feel it in his gut. This was bad. Much worse than Alex getting away. Dan was down. He had a man down on his watch, the worst possible outcome ever. He heard a groan. Turning toward the tree line, he saw Dan. "Call nine-one-one. Dan is down! Repeat—Dan is down!

CHAPTER TWENTY-ONE

"Holy shit, Leo! I mean, what the hell?" Alex screamed into the phone as she flew down the road.

"Thank God, you're okay! I thought they got you or something. What happened?"

"I was on my way out when something exploded behind me. I have no idea what happened." She could hear sirens advancing. She slowed the car to a more normal speed and flicked her headlights on. Seconds later, several fire engines rounded the curve ahead of her and screamed by.

"What's going on?" Leo demanded.

"Fire engines, but the cops can't be far behind. I'm a minute out." She rang off. Her heart was pounding out of her chest. What the hell had happened? One minute she was driving, and the next, the world had exploded behind her. A picture of Mitch running to the edge of the drive flashed before her eyes. She fumbled with the turn signal as she turned into the Sterling's driveway. Her hands were shaking.

This one was shorter than Drake's, and the house was immediately visible. She pulled over to the garage where the door to the third bay rose slowly. She pulled forward and then reversed into the bay. She turned the car off and took a second to get her bearings. She needed to stop her hands from shaking. She flexed her fingers. She didn't need to wipe anything down because she still wore her gloves. She let out a deep breath and grabbed her backpack.

Her clothes and tools were all over the passenger seat and the floor. They must have fallen out when she fish-tailed around the driveway. She hastily leaned over and pushed everything back into the bag, but the strap of the backpack got stuck under the passenger seat. She cursed loudly and then scooted out of the car.

Alex went around to the passenger side and pulled open the door. She unhooked the strap from the bottom of the passenger seat. She put her hand under the seat and felt around to be sure she hadn't left anything behind. Her fingers closed on what felt like a tube of some kind. Great, she'd almost left her lip balm behind.

Her phone buzzed in her pocket, surprising her so she whacked her head on the dash. "Shit." She grabbed the tube and put it in her bag while she glanced at her cell phone screen. Leo was trying to rush her. His text was wasted. She was already going as fast as she could.

She stood up and then quietly closed the car door after making sure she left the key on the dash. She was sure there was damage to the car, but there was nothing she could do about it.

Going over to the side door of the garage, she let herself out. As promised, the lights were off. She slid through the darkness down the drive and out through the gate. About a quarter mile down on the left, Leo was wait-ing. She double-timed it to the car and hopped in.

"Please tell me you have a clue what happened back there?" she said as she buckled herself in.

Leo pulled away from the side of the road. "No. I was hoping you could tell me. Is there any possibility you could have done anything to set off that explosion?"

"I've gone over it again and again, and there is no way I did anything that would cause anything to explode. I was just driving down the driveway." She tried to take a breath and calm down again. "Could it be a gas pipe or something like that?" she asked.

Leo shot her a look. "Be one hell of a coincidence for a gas pipe to blow the exact moment you're stealing the car. I don't believe in coincidence, lass, and neither do you."

"But Leo, who would want to blow the car up? Why would they blow it up?"

"I don't know, but I've got a bad feeling in my gut."

"Me, too." She leaned back in her seat and closed her eyes for a second, but all she could see was the fireball and then Mitch's face.

Leo merged onto the expressway. "We stick to the plan. I'll drop you at LaGuardia Airport and then I'll head to Newark Airport. We'll give it a couple weeks to cool down, and then we'll hook up again back in Europe."

She was about to agree when a new thought hit her like a sledgehammer. "Oh, my God," she blurted.

Leo whipped around to see her face and then went back to watching the road. "What? What's wrong?"

"He knows my name, Leo, my real name." It came out as a whisper. She couldn't get her vocal chords to work.

"He knows your name," Leo repeated. She could tell by his tone that he was stunned. "The security guy, that's who you mean, right? Mitch Callahan. He knows your real name?"

She ran her hands over her face. "Yes."

"When were you going to tell me this?" Leo's face turned gray before her eyes.

"I..." She paused and then decided she might as well tell him the truth, "I wasn't going to if things went off without a hitch. It wouldn't have mattered. But now..."

"I see." Leo was livid. His knuckles had turned white on the steering wheel.

"I know I should have told you. I just...didn't think..."

Leo swallowed hard. "No, you certainly didn't." He avoided looking at her.

She wanted to say something, anything, to make it better, but there was nothing to say. She stayed silent. She had put Leo in danger for her own ego. She should have waited like Leo wanted, stole the car back once Drake was gone. It would have been safer for both of them.

But after yesterday, she'd been humiliated and wanted revenge. Whatever caused the explosion, it was sure to blow back on her. Leo was going to be collateral damage, and it was all her fault. Some revenge.

CHAPTER TWENTY-TWO

J ake looked up from the screen as Mitch entered the boardroom and barked, "Anything?"

He shook his head. "No word yet on Dan."

"That asshole Drake won't talk to me yet. He's doing "damage control" with all his high society guests." Mitch slammed the table with his hand. "What the fuck was he thinking putting the prototype in the car?"

Jake just shook his head. Mitch drew in enough oxygen to fill his lungs to the max and then let it out slowly. He needed to be in control. As much as he wanted to kill his client, anger wasn't going to solve this problem.

"How about the guests? Everyone is okay?"

"A few older ladies seemed to have a few moments of heart palpitations but that's about it. We got the names and contact information for everyone. We should be good that way. There was a slight bit of damage on a few of the guests' cars but Drake has already promised to have it all fixed."

"Good," Mitch said as he walked around the table and sat down next to Jake in front of the security monitors. He reached back and grabbed a couple of bottles of water from the mini fridge. He dropped one on the table in front of Jake and then opened his own before downing half the bottle in one swig.

"I talked to the fire chief and the police chief. Nothing more to be learned from them tonight. Maybe once they get their reports back on the bomb, but I don't think it's going to yield any major surprise. I looked at the remnants of the IED, and I think you're right. It was made to go off when she went down the driveway."

Jake nodded but continued to study the screens in front of him.

"What about this?" Mitch asked as he pointed at the screens.

"I've watched everything from yesterday at about five p.m. onward. She didn't get anywhere near the area where the bomb went off. I've fast forwarded through it a couple of times just to be sure. I mean, I guess you could watch it in real time just to be absolutely certain. I'm ninety-nine-point-nine percent sure. Even when she was parking cars, she wasn't in that area."

"That's what I thought. I didn't figure she planted it. There's got to be more going on here." Mitch shook his head slightly as he leaned back in his chair.

"Whaddya mean?"

"Alex isn't on film planting the bomb. The spot where the IED was hidden was out of any camera range, but she would've had to pass by one of the cameras to get there. And why set off an IED? She was already clear of the garage and going down the driveway."

"A distraction maybe or to slow down anyone who was chasing her?" Jake suggested.

"Maybe." He wasn't convinced. He'd seen the expression on her face when the explosion happened. She'd been as shocked as he was. He was sure of it. "It seems like overkill, doesn't it? She was stealing the car. She didn't need a distraction. She already had us fooled." And that still rankled him in all kinds of ways. It was a huge blow to his ego. He'd thought he was so smart, but she had him fooled.

"Why did she steal the car? Did she know the prototype was in it?" Jake asked. "It's pretty damn easy to track down a stolen Ford GT. There just aren't that many out there. Hell, you couldn't get one today if you tried. Seems odd."

"I agree," Mitch said as he stood up, "but I'm pretty sure Drake knows, and he'd better be in a sharing mood because I am fucking done waiting. Check the cameras again for *anyone* disappearing into the area where the IED was planted. That includes our guys. I want to know how we, *how I* could have missed this."

He stalked out of the room and went across the hall to Drake's office. Drake was on the phone and sent Mitch a dismissive look, but Mitch refused to leave. He stood squarely in front of Drake's desk and waited for him to get off the phone. Drake got the message and wound up his call.

"I assume you must have some news about my car," Drake said as he rose from his chair.

"No. No news. And Dan's condition is still unknown. They took him in for surgery a couple of hours ago. Thanks for asking."

Drake frowned. "What about the thief? Are you tracking her?"

"No."

Drake raised an eyebrow. "What do you mean, no? I expected you to be on this. You said you wouldn't let her off the property, and now you can't catch her?" Drake's voice was getting louder. "You promised me you could do this job. I thought you let her get away on purpose. That you had some master plan to follow her back to Tolliver and who's behind this."

Most would crumble when Drake thundered at them. Mitch stood calmly and waited. Years in the military had toughened him up. There wasn't much in the way of yelling that he paid attention to these days.

"Are you finished?" he asked calmly. Drake's lips curled, but Mitch cut him off. "I did have everything under control, and I would have had her if she'd done what she was supposed to do, but she didn't. So tell me. How did she know the prototype was in the car?"

Drake stayed silent but ran his hands over his face. Then he moved from behind his desk to the bar and poured himself a healthy dose of Scotch. He downed it in one swallow.

Mitch demanded, "What? What aren't you telling me?"

"The car isn't mine."

"What? Who owns the car?"

"Diana Sterling. She gave it to me. Well sort of. She asked for it back when we...parted ways. I refused." He grimaced. "So, technically, since it was never signed over to me, it's not my car." Drake poured himself another shot of whiskey and downed it like the first.

Mitch could tell it cost Drake a lot to admit that to him. "I see."

"I guess the gentlemanly thing to do would have been to return it, but I wasn't particularly feeling like a gentleman. I'd just been dumped for the ex-husband who cheated on her. Who does that?" He was gripping the empty glass so hard his knuckles were white.

"So you held on to the car and Al—it was stolen."

Mitch had almost said her name but had stopped himself. He wasn't altogether sure why. It just seemed like a betrayal of some kind. Who was he kidding? This whole mess was based on betrayal by the sound of it.

"Yes. She gave the car to me in a momentary lapse in judgement, or so she said. Now, she and her husband have patched things up and she wants it back. Now I have to tell Diana that the car she had ordered for her husband, the one that took years to get, is gone." He put the glass firmly down on the counter.

Ouch. Well that sucked big time *but too fucking bad.* Mitch wasn't in a sympathetic mood. "Why was the proto-type in the car?"

Drake grimaced again. "When we discussed the idea of letting the thief break in, you agreed but had reserva-tions. It made me…less confident about your security. I decided yesterday that instead of keeping the prototype in the safe, I would move it. Just in case things didn't go according to plan."

Mitch's gut instantly twisted into knots.

"Best hiding place. No one would look for it there, and I thought with all the security in place, the car would be safe."

Mitch fisted his hands to stop himself from calling Drake every curse word he knew. He clamped his jaws together, but in the end, it was too much for him. "You didn't trust me and ended up screwing us both in the process. Un-fucking-believable."

"Yes, well my instincts were correct as it turns out. Things didn't go according to plan and, now, not only is the car gone, but my prototype is missing, and as you so willingly pointed out earlier, one of my employees is hurt. So, what are you going to do about it?"

Mitch clenched and unclenched his jaw. "I'm working

on it. The car won't be easy to hide. I already reported it to the police, and they put a BOLO out on it. I have a couple of guys looking for the thief at the airstrips around here. I called my brothers. They have people going to LaGuardia, Newark, and JFK. I don't think she'll fly out if she has the car, but she's been unpredictable so far." Understatement of the century.

"What are you doing to find the mole?" Drake asked.

"What mole?" Mitch asked.

"As you pointed out, how did she know I put the prototype in the car? She had to have access to the security system."

"I had access to the security system, and I didn't know you moved it," Mitch pointed out.

Drake frowned. "You should have known."

"You expect me to review every hour of video every day to see what goes on inside the house? The system is there to tell me if someone breaks in. It's not there to watch every person's movement every hour of the day. A better question is, who did you tell that you moved it? Did anyone see you?"

Drake glared at Mitch. "I didn't tell anyone, and no one saw me. She must have had access for her to know I put the prototype in the car. You tell me it can't be done from the outside without you knowing, so she must have had someone on the inside."

"You still think the prototype was the target?"

"Why? Don't you?"

Mitch paused. "I don't believe in coincidence, but I'm having a hard time believing that she knew the prototype was in the car. How long before she broke in did you put it there?"

"Late last night."

"There's no possible way she could have planned to

break into the garage in less than twenty-four hours. She signed up to be part of the valet service hours before that, and she obviously knew what tools she would need to hit the garage before she arrived here. I think the car was her target. I don't think she knew about the prototype."

"Well, I don't believe in coincidences either. Your thief ended up with my prototype." Drake moved to stand directly across from Mitch. "We both know Tolliver is up to something, and it's bloody unlikely there just happens to be two thieves in the area, so she must have been after the prototype."

Mitch chose his words carefully. "I'm not sure what's really going on, but I can prove she had nothing to do with the explosion. She was nowhere near it." He hesitated. "And I saw her face when the bomb went off. She was shocked. If she faked that level of fear, then she deserves an Oscar."

Drake opened his mouth and then snapped it shut. He sat down hard in his chair. "What's your theory then?"

"I'm not sure." He shook his head. "No matter how I move the pieces around, they just don't fit in the puzzle. The thief didn't know about the bomb, so who planted it? If she was only after the car, was it a coincidence she came on the same day the person who planted the bomb decided to use it? Were they partners? What was the purpose of the bomb? How is Tolliver involved? Is he involved at all? None of it makes sense, but you can be sure I'm going to figure it out."

"Fine. I'll give you some leeway on this, but I want hourly updates. I want all hands on deck looking for that car and prototype. Now"—Drake picked up his cell phone off the desk—"I have to call Diana, so if you'll excuse me."

Mitch nodded, left the office, and then walked back across the hall to the dining room.

Jake gave him a small smile as he entered the room. "You still have your head. That's good."

"Yeah, but not by much."

"Dan is out of surgery. They took out his spleen."

"Okay, I want to go talk to him as soon as possible. We need to figure out what went on out there."

Jake took a slug from a water bottle. "The doctor said he'd be out for a while."

"Well, maybe we should swing by and wake him up. Text the police chief and tell him we need to talk to Dan quick-time. See if he can exert some pressure with the doctors."

"Sure, boss." Jake grabbed his phone.

"Do it on the way. We're going to see Dan whether they like it or not."

"Where do you think nurses get their shoes? My aunt was a nurse, and she would always sneak up on us and catch us in the act whenever we were misbehaving, which was a lot." Jake shot a quick look over his shoulder as they walked by the nurses' station. "I have a built-in fear of nurses."

Mitch chuckled. "I'll remember that. You never know who will show up at your door next Halloween."

They paused in the hallway outside of Dan's room. He'd just come down from recovery.

Jake said, "The chief called ahead. Nurse Ratchet back there gave us five minutes, but you'd better use 'em wisely. She's already frowning at us."

Mitch shook his head. "You sure you're an ex-SEAL?" he asked as he went into Dan's room. Jake ignored him and walked over to the far side of the bed. Mitch moved to stand beside Dan.

He was hooked to several monitors. There were wires and tubes in all kinds of places. It made Mitch want to turn on his heel and run. On the drive over he'd been questioning if Dan might have something to do with all this, but seeing Dan like this, he just couldn't make it work.

The last person he'd seen this way was his mom. She died a few years ago, but the memories swamped him as he stood there. A lump was building in his throat. He cleared it and reached out and touched Dan's shoulder.

"Dan," he called softly. There was no response. "Dan," he said louder this time. Dan's eyelids' fluttered but remained closed. "Dan," he said again in a firm voice, and Dan's eyes opened.

"Mmish," he mumbled and then his eyes closed slowly.

"Yeah, that's right it's Mitch and Jake. We need to talk to you, buddy." Mitch put his hand on Dan's shoulder and gave him a small nudge.

Dan's eyes fluttered. "Mish..."

"Dan, do you know where you are? Do you remember what happened?"

"My...fault."

"No, Dan. It wasn't your fault. I need you to concentrate, though. Did you see anything? Do you remember anything?" Mitch leaned over the edge of the bed so he could catch any word that Dan uttered.

"Bomb."

"Yes, a bomb went off. You got hurt, but you're on the mend. Did you notice anything? Dan?"

"Wasn't supposed...to happen...that way." Dan's voice was soft and hard to hear.

Jake put his hand on Dan's arm. "You're right, dude, it wasn't supposed to happen the way it did. She was supposed to go for the safe. But did you see anyone else? Anything else?"

"I...lost..." Dan's voice faded out entirely, and his eyes closed.

"Dan? What did you lose, Dan?" Mitch nudged him again in the arm, but his eyes remained closed. He tried again. "Dan? You gotta talk to me. What happened to you?"

Dan opened his eyes again. "Sorry," he mumbled.

"Dan." Mitch gave him a bit of a harder nudge.

"That's enough, gentlemen," a firm voice stated behind them.

Mitch straightened up and turned around. Nurse Ratchet. He glanced at her name tag. Nurse Wilson was her real name. "Ms. Wilson, we're just trying to get some information from Dan. It's part of an ongoing investigation."

"I don't care." She moved closer to the end of the bed. "This man needs his rest. It's almost two a.m., well past visiting hours. You cannot ask him anything else tonight. You need to leave."

Mitch gave the nurse one of his best smiles. "I know we're bending the rules here a bit, but we won't be more than a couple of minutes, and then we'll be out of your hair."

"You'll be out of my hair now," she said firmly. When she shot Jake a look, he took a step back from the bed. She turned to Mitch. "You need to leave. I will call security if necessary. I did as the chief asked. You had your five minutes. This man needs his rest now. You can question him later this morning *if* he's up to it." She planted her fists on her hips. "Time to go," she said with more force. Mitch had the distinct impression that, given the opportunity, Nurse Wilson would grab them both by their ears and throw them out of the building on her own.

"Uh, okay then." Jake took great pains to stay as far

away from the nurse as possible, hugging the wall as he rounded the end of the bed where she was standing. "Uh, I'll just wait for you in the hallway," he called as he went past the nurse and almost ran out the door.

"You need to go as well."

"I understand, but I need answers."

The nurse frowned at Mitch. "I don't want to call security, but I will if I have to. You are disturbing him, and he needs his rest. You can come back in the morning, but it's time you left."

Mitch opened his mouth to argue again but changed his mind. Dan was still out of it and not very helpful. Maybe tomorrow he would be up for a longer chat. "Fine, I'm going, but I'm going to pop by tomorrow."

"Fine," said the nurse. Mitch walked through the doorway and out into the hall. She bustled out the door and closed it after her, giving Mitch and Jake a narrowed-eyed look before she marched down the hallway.

"She's one scary nurse," Jake mumbled as he and Mitch stood waiting for the elevator.

Mitch laughed. "You never went to Catholic school growing up, did you? She's a pussy cat compared to the nuns who taught me."

Jake shuddered a bit. "Better you than me."

They stepped onto the elevator, and Jake hit the button for the lobby. Mitch's phone vibrated. He pulled it out of his pocket and read a text. "Drake wants us to meet him at the Sterling residence. Do you know where that is?"

"Yeah, just down the way from Drake's. Does he say why?"

Mitch shook his head. He was exhausted. He'd been up since dawn, and with this mess, he wouldn't see his bed for quite a few more hours. He didn't want any more surprises. He'd had his fill today, and none of them had been good.

Ten minutes later, they pulled in front of the Sterling place and got out of the car. Drake was speaking with Diana Sterling in front the garage. Mitch could see a Ford GT parked in the bay.

"Is that the car?" Jake asked.

"Yeah, I think so. How many GTs could there be here? It's a rare car." Mitch prayed it was Drake's, or rather Diana's, car. Then maybe the nightmare would be somewhat over. Drake would have the prototype back.

Mitch and Jake walked over to Drake. Mitch nodded in Drake's direction and then smiled at Diana Sterling. Drake waved at them and said, "Diana, this is the head of my security team, Mitch Callahan, and one of his team, Jake Boxer."

"Ms. Sterling," Mitch said.

"Ma'am." Jake nodded in her direction.

"Diana, can you tell them what you told me please?"

Diana Sterling gave a large sigh. "Really, Jameson, can't you just tell them? I don't want..." Whatever she was going to say, she stopped at the look on Drake's face. "Very well," she said with another large sigh. "I was telling Jameson that I hired someone to get my car back after he refused to give it to me." She shot him a hard look and then frowned. "Really, it would have been so much simpler if you would have been a gentleman about it, Jameson."

"I didn't feel like being a gentleman, Diana. You—" He clamped his jaws together.

She shook her head. "The man I spoke to said his name was John. He had a bit of an accent, but I couldn't tell you from where. I only spoke to him over the phone, so I can't tell you what he looked like. I can give you the number, though." She reached into her pocket and produced a slip of paper with a phone number written on it.

A burner phone, no doubt, but Mitch reached out and took the piece of paper. Nodding his thanks, he slipped it into his pocket. "So, you never saw the man. You just communicated by phone. Do you know anything about the thief?"

"No. Just that it was a woman. He referred to her as 'she' when he spoke of her."

No surprise there. Alex had been hired to get the car back, which is why she'd been in the garage. She had accomplished her goal. "Is there any video surveillance of her returning the car?" Mitch asked as he pointed toward a camera that was attached to the corner of the garage.

Diana looked puzzled. "Oh, no. That was part of the deal. Lights off, and no cameras either."

Of course, it was. She was too smart for that. Mitch sighed silently.

"How did she get it in here?" Jake asked.

"I left the gate open for her. I told John that I wanted it back before today. He said they would do their best, and then he called me back and told me to leave the gate open and have a garage door open for her to deliver the car. And then he said about the lights and cameras." Diana kept intertwining her fingers and twisting them.

"When did he tell you this?" Mitch asked.

"Yesterday morning. He called me."

"Okay."

Diana's fingers flitted about, trembling when she touched her hair. She stepped back. "If that's all, I'd like to go in before... I'd like to go in."

Mitch smiled gently. "I just have a couple more questions, and then I need to examine the car."

"Fine," Diana snapped. Her patience was obviously wearing thin.

"How did you find this John person?"

Diana Sterling's hands flew to her hair again and then came back down and twisted in knots. "From a friend. I can't say more."

Mitch knew immediately if he pushed her, Diana would stop talking and run into the house, so he tried another tactic. "Did your friend give you a phone number for John?"

"No. My friend told me to place an ad on Craig's List for a repo man to help me with a problem, so that's what I did. I really need to be getting back." She shot a glance at the front door. It was clear she was afraid her husband would come out and join them any minute.

"Okay. I'm just going to take a quick peek at the car, and then we'll go."

Mitch glanced at Drake who shook his head. The prototype wasn't in the car. He knew it was too much to hope for. At least now they knew what had happened to the car. It didn't solve the mystery, though. He still had no idea how Alex had known the prototype would be in the car, or if she was just after the car and got the prototype by accident.

Mitch went to the driver's side, and Jake went to the passenger side. They opened the doors. Then they leaned in and did a visual inspection of the car.

"What are the chances she'll let us do forensics on the car?" Jake asked as he squatted down on his haunches.

"Zero. Feel free to use your hands."

Jake nodded and started running his hands over the seat and checking the whole passenger side area. Mitch did the same with the driver's side. They both came up empty. She had cleaned out the car and left it in pristine condition. Nothing in the glove box. Nothing on the floors. If he had to guess, she probably had worn gloves and possibly wiped it down. Stepping back out of the car, he shut the door. In the brightly lit garage, he could see chips in the paint and a few dings where debris from the bomb must have hit. He was willing to bet Diana hadn't looked closely at the car yet. She was going to lose her mind when she saw the damage. No way to hide that.

"Okay, we're finished." He walked over and offered his hand to Diana. "Mrs. Sterling, thank you for your help. Sorry we had to meet under these circumstances."

She shook his hand and nodded. She did the same with Jake and then turned to go.

"If you can think of anything else about John or the thief, please be in touch," Mitch said.

Diana frowned but nodded. "Jameson," she said before turning and mounting the stairs to her front door. She opened it and walked through without a backward glance.

Drake turned to Mitch. "I'll see you in my office in ten minutes. I want an update." He turned on his heel and strode over to his Mercedes. His driver opened the back door while his security detail kept watch. They nodded to Mitch and then got into the car after Drake. A minute later, the car drove off.

"Well, shit," Jake mumbled as they walked back to the car. "I was hoping this would be the end of it when I saw that car."

"You and me both, but I couldn't be that lucky." Mitch opened the driver's side door and climbed in. "Somehow, this is all just the beginning of one big mess. I can feel it in my gut."

CHAPTER TWENTY-THREE

Alex pulled off her wig and tucked it into her backpack. Then she took off the vest she'd been wearing as part of her valet uniform. Now the white blouse and black pants she was wearing no longer looked like a uniform. She reached behind her and grabbed a black blazer and a short brown wig off the back seat. By the time she got out of the car, she would look like every other woman with short brown hair in New York.

She glanced at Leo, but his entire focus was on the road ahead. Glancing at her watch, Alex noted they were making good time. It was only slightly after two a.m. They'd taken some back roads as a precaution, but they were coming up to the city. Alex couldn't take anymore silence.

"I can't use the original exit strategy. He has my name, and he can find a picture. It's too dangerous for me to go to an airport now, at least one in the New York area. You're still good, though. He doesn't know about you. You can still fly out of Newark. We'll meet up, just maybe in a couple of months instead of a few weeks. That will give me plenty of time to get out of town." She was nervous. Leo never got mad at her. He was really the only parent she'd ever known, and he was silent. It was making her crazy. "I have another plan in place just in case things went to hell. I think this qualifies. Like I said, it will take longer, but it should be—"

"Stop talking, lass. You're making it hard for me to think."

Leo had finally spoken to her but hadn't yelled. A weight lifted from her chest that was immediately replaced by guilt. Once again, she was thinking of herself. She needed to make sure Leo was okay, no matter what. This was all on her.

"We don't know what Callahan knows. We know he has your first name but not if he has your last. We have no idea if he has my name or not. If or when he talks to Diana Sterling, he's going to find out I exist. I didn't use my real name and we never met in person. There shouldn't be a way to trace me but, still, he's going to find out about me. It doesn't leave us with much in the way of choice. We can drive down to D.C. or go to Baltimore and catch a flight there. It should be far enough."

She laced her fingers together and gripped her hands. "The thing is, the longer we drive, the more time he has to figure things out and get organized. I think"—she took a breath—"I think you should still fly out tonight. Go to Newark. Callahan will take a little while to figure out what happened. The explosion will buy you a bit of time. He'll talk to the Sterlings and find out about you, but you're using a different alias than the one you gave Diana Sterling. He won't have a picture of you."

Even now, Leo was wearing a ball cap pulled low and a fake mustache. By the time he got to the airport, he would be wearing something different again. "Fly out tonight."

"And what are you going to do? I've not ever left you behind, and I won't start now." Leo shook his head.

She swallowed the huge lump that sat in her throat and brushed an errant tear off her cheek. Leo was the sweetest man ever. She loved him like the father figure he was to her and, thankfully, he still loved her, too. "I'll be okay. New York is a big city, and I have connections there."

Leo glanced at her quickly. "Are you sure?"

She shrugged. "My choices might be a bit limited at the moment." She squared her shoulders. "It's more important to me that you get out of town. You need to get back to your nonna. Someone needs to look after her. Besides, I need you far away from this mess so you can help me if I need it.

"That explosion wasn't a coincidence, and whatever or whoever caused it, chances are good it's going to come back on me. I'm going to be hotter than hell for the next while, which means I'll need outside support." She reached over to touch Leo's arm, but he caught her hand and squeezed it.

They drove in silence the rest of the way into New York City. Alex's stomach was tied in knots. She was worried about Leo getting out. She wouldn't be able to live with herself if he got busted for helping her.

As they crossed the bridge into Manhattan, Leo asked, "Where do you want me to let you out?"

"Anywhere you like. I'm fine."

He nodded. "I don't like leaving you behind. I feel like I'm abandoning you. It just doesn't sit right with me."

"Leo, whatever happens to me is my own fault. You've been trying to convince me to stop for months. I took one risk too many, and it's not paying off. I just don't want you dragged down into whatever kinda mess this becomes." She stuck a false smile on her face. "Maybe we're panicking for nothing. Maybe the explosion was an accident, and it has nothing to do with me stealing the car."

Leo shot her a frown. "Ducks, I'd love to believe that, but you and me both know that's not the truth."

She sighed and worried her lip between her teeth. "We can always hope, Leo. Either way, I have connections that can get me out of most things. It's important to me you're safe. You've been nothing but good to me, Leo. We made a fantastic team."

"Made? What's the made business? We *make* a fantastic team."

She smiled ruefully. "I think we might have just gone into retirement, which is what you wanted, so it's all good, right?"

Leo frowned again and then brightened. "You can come visit me and my nonna in Italy. You haven't eaten until you've had dinner made by my nonna."

She tried for another smile. "I'm looking forward to that." She saw an opening at the curb ahead. "Pull in there." As the car moved into the spot, she said, "Let me know when you're out safe. I have my burner. I'll see you in the usual spot three months from today."

When Leo turned to her, she gave him a peck on the cheek and then grabbed her bag and hopped out of the car. She went around to the trunk and pulled out her luggage. She closed the trunk lid, walked away from the car, and moved down the sidewalk without looking back. She was afraid if she did, it would be the last time she ever saw him.

She navigated her way through the streets, keeping her head down and an eye out for anything unusual. She made a few loops and turns to see if she was being followed, but it seemed all clear to her. Finally, she made her way to her flop house.

No one except Lacy knew she had a bolt-hole in New York. She had never even told Leo. She approached the building and dashed inside at the last second. The lobby looked the same as it had the day she bought the condo. She went over to the elevator and hit the button and went up to the twenty-fourth floor.

After the doors opened, she took a brief look around and got out. She went down the hall to her place. She dug in her luggage and pulled out her keys. She unlocked the door, and once she let herself in, closed the door and leaned against it. Home sweet home, at least for the next while.

She kicked off her shoes and pulled off her wig. She was in dire need of a shower. She walked through the living room, pulling the white sheet covers off the furniture as she went. She threw them in a pile in the corner. Sneezing from the dust, she made her way into the bedroom and did the same there. By the time she got into the shower a few minutes later, she was in the middle of a sneezing frenzy.

She let the hot spray pound onto her shoulders. Her whole body hurt. She tried to swallow the tears when they came, but it was too much. The last twenty-four hours had been rough. She was an emotional wreck, as well as a physical one. She sobbed as she stood under the spray. It was bad that she put Leo in jeopardy tonight because of her ego. It was worse that she was not only humiliated and betrayed by a man like all those women she did jobs for, but she was starting to suspect she was in love with him.

CHAPTER TWENTY-FOUR

Mitch sat his elbows on his desk and rubbed his eyes with the fleshy part of his palms. How could it be less than twenty-four hours since the shit hit the fan? He was exhausted. He'd gone back to his room at the estate after another dressing down from Drake and had a shower. He'd tried to catch a few hours' sleep, but every time he closed his eyes, he either saw Alex's face filled with horror when he'd said her name or Alex's shocked expression just after the bomb went off.

He consoled himself with the fact that she was okay. If she never believed he hadn't intentionally seduced her on the yacht to humiliate and betray her, he'd have to live with it. Her being alive was the important thing. It would be nice to see her again just to confirm that fact.

He'd gotten up after a few hours and driven into the city. He needed to be at his own office with his brothers. He hated to admit it, but he needed the support. Besides, Jake could handle managing the cleanup and anything else that needed to be done out at Drake's.

He sighed as a cup of black coffee appeared directly in front of him. "Drink up. It's going to be a long day," Logan said as he sat in one of the visitor chairs in Mitch's office.

"Thanks." Mitch picked up the mug and leaned back in his chair. He glanced over his shoulder out the window at the street. West 48th Street had changed drastically since their father had bought the buildings back in the seventies.

He remembered visiting his dad at work but not being allowed to go outside to the street for any reason. It was a dangerous neighborhood then. Hell's Kitchen had been gang territory back in the day, and although gentrification had started in the seventies with people like his dad, things didn't really pick up until the nineties. Even then it wasn't really until the mid-oughts that real estate really took off. Now, Mitch and his brothers could never purchase this size office space here, let alone own a couple of buildings.

Gage walked into Mitch's office and plopped down in the other visitor's chair across from Mitch. He leaned back in his seat and looked around. "Tell me again how you ended up with the nicest office?"

Mitch smiled slightly as he looked at his space. His back was to the wall with his desk and visitor chairs in front of him. The door was in the far right corner. The two huge windows that flooded the space with light made up most of the left wall. The floors were the original hardwood, and the mantel over the working fireplace that was on the opposite wall from his desk was hand carved. The buttery brown leather couch that was in front of the fireplace was long enough for him to sleep on, and it was comfortable, too. "You two wanted bigger spaces. I don't need that much space."

"I don't recall saying I needed more space," Logan said

as he eyed his brother. "I seem to recall you telling me where my furniture had been delivered. I'm pretty sure we never had a discussion about offices."

Mitch shrugged. "Oh, I thought you wanted Dad's old office."

Gage grinned. "I think we got played, Logan. Not sure how he did it, but he arranged the whole thing. We're gonna have to keep a closer eye on this guy."

"Duly noted." Logan nodded and took a sip of his coffee, sizing his brother Mitch up over the rim. "So, where do we stand with this mess?"

Mitch winced.

"I didn't mean to imply it was your fault." Logan tried to quickly assure him while a look of guilt flashed over his face.

"But it is my fault." Mitch knew it in every cell of his body. It was his responsibility, so it was his fault.

"Bullshit." Gage shifted in his chair until he was leaning forward. "Drake didn't give you the whole picture. And the stupid asshole put the prototype in the car. If he had trusted you in the first place like he should've, the prototype would still be locked in the safe. Hell, if he'd given the car back like he should've, then the whole thing wouldn't have happened."

"But it did happen, and now I have to figure out how to clean up this mess before it ends up destroying everything we've built here." Mitch took a sip of coffee and swore. "Damn, that's hot. How much sugar did you put in there, Logan?"

Logan gave him a small smile. "Just enough."

Mitch didn't like the look of the smile. He'd be making his own coffee from now on. Logan's revenge had always been brutal when they were kids. If Logan thought he was cheated out of the office, vengeance would be in the cards.

"We," said Logan.

Mitch looked up at him puzzled. "I said 'we've built.'"

"No. I mean 'we' have to figure this mess out. You were a SEAL, so I know you get being a team player. We're your family and your team. We all have to work to sort this out. We took the job on. We all agreed on it, not just you. I've read the reports on everything, excellent by the way. I'm assuming you had Jake do it."

Mitch tried to look insulted but couldn't pull it off. He made Jake write every report, just like when they were in the SEALs. Mitch sucked at writing, period.

Logan set his coffee cup on a coaster on the desk. "You did it right. Even I can tell that, and I don't have the experience you and Gage have. You didn't screw up. It's not on you. It's on us, so please just accept that so we can plan together."

Mitch was stunned into silence. He and Logan had never really gotten along. Logan had always been on his case about being a slacker and lazy. Now, all of a sudden, he was saying all the right things.

He glanced at Gage, but his brother's face was impassive. Logan wouldn't have come out with that speech on his own. No way, but he appreciated the sentiment behind it. He could tell Logan meant it. "Thanks." It was all he could trust himself to say. He wanted to ask why the change of heart, but it would lead nowhere good, so it was best left alone.

"Now, fill us in on the latest, little brother, and let's make a game plan," Gage said as he leaned back in his chair and put his feet up on the edge of Mitch's desk.

"I already told you about finding the car. Drake tore another strip off me for that whole debacle. Jake went back to see Dan at the hospital this morning. He was still pretty doped up. Jake said it was hard to get anything out of him.

Dan doesn't remember anything after yesterday afternoon. He has no memory of the explosion. He doesn't remember standing guard or the party at all. Jake says Dan had no idea the car was stolen."

"What does the doctor say?" Logan jotted something down on a pad of paper he had magically produced somehow. Once a lawyer always a lawyer.

Mitch shook his head. "The doctor agrees that it could be possible. Dan doesn't have any head injuries, but given his proximity to the explosion…" He shrugged.

"Anything is possible," Logan finished for him. "The doctor is trying to cover his ass just in case something turns up later. Jake won't get anything definitive from him either way. Doctors hate to be pinned down. Have Jake make another run at Dan later today. Tell him to find out when the next round of medication is to be given and show up about half hour before. Pain tends to clear the mind a bit, but also distract. Patients tend to tell the truth a bit more when they are in pain and waiting for their meds. If you can get the doctor to hold off a bit on the medication, all the better."

Gage and Mitch exchanged a look. Gage chuckled. "That's pretty cold. You lawyers are a scary lot."

Logan snorted. "Says the man who worked in naval intelligence. Bit of pot and kettle, isn't it?"

Gage grinned at his brother. "Maybe, but it's classified."

Logan glanced at his watch. "I have a couple other clients I have to check in with about a few things. Nothing major since it's Sunday, but there were a few minor fires I put out last week, so I want to make sure all is running smoothly. After that, we're going to continue doing a deep dive for information on Tolliver." Logan stood up. "I'll check back with you in a couple of hours."

"Sure." Gage gave him a wave.

Logan grabbed his coffee and left the office.

"I wasn't kidding. He's a bit scary when he's in lawyer mode," Gage said as he readjusted his feet on the desk.

"Logan is always Logan. Very 'stick up his ass' efficient." Mitch took another sip of coffee and promptly spit it back into the cup. It was too sweet to drink.

"Be nice. He's your brother, and that anal-retentive nature of his is what makes him such a good lawyer. Be thankful he's on our side."

Mitch grimaced. It was true. Logan had tried to extend the olive branch, and he was being a prick about it. Some things just didn't change, no matter how old he got.

Gage took a swig of his coffee, then asked, "So, any ideas how we find your thief?"

"No. Not a one. It's like she disappeared into thin air. She knows that I know her real first name, but not her last. She'd think it would be a gamble to try and use the airports. Unless she has fake ID to go with her many disguises, then I guess anything is possible. Did you hear anything from the guys you have at the airports?"

Gage nodded. "They got nothing. There were a couple of women that looked like they could have been her but turned out to be false alarms. She might have slipped past us. Who knows?"

"Great. Doesn't leave us with much." Mitch rubbed his face with both hands.

"How did Diana Sterling hire Alex in the first place?"

"Through an ad on Craig's List but it's really word of mouth. My understanding is Diana was told to place an ad on Craig's list that asked for a repo man to help with a problem. A man contacted her, and she worked out the details with him."

"But how did Diana Sterling know to do that? Where did she hear about Alex?"

"From a friend."

Gage frowned. "What friend?"

Mitch looked at his brother. "I have no idea. But I'm sure as hell gonna find out."

CHAPTER TWENTY-FIVE

A lex paced back and forth in front of the TV in her apartment. The commercial was still on, and she wanted to throw the remote at the TV. The anchor had said they had new details on the Hamptons Bombing. That's what they were calling it. And then they went to a commercial break. It was excruciating for her. The commercial ended, and she flopped down on the sofa across from the screen. She put down the remote and grabbed her mug of tea, cupping it in both hands.

The blond talking head smiled at the camera. "Late yesterday afternoon, during the annual Kickoff to Summer party thrown by well-known businessman Jameson Drake, a bomb went off. Police say it was part of a larger plan to steal from Mr. Drake. Drake, who is best known for his real estate holdings, is also a big name in business circles for investing in technology start-ups. The police believe that a thief or thieves were using the bomb to distract Mr. Drake's security so they could rob Drake.

"Although the thieves got away empty-handed, one of Drake's security team was hurt in the blast. His name has not been released, but he is currently in the Hamptons General Hospital in serious condition. A spokesperson for Drake has said that Mr. Drake is relieved that nothing was taken, but he is very upset that one of his employees was hurt. He is offering a reward for any information that leads to the capture of the thief or thieves. It is thought that the police do not have a suspect in custody at this time but are searching for a woman whom they believe may be responsible for the bombing."

The male talking head started speaking. "In other news..." Alex dropped the mug on the table with a clunk and picked up the remote. After turning off the TV, she threw the remote down on the table and then hopped up and resumed her pacing.

She was breathing rapidly. Her heart was double-timing it in her chest. The cops thought she'd planted the bomb. Someone got hurt. Had to be the first guy that shot out of the bushes at her. She couldn't believe it. She would never in a million years plant a bomb. One of Mitch's team was hurt. She was glad it wasn't Mitch. She never wanted to see him again, but the pain in her chest eased slightly at the knowledge he was safe.

She took a deep breath. What should she do? Better question was, what could she do? She hadn't planted the bomb. The news station obviously didn't have the scoop on the car she'd stolen or else they would've mentioned it. No surprise there. It was amazing what information could be held back when powerful people were involved. Between the Sterlings and Drake, no one wanted the true story of the car out there, so they squashed it. That was probably a good thing for her. But the cops had to know, so maybe not.

She did not want to be held responsible for a bomb that hurt someone. She should run. Get as far away as possible and do it as quickly as possible. Except Mitch knew her name, and there was no way on God's green earth he was going to let it go. Not ever. Especially since someone got hurt on his watch. She understood him well enough to grasp that instantly.

She walked over to what passed for the kitchen of her apartment and leaned on the island. Grabbing her phone, she dialed a number from memory. She had thought she would call Lacy so they could catch up. Now she desperately needed her friend's help.

"Hey. Just hanging out. It's raining here. Call me." Alex had made her voice very casual but she knew Lacy would understand as soon as she heard the message. They had worked out the simple code when they were in high school. "Rain" meant trouble and "hanging" meant grounded when they were teens. Now hanging meant stuck. She only hoped Lacy would get the message quickly. She needed to find a way out of this mess before it literally came banging on her door.

Her phone buzzed. It was a text from Lacy. *Our usual spot in a half hour?* Alex immediately responded with a happy face emoji. Thank God, Lacy was in the city and could meet her. She went into the bathroom and opened the closet. She pulled out the long black hair wig and then grabbed some large sunglasses off the shelf.

"These should do," she mumbled to herself. She put them on the counter and then went into her bedroom and changed into a pair of black leggings and a black T-shirt. With the black wig and glasses, it would be hard to recognize her. She added a black dog collar around her neck, some large silver stud earrings and some funky chunky silver rings and bracelets.

Once she put on the wig, she did her makeup. Light foundation, much lighter than her skin tone, with lots of black eyeliner and dark lipstick. Then she grabbed the sunglasses and went out to the hall closet. She pulled on a pair of knee-high black lace-up boots that had big silver buckles. She stood back and admired the effect in the mirror in her foyer. As expected, she looked like every other goth type in Manhattan. More importantly, she didn't remotely look like herself.

She left her building and walked east toward the rendezvous point. She thought about grabbing the subway or a cab, but decided against it. Uber was out, too. She didn't want to have to speak to anyone, and she didn't want to get trapped on mass transit. It took her longer than she thought, so when she walked into the designated Starbucks, she was already five minutes late.

She did a quick scan of the room while she stood in line. It was filled with people looking at screens. They were either working on their laptops or using their phones. She could walk through naked, and the only ones that would notice would be the baristas, which is exactly why she liked Starbucks. No one paid any attention to who was around them.

She got her skinny decaf no-whip mocha and claimed a table in the corner. She sat down with her back to the wall and watched the door. Lacy walked through about two minutes later. She went to the counter and ordered a drink. It took about five minutes and some back and forth between Lacy and the barista before she finally had her drink and made her way over to Alex's table.

"Hello. How are you?" she said low as she sat down. She shed her coat and got out her tablet. "In case I need to take notes." Then she took a sip of her drink. "Okay, I'm ready. Fill me in."

Alex smiled. "It's nice to see you, too." She knew Lacy

was only following the rules, but it still seemed odd not to greet her best friend with a hug.

"You know the rules. Do nothing to draw attention. People notice hugging." Then Lacy did smile. "I gotta say, it took me a couple of minutes before I realized it was you. That look totally works. I wouldn't have been able to pick you out of crowd if I didn't know to look for you."

"Good to know it's working." Alex's shoulders started to relax just a fraction. Just seeing Lacy was making her feel better. She'd been feeling sick ever since the news report.

"So, what's going on?" Lacy murmured as she set up her tablet.

"I...I'm not sure where to start." Alex took a breath and then another. Then she spoke in a quiet voice, "Okay, so I had a client, and the job went sideways. I'm worried that I'll be blamed for something I didn't do. I need to know what my options are."

Lacy nodded. "All right, start at the beginning and tell me everything."

Alex laid it out in detail. When she got to the part about the yacht, she hesitated, but then found herself spilling everything. Lacy was her best friend, and she needed that right now just as much as a lawyer.

Her cheeks got hot as she talked about it. She was glad her sunglasses covered most of her face. It was...humiliating to have let her guard down so far. She had almost gotten caught because of it. In fact, she still might. She was hating herself for losing control that afternoon.

Lacy was silent for a minute, then reached across the table and squeezed her hand. After a minute, she brought her hand back and cleared her throat. She was back in lawyer mode.

"I am assuming you're wondering your culpability in

all this." At Alex's nod, she continued, "Well, the car is a non-starter. It's still in Diana Sterling's name, so it's hers. You were acting on her behalf to repossess the vehicle, so they can't get you for grand theft."

"Exactly! That's what I am, an Asset Repossession Specialist Extraordinaire. That's why people hire me." Alex grinned.

Lacy frowned. "You know the acronym for that is ARSE, don't you?"

Alex glared at Lacy. "Yes, thanks, and thanks for pointing that out," she huffed.

"Just sayin'," Lacy mumbled before continuing. "They can try for breaking and entering, but again you were acting on her behalf as a repossession agent. They could give you a hard time about not having the correct paperwork for that...but it's not a serious thing."

"What about the bomb and the guy who got hurt?"

"Well, you had nothing to do with it, so none of that is on you."

Alex relaxed even more. "Great, so I'm in the clear."

Lacy put up her hand. "I didn't say that. Legally speaking, you should present yourself to the police and explain your part in everything so they can clear you as a suspect."

"I can't do that. There's no way. I mean, they'll know my real name, and what if they find out about...other repossessions I've done? Yeah, no, there's no way I'm going to the cops." She was shaking her head.

"Okay, calm down. You don't have to come forward, but until they figure out who the bomber is, the pressure is going to be on. Telling your story would most likely get you off the hook."

"Most likely? What do you mean, most likely? I had nothing to do with the bomb." Her voice had gotten louder, and Lacy immediately shushed her.

"You need to relax. Take a breath. Right now, you are probably their only suspect. You would need to convince them you had nothing to do with it since it might be hard for them to believe you broke in on the same day, at the same time, as a bomb went off and had nothing to do with it. Cops are big on coincidence."

Alex jerked upright in her seat.

"What is it?" Lacy asked.

Alex took a sip of her drink to buy time before she answered. "You're right. It is a huge coincidence. Too big. I hadn't really thought about it before but...I think someone used me as the distraction, or at least part of it." She turned to look out the window, but she wasn't seeing the sidewalk, she was trying to wrap her brain around this new idea.

Lacy sat back in her chair and smoothed her hair back. She took a sip of her drink. "It's certainly possible."

"But that would mean someone knew I would be breaking—that is, I would be there on that day. I wasn't sure I was going to do it Saturday until the day before. It was always the plan to go in during the party if possible, but several things happened that could have altered that plan. So, someone close to me had to be involved." As she took another sip of her drink, her hand shook a bit. There was a mole in her operation.

Lacy leaned forward on the table. "Walk me through it. Who knew you would be going for the car yesterday?"

"Leo, of course, but it goes without saying that he would never set me up. He's the one who taught me everything I know."

"Okay, not Leo. Who else?"

"No one, really." An image of Mitch rose in her mind. He knew she would do it, especially after what had happened between them. He knew she would be determined to go through with it, just to get back at him. He would have done the same if she'd gotten one over on him. And he knew her real name. Maybe he knew her whole story. Could he have set her up? What did he get out of it?

"What about the client? Did Diana Sterling know you would be getting her car back yesterday?" Lacy asked.

"Yes. She asked Leo if we could get it this weekend because she wanted to give it to her husband today. But why would she set me up? I've never met her. I listened in on the phone conversation she had with Leo, but she has no clue who I am."

Lacy shook her head. "I don't know. I'm not sure who wanted to set you up, but it looks like someone did."

Alex took another sip of her drink. She was getting a headache. This was going from bad to worse for her.

"So, you don't want to go to the cops, I get that, but you need to clear your name somehow, otherwise they'll still be looking for you. And the longer they do, the more poking around they do on you, the more likely your whole career comes to light. It's a big risk."

"I can't go to the cops. Too many questions there are no easy answers for." She shook her head again.

"What about going to the security guy? You two have a sort of relationship. He knows you're a thief. From what you've said, his reputation is riding on this. He may be willing to listen to you and run interference with the cops."

"Why would he do that?" She could picture Mitch being pissed at her, but she couldn't see him willingly help her out at this point. She'd gotten away with the car, which made him look bad.

"Because he needs to know who placed the bomb if he's going to save his reputation. Word will get out that all this happened on his watch. He needs to keep it as quiet as possible, and he needs answers as soon as possible."

She looked at her friend. She hated the idea of seeing Mitch again. She wanted nothing to do with him. She was humiliated. He'd gotten close to her and then betrayed her. No, there was no way she wanted to see him. But the logic of Lacy's argument couldn't be denied. And she needed to clear her name quickly so the cops would stop poking around in her life. She worried her lip between her teeth. "Could you be there with me?"

"Of course. We'll set up a place and time of our choosing. He'll adapt." Lacy gave her an encouraging nod. "I think this is your best way out."

Alex drew a deep breath and released it. "Okay. I'll call him. Where should we meet?"

"Central Park. By the Ladies Pavilion off 77th street. It's as good a place as any. He's familiar with the city?"

"Yes. His family company is on West 48th street. Callahan Security. He and his brothers, Logan and Gage, spent a lot of time in the city when they were growing up while their father was building the business."

"Wait. Did you say Logan Callahan?"

"Yes, why? Do you know him?"

Lacy's lips tightened into a thin line. "Unfortunately. We've gone head to head a few times. He's a bastard in court, and out of it."

"Great." Alex's shoulders drooped.

Lacy leaned across the table. "Don't worry, I can handle Logan Callahan. You probably won't ever meet him. It's Mitch you have to deal with. Make the phone call, and let's get the ball rolling. The sooner we get this done, the faster you'll be able to get out of town."

CHAPTER TWENTY-SIX

M itch hit the bag one last time and sent it flying. He was dripping with sweat, but his brain didn't feel any clearer. His jaw was still clenched together like it was wired shut. So much for the idea that exercise would help. He sat down hard on the bench and mopped his face with a towel. He dropped the towel beside him and opened his water bottle. After downing the contents, he looked around the room.

The advantage to owning the building and a couple more on the block was that his dad, and now he and his brothers, could do whatever they wanted with it. Turns out they all wanted a gym, so they turned the fourth floor into a gym.

The hardwood floors gleamed under the lights. The heavy bag and speed bag were in the corner next to where he was sitting. Across the room were the weight machines, and in between was the free weight area. There were even yoga mats and exercise balls in the corner.

Logan had been in charge of the remodel and putting the gym together. He'd done an excellent job. It rivaled a lot of the major chains in the city. Mitch didn't want to know how much it had cost. Logan had said it was an investment. If they were going to be doing security work that involved personal security and things like kidnap and ransom, they were going to need their operators to be in shape, and it was cheaper to offer them a place to work out than to pay their gym memberships.

Mitch got up and started walking toward the door to the showers. Logan hadn't skimped there either. They were first rate, with a steam room to boot.

"Yo, Mitch, call for you." Dex's voice came through the speakers. "Line two."

Logan had also made sure the whole building was wired to a communication system. There was no hiding. Mitch did an about face and picked up the receiver on the wall.

"Callahan." He was greeted with silence. "Hello?" He looked at the phone and realized he hadn't hit the line button. "Fuck," he snarled as he hit the button.

"And here I thought you might want to talk to me." Alex's voice hit him like a bullet to his Kevlar vest.

"Goddammit, Alex? Where the fuck are you? What the hell did you do?" he roared into the phone. A dial tone buzzed in his ear. "What?" He looked at the phone. She'd hung up on him. He wanted to crush the receiver into the wall. He gritted his teeth and hit the intercom button.

"Yo," Dex answered.

"I need you to get that call back," Mitch growled.

"No can do. The call came in from a private number."

Mitch heard cracking sounds and realized he was crushing the receiver. He loosened his grip. "There's no way to trace it?"

"I can try, but it's illegal," Dex responded.

"Do it anyway."

Dex sighed. "Can't. Your brother specifically forbade me to do that or anything like it, and I quote, 'No matter what either of my brothers say. They may threaten bodily harm, but I cut the checks. You want to get paid, nothing illegal.'"

Mitch was speechless. He was going to kill Logan. It was that simple. He slammed the receiver down on the wall handset. It bounced out, smashed into the wall, and hung from the cord. He picked it up and banged it back in place, sending bits of plastic flying. It immediately rang. He picked it up.

"Line two," Dex said.

He hit the button. "Callahan," he barked.

"If you're going to yell at me, I'm going to hang up on you. Do we have an understanding?" Alex's voice bounced around his brain as he tried to rein in his anger.

"Yes," he managed to ground out.

"Okay good. Here's the deal. We need to talk."

"Yes, we do. You need to answer some questions. Namely, what the hell were you thinking?" he bellowed.

There was an exaggerated sigh from the other end. "Do I need to hang up again?"

Mitch hit the wall with his hand, making his palm sting. "No. Don't hang up," he demanded. And then in a calmer voice he repeated, "Don't hang up." He took a deep breath. "Okay then, let's talk. Are you willing to answer some questions?"

"No. Not on the phone. I want to speak to you in person."

That threw him. He never expected she would want to see him face-to-face. His gut clenched. "Okay, where?"

"The Ladies Pavilion in Central Park. One hour. No cops." And then she was gone.

Mitch hung up what was left of the phone, spun on his

heel, and jogged over to the showers. Five minutes later, he was down on the second floor, heading toward his office. "Gage, Logan?" he yelled as he stalked down the hallway. Heads popped out of several doorways, but none of them were his brothers. He was about to yell again when Logan appeared from the hallway beside him. "There's no need to bellow. We have a completely functioning intercom system, not to mention we all have cell phones."

"Cut the shit. Where's Gage? Alex called, and she wants to meet."

Gage walked up from behind him. "What? She called? That's...unexpected."

"Yeah, my thoughts exactly," Mitch agreed. "I don't know what she's up to, but she wants to meet in person."

"Let me call the Police Chief from the Hamptons. I'm sure he'll want to be here for the sit-down," Logan said as he turned toward his office.

"No. No cops. She specified." And he wouldn't have time anyway. "She wants to meet at the Ladies Pavilion in Central Park, in"—Mitch glanced at his watch—"forty-nine minutes. Where the hell is the Ladies Pavilion?"

Gage shook his head. Zane, who had wandered over from his desk, shrugged. Both Dragan and Dex shook their heads as well.

"Seriously?" Logan asked. "It's off the 77th street entrance on the west side of the park by the lake."

"How do you know where it is?" Mitch asked and then immediately waved his hand. "You know what? I don't care. We need to make a game plan." He started moving toward the boardroom. The rest of the guys followed him down the hallway.

"How many do you want to take with you?" Gage asked as he sat down at the table. He opened the room's laptop and started typing away. The screen lit up and, within seconds, there was a satellite image of Central Park with a focus on the Ladies Pavilion. "It's got the lake on one side but several pathways on the other. I think three should do it. We can grab her and bring her back here. What do you think, Mitch?"

Before Mitch could say anything, Logan spoke up. "There will be no grabbing of anyone. It's great that she wants to talk, but technically you have no proof of wrong-doing at this moment. She's a person of interest. The cops would like to speak to her, but no one is arresting her or scooping her up. You'd be guilty of kidnapping."

Mitch looked at Gage. "Why did he have to be a lawyer? He makes everything so fucking difficult."

Gage smiled.

Logan shot his brother a look. "I'm trying to keep your ass out of jail. If you grab her and she presses charges, our reputation goes downhill in one hell of a hurry. So, let's be rational and come up with a legal solution."

Logan's reminder about the company's reputation hit him like a fist to the gut. Him taking this case was the sole reason they were in this mess to begin with. He wanted to yell at his brother, but Logan was right. They had to do this by the book. They were already on thin ice. "Okay, Logan, what do you suggest?"

"You and I will go. I'll keep you out of legal trouble, and you find out what you need to know. Ten to one she's bringing a lawyer anyway."

"Alex? No way. Why would she bring a lawyer to talk with me?" Mitch asked.

Logan snorted. "Whenever anyone says they want to meet to talk and it involves a legal situation, they always bring their lawyer."

Gage looked at Mitch. "Sounds reasonable to me. She doesn't pose a threat." He grinned. "Or at least not one that you can't handle. The two of you should be fine on your own. In the meantime, I'm going to take a crack at Drake, find out if there's anything else he knows that he didn't feel like sharing. Does that work for you two?"

Both Mitch and Logan nodded.

"Dragan," Mitch said, "I want you to dig deeper on Drake and this Tolliver guy. Find out everything you can. Every detail. I want to know who their first crushes were, got it?"

Dragan unfolded his six-foot-four-inch frame from the chair. "I'll start with Tolliver," he said with his usual rumble.

"Dex, do me a favor and get Diana Sterling on the line asap. We need her to answer some more questions. She's been dodging us. I don't care how you do it, but get it done."

Dex nodded. "Yes, sir."

Mitch turned to Zane. " I need you to drive. Parking will be a nightmare. I want you to pull up as near as you can to the 77th Street entrance and keep the engine running. Just in case."

Zane gave him a nod and left the room.

Gage pointedly looked at his watch. "You two need to go if you're going to make it on time."

Mitch nodded. "You need to change quick time, Logan?"

"Change? Why would I change?" Logan looked down at his gray Zegna pants and white Eton shirt with red Armani tie.

Mitch sighed loudly. "You think you're going to blend in wearing that in Central Park on a Sunday? Put on some jeans." Mitch pointed to his own jeans and black T-shirt.

"I don't think there's any need to blend in," Logan responded.

"Oh, for Christ sake, just lose the tie," Mitch snarled as he stormed out of the room. He just didn't understand his brother. Logan was so uptight and by the book, it drove Mitch crazy. Thinking outside the box just didn't exist in Logan's world. Logan had been more willing to get into trouble when they were kids, at least with Gage, but not so much with Mitch.

He punched the elevator button with more force than necessary and then stalked on when the doors opened. He pushed the button for the ground floor and caught his reflection in the elevator doors. Once again, he was reminded of how much he was the outsider. His looks, his attitude, none of it was like his brothers', or at least that's what they made him believe. Well, the hell with that. It didn't matter, now. He was going to finish this job if it killed him.

The elevator doors opened, and Logan was standing there waiting for him. It pissed him off all the more. He started to walk by his brother, but Logan caught his arm. "I don't know what I did to piss you off this time, but you need to take a breather. You need your head on straight before we meet with this woman."

He pulled his arm out of Logan's grasp. "Don't worry about me. I've held it together while being shot at by rocket launchers, so I think it would take a bit more than meeting one woman in Central Park to throw me off my game." He walked out the front door of the building and climbed in the SUV that was waiting at the curb. As soon as Logan climbed into the front seat, Zane took off and headed uptown.

Zane and Logan started discussing business and the new software that Logan was testing. Mitch tuned them out and tried to get himself under control. Who was he kidding? He was totally wound up. He didn't know what he was going to do when he saw Alex, hug her or strangle her. He needed to focus.

He tried a couple of breathing exercises, but it was no use. He was pissed. No, he was damn mad. Mad that Alex had put him in this position, mad that he'd let her, but mostly mad he hadn't been able to stop it all from happening. He was an ex-SEAL, for crying out loud. This should have been child's play for him. He'd planned more intense missions, deadlier missions, than this, and still he couldn't manage one man's security.

Maybe he should get out. Wrap this shit up and quit. Logan and Gage could run Callahan security on their own. They had Dex, Dragan, and Zane to help them, not to mention the guys they had out on jobs. They'd be fine. But would he? He didn't have an answer, and that scared him.

Zane pulled up at the curb by the 77th Street entrance. "You got two minutes."

Logan looked over his shoulder at Mitch. "Ready?"

"Yeah. It's going to be a walk in the park."

CHAPTER TWENTY-SEVEN

"Are you sure this is a good idea?" Alex asked for the umpteenth time as she paced back and forth inside the pavilion.

"It's the only choice you have that might get you out of the picture without involving the cops." Lacy smoothed back her hair in a ponytail. "You're making me nervous with all your marching," she said. "Did you know this is actually an old trolley shelter from the turn of the century? It was built to give people a place to wait out the weather after their visit to the park." Lacy ran her hand over the scrolling wrought iron. "It's beautiful. Look at the gold leaf. Bus shelters have certainly come down in the world since then."

"Yeah, well, we don't have to ride horses to get around, so there's that," Alex said as she brushed the long black hair from her face. The heat was making her scalp sweat under the wig. She ran a finger under the dog collar around her neck. Of all days to choose an all-black disguise. She'd debated changing it when she and Lacy were waiting to meet Mitch but decided against it. She was regretting that decision now.

"True." Lacy sighed. "You know hanging up on him might have been a bit over the top. Poking the bear and all that."

"Mitch was going to yell at me and not listen to a word I said, so I didn't give him that option. Giving people limited options always works better for me."

"Well, let's hope the bear isn't too pissed off. If he shows up with the cops, there's not much we can do."

Alex frowned. "We can run." Then she glanced at her friend. Lacy was wearing a gray pencil skirt with a white sleeveless tank and a pair of black spike heels. "I can run," she amended. "You can smooth things over for me, also known as buy me time so I can escape."

Lacy snorted in response. "Thanks. Leave me holding the bag."

"Isn't that what lawyers do?" Alex asked innocently. Then she stilled.

Mitch and someone else were coming down the path. It had to be one of his brothers. They had a similar walk. Their coloring was different, but the facial structure was the same. Two very good-looking men. She wondered if it was Logan or Gage.

Her stomach twisted into knots. Heat rolled up her neck into her cheeks. Humiliation washed over her in waves. This man had seen her naked. He'd had his fingers inside of her, and if she'd had her way, much more. She'd been such a fool. She swallowed hard and willed the color back out of her cheeks. She was going to get this mess sorted out, and then she was never going to see Mitch Callahan again.

Lacy must have noticed her reaction because she turned around and promptly said, "Son of a bitch."

"What?" Alex asked quietly, almost without moving her lips. She didn't want Mitch to hear them speaking. It was a system they'd worked out at boarding school so they could talk during study hall and when they were sneaking out at night so they wouldn't get caught.

"Logan Callahan." Lacy's answer was barely a whisper.

"And?"

"He's a major pain in the ass, but like I said before, I can handle him."

"Fabulous." Alex moaned. The men stopped at the entrance to the trolley shelter.

"Ladies," Logan said, "mind if we join you?"

Alex just stared at Mitch. He looked exhausted and more than a little pissed off. But he was in one piece, and the tightness in her chest eased just a fraction. She quickly reminded herself this was the man who used her, who wormed his way into her heart only to betray her. She made sure she was close to the exit on the opposite side, so if worse came to worse, she could make a break for it. Mitch came up the stairs and stood a few feet from Alex. Logan followed his brother and stood opposite Lacy.

Logan smiled. "Ms. Carmichael. Always nice to see you."

"Mr. Callahan. I wish I could say the same."

"You two know each other?" Mitch asked.

Lacy said, "Your brother and I have met a few times. Always on opposite sides of the negotiation. Looks like today will be no different."

"Yes, here we are again," Logan agreed.

"So, here are the rules." Lacy moved to lean against the pavilion wall as she ticked the points off on her fingers. "You can ask questions, but this is an off-the-record meeting and anything my client says is not admissible in court. She will not answer any questions about her past or her future plans. She will not—"

"Why did you do it?" Mitch asked, his expression guarded.

Alex wanted to throw up. She wanted to run. She wanted to be anywhere but here. She hadn't realized how much she didn't want to see Mitch until this very moment. She felt...exposed. "I, uh..." She cleared her throat and started again. "I was hired to steal, that is retrieve, the car and return it to its rightful owner." She met Mitch's eyes. She saw something, some emotion, flash in them, but it was gone too fast for her to identify it.

"I meant, why did you take the prototype?"

"What? What prototype? I took the car, and that's it. I had nothing to do with the bomb or anything else. Just the car."

Logan snorted. "You expect us to believe it was a coincidence that you happened to be stealing the car on the same day as someone else set off a bomb? And you didn't know about it?"

Alex met Logan's stare head on. "I don't expect you to believe anything. I am merely stating the truth."

Lacy glared at Logan. "My client had nothing to do with the bomb or whatever this prototype thing is. She was retrieving the car for the owner."

"So, that's your client's story?" Logan scoffed. "What? She's a repo guy now? You know we could call the cops and have her arrested for breaking and entering and grand theft auto."

"In your dreams, Callahan," Lacy shot back. "Your man Drake never owned the car. He was asked for it back, but he refused, so Ms. Sterling had no choice but to hire my client to retrieve it. You can't get anywhere near grand theft or B and E, and you know it. Nice try."

"I think I can prove it," Logan challenged. He went on, but Alex tuned out the next bit because Mitch moved over to stand directly in front of her.

"Where's the prototype, Alex?" His eyes bored into hers.

"I—I don't know what you're talking about." When he looked at her like that, it was like he could see her soul. She wanted to look away, but she couldn't seem to do it. "I took the car and only the car. I don't know anything about a prototype."

Suddenly there was a *tinging* sound like metal on metal. Alex turned to see what it was, but Mitch hit her square in the chest, knocking her backward out of the pavilion and into the dirt. She landed hard flat on her back, and her head hit with a thunk. She saw stars. Mitch landed on top of her, knocking the breath out of her lungs. She couldn't speak. She blinked rapidly. The sound happened again and then again. The fog lifted in her brain. Bullets. Someone was shooting at them using a suppressor.

There was a puff of dirt next to her and Mitch rolled them into the bushes behind the pavilion. He kept her covered with his body. She fought to get Mitch off. She needed to sit up to catch her breath. Her arms flailed as she tried to move him.

"Stop moving. They'll see us," Mitch hissed in her ear. He was peering through the bushes in what she assumed was the direction the shots came from. She hit him again. The world was turning black. Her vision was tunneling.

"Alex. Alex. Oh, my God, Alex, honey. Breathe. Just breathe." Mitch shifted his weight, and suddenly her lungs found oxygen. She took in a big gulp of air and then another. It was like heaven.

"I couldn't breathe. Couldn't get air into my lungs."

"Shhh," he hissed at her. "I can't see where the shooter is. I don't know if he's gone."

The sound of a groan met their ears. "Logan?" Mitch yelled. There was an edge of panic to his voice. So much for being quiet, but she understood. Panic was crushing her chest again.

"Lacy?" she squeaked. It should have come out as a yell, but terror had made her throat close over. If Lacy was hurt or...worse, she wouldn't ever forgive herself. She tried again. "Lacy?" It was louder this time, but still not the yell she was hoping for.

"Yeah," came a muffled reply. Then, "Get off me! You're crushing me!"

She'd know Lacy's voice anywhere. Thank God, she was okay. More than okay. She was yelling at Logan, so she was in fine shape and very pissed off by the sounds of things.

"Logan?" Mitch called.

"Ye—uh." They heard a thunk and another groan.

"Logan!" Mitch slid off Alex and soldier-crawled across the dirt to the pavilion. He pulled himself up the stairs on his belly. Lacy stood up. Mitch told her to get back down, but she snorted at him.

"The shooter is long gone," she said as she tried to wipe the dirt off her blouse and skirt.

Alex got up and walked over to Lacy. Logan was sitting up against the inside of the pavilion.

"Are you all right?" Alex asked him. He gave her a quick nod.

"He's fine. He's just winded. I hit him so he'd get off me. He was crushing me. I couldn't breathe," Lacy said as she continued to brush the dirt off her clothing.

Alex nodded. She knew what that felt like. She looked around. "Wait. Where did Mitch go? He was just here."

Logan nodded toward the direction the shooter had been. "He went to check it out." Logan finally got to his feet and started brushing himself off. "And you're welcome," he said to Lacy.

"For what? Almost crushing me?" she retorted.

Logan shot her a look as he continued to brush at his pants. "For saving your life. Standing still while people are shooting at you is not the best idea. You could have easily been killed."

Lacy rolled her eyes and then smoothed back her hair. "I wasn't the target. And to be frank, your reaction time was slow, so if I had been the target, I would have been dead."

"She's right," Mitch agreed as he walked back onto the pavilion. He shot a glance at Logan's face and quickly amended, "About the shooter that is. Whoever it was, they're not very good, or at least not as good as they should have been to try for that shot. There's a lot of trees and bushes between here and where they were standing by the wall. It provides great cover but makes the shot harder. Amateurs for sure."

"So," Logan asked, "who were they shooting at and why did they stop?"

Mitch halfheartedly brushed off the front of his shirt. "Not sure, but let's not stay and find out." He grabbed Alex by the arm and started to walk out of the pavilion. "We have an SUV waiting. Let's go."

"Uh, no. I'm not going with you." She pulled her arm away.

Lacy grabbed Alex's other arm. "My client—"

Mitch whirled around. "Your client almost got killed two minutes ago. We have no idea who the shooter is or why they're shooting. Your client needs to get to safety. Now."

"My client can keep herself safe," Lacy stated firmly.

"Can she now?" Mitch snorted. "Is that why my brother and I had to take both you and your client down so you two wouldn't get shot? If we hadn't been here, you two would have been dead."

Alex saw red. Just like before. Mitch thought she was weak. She might have fallen for his smile and banter, but she sure as shit wasn't weak. She got right up in his face. "Oh, really? No one shot at me or Lacy all day until we met with you two. Did you even consider that? We were just fine until now, so maybe it's you two that the shooter is after. Either way, I'm not going with you. I can take care of myself."

Mitch fisted his hands. The pulse in his neck was slow and steady unlike hers, which had skyrocketed.

"It's dangerous to stay here. We've no idea if the shooter is gone for good or just in hiding. We need to move now." Mitch didn't take his eyes from hers, and the fire burning in their depths just stoked her anger more. If he wanted a fight, she was willing.

Logan broke in, "I think we can come to an arrangement."

She looked over at him to find him leaning nonchalantly against the entry to the pavilion. His clothes looked impeccable once again. How the hell did he do that?

"What are you thinking?" Lacy asked.

"Let's agree to you ladies accompanying us down to our office to continue the interview." Lacy opened her mouth, but Logan put up his hands to cut her off. "You may leave at any time. We will not call the police, and the interview will remain informal."

Lacy's eyes narrowed. "Absolutely no recording of the conversations that occur in any way, shape, or form. Nothing is admissible. And no tracking devices or any kind of location devices will be planted on myself or my client in the room. We will not be followed when we leave."

Logan nodded, but Mitch remained silent. "Mitch," Logan said, warning in his voice.

Mitch spoke through his teeth, "Fine."

"Great. Let's go." Logan signaled that Lacy should precede him out of the pavilion. She sighed heavily and grabbed Alex by the arm. Mitch took the lead and Logan brought up the rear as they headed up the path to the street.

"Are you sure about this?" Alex asked Lacy in a whisper.

"No. But we really don't have a choice. You want to clear your name, and this is still your best shot. Just choose your words carefully. They'll record it."

"They just agreed—"

"Logan agreed. Mitch grunted his assent. I'm willing to bet there will be others who will make it happen without telling Logan. Plausible deniability."

Alex rubbed her face with her hands. "Well, fuck."

"Yes. That pretty much sums it up," Lacy agreed.

They came out of the path and hit the sidewalk. Mitch ushered them into the SUV, and he and Logan hopped in the other side. Somehow Alex managed to get sandwiched in the middle between Lacy and Mitch. When her thigh brushed his, she tried to scooch over, but no matter how much she moved, she couldn't get away from his touch. It was as if he was following her. She wanted the ride to be over. Heat crawled up her cheeks again. Would this humiliation ever go away?

The worst part was when his arm brushed her breast by accident when he took a phone from Logan. Heat started blooming in other places. She remembered how good he felt beneath her, how hot his kisses were. Her fingers tingled with the memory of his chest muscles rippling under them. She was getting hotter by the second. She needed to get away from this man. She glanced up, and their eyes locked. His gray ones went from cold hard steel to smoky. He knew what she was feeling, and he was feeling it, too.

When the truck jerked to a stop, she pushed Lacy out onto the sidewalk. They were ushered into the building quickly, and she stumbled a bit as she entered the lobby. She was surprised when she looked around. She had figured them for a modern look, all glass and chrome.

Instead, the lobby was small and intimate. Two women were sitting behind a tall desk with a gleaming wooden surface. The lighting was soft. The walls were what she would call greige, a mixture of gray and beige. The artwork was a mash-up of modern and classic pieces, but all of them were originals. It could have been a doctor's office except for the discreet cameras in the ceiling and the hidden door that blended into the woodwork perfectly. Her life as a thief taught her what to look for, so she recognized the signs.

The entry doors were bulletproof glass, and she had no doubt a steel one would slide out if a panic button was hit. She also knew each woman would be an excellent shot and have at least one gun in a drawer close by.

When they stepped onto an elevator, Alex immediately cased the place. It looked very posh with fancy buttons. *Five floors.* Expensive wood paneling *with no hand holds. Hard to climb out of the top. Camera in the ceiling.* There was no doubt in her mind that the elevator could be controlled from the desk below as well as a desk on any floor. They would be able to shut it down at will.

The doors opened on the second floor. Again, there was a welcome desk done in wood with a glass wall behind it. The space behind the glass was done tastefully like the lobby. Browns and greys with touches of color here and there. Fresh flowers. Original artwork. The hardwood floors gleamed, and the rugs that lay on top were plush with calming patterns. The whole place spoke class.

Logan had to have been the one who oversaw the decorating. No way did Mitch have a hand in this. It was just way too classy, too upscale for him. It had all the right touches. She glanced over at Logan. Definitely his style. Made her wonder what the rest of the building was like.

"You own the whole building, correct?" she asked Logan.

Mitch brushed by them and continued through the glass doors down the hallway.

"Yes, we do." He held the door open for her.

"What's on the other floors?"

"Why? Are you planning your escape?" He looked amused, and she made a face but mostly because she was. It was second nature. She couldn't help it.

"The third floor is more office space similar to this one. The fourth is the gym and the fifth is living space, a kitchen, great room area, some bedrooms, that type of thing."

"Do people live here?"

"Someone is always here but no, no one lives here full-time. It's more for the guys to grab a bite or catch some sleep if they are on a job and don't have much time off."

He tried to usher her through the door, but she balked. Lacy glanced at her.

"Let's talk on the fifth floor. I'm hungry," Alex said.

Logan's expression flickered for a second, but then his face returned to neutral. "We can certainly order in if you like."

"That's great, but I'd like to talk in a more comfortable setting." Alex smiled up at him.

Logan frowned but nodded. "Give me a minute." He walked through the doors and down the hallway. He disappeared into the same room as Mitch.

"What's going on?" Lacy asked.

"Well, if they're going to record us or play other games, might as well make it more complicated for them. Besides, I gotta say my ass hurts. Mitch crushed me, and I'm bruised all over. I can't bear the thought of sitting on a hard chair in a conference room for the next few hours, but I'm not telling him that," Alex said quietly.

Lacy rubbed her thigh and made a face. "I agree. Comfortable furniture does sound better. I'm feeling somewhat beaten up myself. It was like being taken down by a rock wall. I'm going to need a bath tonight. I'm starting to stiffen up."

Alex nodded. "Besides, I'm starving, and there's a kitchen up there. Maybe they have snacks."

Lacy started to laugh, but the sound died in her throat when she saw Logan emerge from the conference room. He did not look happy. And if his expression was dark, Mitch's was positively thunderous. Another man emerged behind them who looked so similar he could only be their brother Gage. His coloring and height was closer to Logan than Mitch, but the animalist way he moved was much more in line with Mitch. His face was blank, but it was almost scarier that way.

"Here it comes," Lacy whispered.

"What?" she said as she glanced at the men advancing toward them.

"The storm, and it's going to be a category five."

CHAPTER TWENTY-EIGHT

Mitch was going to kill Alex, no doubt. He had no idea what this game was about, but he was done playing. They'd just found out that someone had taken a shot at Jake while he was going to see Dan in the hospital again. He was hit, but it was only a graze. Mitch was in no mood for taking any shit from her.

He followed Logan through the door and was about to tear a strip off Alex when Logan put a hand on his chest. His gaze swung to his brother's face. Logan gave him the subtlest head shake. Then he turned toward the women. "Why don't you ladies head on up? Sloan, can you please accompany them and see if they need anything? A drink perhaps or something to eat?"

"Of course, Mr. Callahan." Sloan stood and walked around the desk. She smiled at Alex and Lacy and then led them onto the elevator. Once the doors closed, Logan whirled around and faced his brother. "You cannot go up there screaming. She'll shut down immediately, and we won't get anything out of her."

Mitch's blood went cold. It was just like when they

were kids and Logan used to order him around. He took a step closer to his brother. "Don't you dare tell me how to play this. I've faced off against some of the worst this world has to offer. I can break her."

"Yes, you can. Break. Her." Logan stopped and stared pointedly at his brother.

Mitch frowned, and then he understood what his brother was saying. "That's not what I meant." He scowled.

"Isn't it? I know bull in a china shop is your usual approach, but you can't always do that. Dex told me she hung up on you earlier when you yelled at her. He listened in."

Mitch decided then and there to kill Dex. He clenched his teeth until his jaw hurt.

"Mitch, this has to be done delicately, especially now that they are shooting at Jake in the Hamptons."

"You don't think I know how important this is?" Mitch roared. "That I would risk Jake's safety over my ego?"

Logan leaned back against the wall and folded his arms across his chest. "I'm not questioning your loyalty to your friend. He's mine and Gage's friend, too. We all want to do right by him. But going up there and screaming at Alex is not going to cut it. So, get yourself under control. We need to have a united front and be smart about this."

Mitch's hands were clenched at his sides. He wanted to plant a fist in his brother's face so badly. He could beat his brother to a pulp in a heartbeat. He could make him beg for mercy in about two minutes. Logan had no idea how much effort it took to keep all that training at bay and not do anything. But deep-down Mitch knew he loved his brother and wouldn't hurt him no matter how much his brother pushed him. And in this case, Logan was right. Again. It pissed him off to no end.

Gage put a hand on Mitch's back. "I know," was all he said. Gage had always known how Mitch felt around him and Logan. He'd been the peacemaker for years. He also knew what Mitch was capable of and that Logan had no idea how lucky he was that Mitch didn't decide to forget they were brothers.

"Okay, let's do it," Gage said as he hit the button for the elevator. Mitch took a deep breath and rolled his shoulders. He tried to clear his mind like he did before each mission. He had to be clear and focused to react fast.

Jake came to mind. Mitch had left him with Drake. He was fine, but still. It was on Mitch if anything happened to his people. He had to get this case figured out before someone else got seriously hurt.

He stepped onto the elevator and tried not to think about Alex almost getting shot in the park. It had been an instantaneous reaction to cover her once he heard the gunfire. Keeping her safe had been the first thing and then tracking the shooter. Fear had hit him like a sledgehammer. It didn't work that way on missions, but the thought of Alex hurt gutted him. He pushed that thought aside as they walked out of the elevator. It wasn't important. He didn't need to understand it, not now. Now he just needed to get answers.

The plush leather cushion sighed as Mitch sat in the chair to the left of Alex and Lacy who were on the matching couch. Both had sunk into the puffy cushions and were munching on cheese and crackers from the plate in front of them on the coffee table. Sloan got up from the couch beside Lacy, and after asking the women if they needed anything else, and being told no, she left.

Logan sat in another overstuffed chair next to the right of Lacy. He grabbed a water bottle off the table and poured himself a glass using one of the clean cups on the coffee table.

"So, how are you ladies feeling now?" Logan asked.

"Fine," Lacy responded. Alex merely waved since her mouth was full of crackers and cheese.

Gage took a bottle and sat on the fireplace hearth that was directly across from the couch. He looked over and caught Mitch's eye. He tilted his head slightly toward the women. Mitch knew he was asking if he could take the lead. He looked down and saw that his fists were clenched and made a concerted effort to open them but when he couldn't, he looked at Gage and gave a slight nod.

He snuck a peek at Alex. She brushed long black strands of hair out of her face. He hadn't seen this wig before today, or the dog collar for that matter. If he didn't know her as well as he did, he never would have been able to pick her out of a crowd. No wonder Interpol had no idea who she was.

Gage cleared his throat. "So, let's get down to it if we could. Alex, can you tell us exactly how you came to be in the garage last night?"

Alex glanced at Lacy who nodded. She took a deep breath and then started to speak.

"So, I got a call from my handler who said we had a job. He told me it was to retrieve something from Jameson Drake. He gave me details, and we worked out a plan. Last night I executed that plan." Alex leaned over and took a sip of water, then sat back and remained silent.

"That's it. That's all you're going to say?" Mitch asked, incredulous.

Alex shrugged. "That's it in a nutshell."

Logan sent Mitch a look, but Mitch ignored it. "Let's get some details. When did you take on the Drake job?"

"Hmm." She closed her eyes in thought. "It was after the…" She paused. "But before I did that side thing for…"

She was being very careful not to divulge details, he noticed.

She opened her eyes again. "So, about a month ago or six weeks ago?"

"How many jobs do you pull a year?"

Lacy leaned forward. "Don't answer that." Alex kept silent.

"Do you know who hired you?" Gage asked.

"Diana Sterling," Alex replied, taking another sip of water.

Mitch ran his hands through his hair. "So, you know the client, but they don't know you."

"Yes, mostly." Alex pulled a pillow onto her lap and started playing with the tassels.

"How long did it take you to plan the job?" Mitch watched her closely.

"The plan is always fluid going in. I don't solidify anything until I get the lay of the land. This time it only took a few days to put it all together."

Mitch frowned. "A few days…"

Gage asked, "What do you mean, mostly? Do people you know, like friends, hire you to steal stuff?"

"Let's get this straight once and for all." She pointed to herself. "I am *the* Asset Repossession Specialist Extraordinaire. My reputation precedes me, so sometimes I work for people I know."

Gage's face broke into a grin. "You know what the acronym is, right?" Alex sent him a black look, but Gage still chuckled. Logan fought to keep from smiling. Mitch saw the humor, but it didn't move him. The only arse in the room was him, by the sounds of things. A few days and, damn, she might have even changed it up after Friday afternoon on the yacht. He was a complete idiot. It had taken him weeks to put together that security plan, but it had only taken her a day to break it.

"So," Gage continued, "Diana Sterling hired you to get the car back. Why didn't she just call the police?"

Alex shot him a look of disbelief. "She'd never ask the cops. It's too humiliating. She wanted it handled quickly and quietly, which is what I specialize in."

"Except for the bomb part," Gage threw in. She frowned at him.

Logan leaned forward in the chair. "No one else approached you about any other job regarding Drake? No one else asked you to steal something for them?"

Alex gritted her teeth. "I do not steal random things. I am an asset reposs—"

"Yes, we heard you the first time," Mitch ground out.

"Well, obviously not because you keep getting it wrong!" she shot back. "Look, I don't just steal random things from people. I don't case their houses and decide I like a painting and take it. That's not me. I am *not* a thief." She looked at all three brothers to make sure they were paying attention. She shot a glance at Lacy, who gave her another slight nod.

"I only retrieve sentimental belongings for people, things they might have given to someone they thought they loved. It's a little different in Diana Sterling's case, but it's the same principle."

The brothers were all looking at her like she was an alien.

"Okay, say person A met person B and fell in love or whatever. They entered into a relationship. Person A then gives B something that is important to her, that has special significance to her. B is thrilled with it and is happy. Then A and B break up for some reason. A who gave B uh, say her grandfather's watch, now wants the watch back but B likes the watch, so he refuses to give it back. A hires me, an asset repossession specialist, to retrieve the watch from B. After all, it's not B's family heirloom, so why should he get to keep the watch? I get the watch from B and give it to A. A is happy, or as happy as a broken-hearted A can be. And B, well B is no worse off than he was before. Make sense?"

The room was silent. Mitch was stunned. Alex wasn't a thief so much as she was a...a what? As asset repossession specialist. He could feel his lips breaking into a smile. All this time, he'd been worried he'd fallen for a thief but, really, she was just out there righting wrongs, as she saw it.

Relief washed over him and then ice water ran through his veins. *Fallen for? No way. No. Back up the bus.* He swallowed hard. Shit. It was true. He'd fallen for her. That's why he'd been so mad that she bested him at Drake's. He didn't want her to be the enemy. And why he'd been so terrified in the park. The thought of her getting hurt had his palms breaking out in a sweat even now. He closed his eyes. Fuck! This was not good. Not good at all.

"So, you are saying you don't know anything about the prototype or the bomb," Gage said. "What did you think was happening when the bomb went off?"

She glanced at Mitch. "I... Honestly, I had no idea. I just got the hell out of there as was my plan. I delivered the car and got out of town. I didn't hear anything about it until much later." She met Mitch's gaze. "I am so sorry one of your men got hurt."

Mitch nodded his thanks.

"I really had nothing to do with it, and I know nothing about it. I—" She paused for a second and then continued. "It occurred to me that someone took advantage of my breaking in to wreak havoc and blame me for it. I don't know why, but if you say this prototype is missing, then maybe they used me and the bomb as a distraction."

Logan spoke up. "We agree with you on part of it. We think the bomb was a distraction, and we know you had nothing to do with it."

Alex's gaze shot back to Mitch. He nodded again. "I've been over the video a million times. I know for a fact you were nowhere near the area the bomb went off before you took the car, so you couldn't have put it there."

She closed her eyes slowly and exhaled. Her shoulders lowered and relaxed. She'd been worried. Really worried. It just solidified his opinion of her more. She was one of the good guys. Even if her methods were questionable, her motives weren't. "Dan getting hurt wasn't your fault."

"Dan. Is that his name? How's he doing?" Lacy asked.

Mitch sat back and linked his hands behind his head. "He lost his spleen, but the doctor says he'll make a full recovery. He says he doesn't remember anything, though, so he's no help."

Logan leaned forward, poured more water into his glass, and then took a drink. "That brings us back to the prototype. Alex, you say you didn't steal it."

"I didn't." She shook her head emphatically.

"Actually, you did." Mitch leaned forward and put his elbows on his knees. "The prototype was in the car, and you...retrieved the car."

"Then it has to still be in the car. I didn't take anything with me except what I brought."

Mitch shook his head. "It's not in the car. I checked, and so did Jake. Not there."

Alex blinked and looked at Lacy. She shrugged. Alex licked her lips. "I swear I didn't take anything from the car. Just my stuff."

"Are you sure you didn't accidently pick it up?" Gage asked as he stood up.

"No. I don't even know what this prototype looks like or what it's for. There was nothing in the car to take, as I recall. It was empty."

Gage walked over to the fridge and grabbed a beer. He held it up and looked around the room. Logan frowned and shook his head. Mitch nodded. Lacy shook her head, but Alex gave a nod.

He got three bottles out of the fridge and took off the tops. "Is it possible that it got mixed in with your stuff somehow?" he asked as he walked across the room and handed Mitch and Alex their beers. He went back and sat down on the fireplace hearth again.

"I don't see how. What does it look like?" Alex took a swig of her beer.

Mitch swallowed a gulp of beer. "It's a memory stick in a circular tube. Silver."

Alex started to shake her head no, but froze.

"What?" Mitch demanded.

"When the bomb went off, I yanked the steering wheel hard and my bag upended. After I pulled the car into Sterling's garage, I went around and stuffed everything back in my bag. I grabbed a tube from under the seat and threw it in my bag. I didn't look at it closely. I just assumed it was my Chapstick, but I guess it could be the tube you're talking about."

Mitch asked. "Where is it now?"

Alex opened her mouth, but closed it. She looked at Lacy. Lacy seemed to understand something from the look they shared because she piped up. "Alex cannot answer that question."

Logan frowned. "Can you go get it and bring it back here?"

"Yes, I guess it's possible." Alex glanced at her watch. "But it will have to be tomorrow."

Mitch stood up. "Why tomorrow? Why can't we get it now?"

"Because it's not available now," Alex said simply.

"It's five p.m. in New York City. What is not available at this hour?" Mitch's frustration was mounting. He needed the prototype back so he could give it to Drake and go out with a win. Then maybe Drake wouldn't tank their company's reputation. As it was, Dex said there were a few clients calling with questions. They couldn't afford to have any client jump ship. The remodel of the space plus all the equipment on the third floor had cost a fortune. Everyone had sunk everything they had into this venture. No way was he going to let it go under without a major fight.

"I'm sorry, but it can't be reached until tomorrow morning. That's just the way it is."

When Mitch took a step forward, Alex stood up to face him. "I'm not trying to be difficult. I'm just being honest. I can't get it until tomorrow morning. I won't tell you where it is because it involves other people. Currently, I know it's safe and they're safe. If we run around and try to find it now, we'll just be attracting attention, and it could put a lot of people in danger. I can go first thing tomorrow morning and get it. I'm sorry, but you'll have to be satisfied with that."

Mitch ground his teeth. So close, and yet it still wasn't in his grasp. He nodded his agreement but moved away from the seating area to walk over to the window. He needed a break. He was tired and frustrated, and he wasn't sure what he was feeling when it came to Alex. Or rather he was afraid of what he was feeling.

"Alex, if you wouldn't mind, I have a few more questions." Logan gestured toward the couch, and Alex sat back down. She reached out and took a long swig of her beer.

"If we go with the idea that you were part of the distraction, then we have to suppose that someone who knew when you would be there set this whole thing up. So, who knew about this job for Sterling and who knew your schedule?"

"Myself, Diana Sterling, and my handler. No one else knew all the details. Diana didn't even know all the details."

Gage frowned and took a drink from his beer. "But no one on that list seems like a decent suspect unless... How well do you know your handler?"

Alex immediately held up her hand. "Stop right there. We've been together for years, since the beginning. He's my rock. He's my partner. I love him to bits, and he loves me. There's absolutely no way he'd do this without telling me."

Mitch felt like he'd just been sucker-punched. Alex had a partner that she loved. He looked over at her. He had no idea what her relationship with the other guy was, but he sure as hell was going to find out.

CHAPTER TWENTY-NINE

"So, you're sure that no one else knew of your plan? Did someone else know about you taking the job?" Gage asked as he got up from the hearth and sat in the chair Mitch had vacated.

"No. No one. I don't talk about my work, and neither does my handler. It's safer for everyone." All this talk about Leo made her mouth dry so she took another sip of beer. She wouldn't give Leo up no matter what.

Logan leaned back in his chair and steepled his fingers together. "Who told Diana Sterling about your services?"

"I can answer that," a man said as he strolled over from the elevator.

Alex whirled around to see who spoke. She'd been so caught up in worrying about Leo, she hadn't heard the elevator ding. The man was tall, over six feet, and lanky. His hair was blond and styled just so. He obviously took pride in his appearance. He was wearing dress pants and a button-down on a Sunday.

"I just got off the phone with her. Took me all after-noon to get her to talk to me, but as luck would have it, she just had another fight with her husband and needed a sympathetic ear."

Gage grinned. "Which you were happy to provide."

He took a small bow. "Which I was very happy to provide." He grinned and brushed a blond curl off his forehead.

"Ladies," Gage said, "this is Dex. He's one of our technical crew but really a jack of all trades. He also happens to be very charming, and the ladies love him."

Dex made another small bow.

"Dex, this is Alex and Lacy," Gage said as he pointed to each one in turn.

"It's nice to meet you both." Dex smiled. "To get back to Diana. You know, she's actually a nice lady. Her husband seems like a huge asshole. Have no idea why she took him back. You women are strange."

"No comment," Alex said.

"What did she say? How did she get Alex's contact information?" Mitch asked from his spot by the window.

He was leaning against the wall, sipping his beer. He appeared relaxed, but after spending time around him, Alex knew that he was stressed out at the moment. Something was bugging him. Their eyes met, but he turned away. Whatever it was, he had no interest in telling her about it. *And she had no interest in hearing it*, she reminded herself.

"Well, now—oh look, snacks." Dex immediately crashed down between Lacy and Alex on the sofa and proceeded to stuff crackers and cheese in his mouth.

Both Alex and Lacy laughed as they got re-situated. "By all means, make yourself comfortable." Alex stole a cracker with a piece of cheese on it from Dex's hand and popped it in her mouth.

"Hey," he called, but his smile said he wasn't remotely upset.

"Dex," barked Mitch.

"Yo," he called back. "Oh, you want the deets. Sure, well Diana Sterling said she first heard about Alex's prowess in getting items back for their rightful owners from her good friend, Monica.

"Monica raved about your work, Alex. According to Diana, Monica thinks you are"—Dex changed his voice so he sounded like a woman—"just an angel. Monica was devastated by the loss of her favorite Matisse to that scoundrel John. Alex bringing it back to her has lifted her spirits and made her feel able to face the world again. She's like a new woman."

Alex laughed. "I remember Monica Moore. She was devastated. Her fiancé was having an affair. Getting the picture back really made her happy. Glad to hear she's doing well."

"I don't suppose Monica Moore would want the prototype?" Logan asked.

Alex tilted her head. "I don't think so. She's always had a trust fund. Her father made millions and handed it down the line. I don't think she's had an actual job, like ever."

Logan stated, "Maybe we're missing something. Let's go over everything again."

Alex groaned. "I'm done. I've already told my story."

"Well, I didn't hear it." Dex gave her a big smile. "I'd love to hear your story." He leaned back on the sofa and put his arm around behind her while he stretched his long legs out in front of him. Mitch made a noise that sounded like a growl, but when she looked over at him, his face was blank. *Weird.*

Lacy started to get up. "I think I'm done as well. I have other things I must attend to."

"Yes. We should be going." Alex rose from the sofa.

"Ladies," Gage said as he stood, "I hate to be the bearer of bad news, but we can't let you leave."

"Excuse me?" Lacy shifted her weight evenly onto both feet, and her hands went to her hips. It was her fighting stance. Alex recognized it right away. "We made a deal that you wouldn't keep us here against our will."

Logan stood up as well. "We're hoping it won't be against your will. But someone out there is shooting at you. We can only assume it's about the prototype. It's not safe for you to go out there on your own. We can protect you here."

Lacy's eyes narrowed slightly. "The problem with your theory is that you can't be sure it was us the shooter was after. We were just fine before you showed up. Maybe this has nothing to do with us, and it's all about you."

"That's a possibility," Logan acknowledged. "However, the fact that Alex was involved, even if by accident, with the bomb going off at Drake's makes it far more likely that someone wants her out of the picture, although for the life of me, I can't figure out why."

Alex swallowed hard. It hadn't really sunk in that someone wanted her dead. The shooting earlier seemed so...random. She hadn't really taken it seriously. Someone wanted her dead. She swayed a bit on her feet. Dex shot off the sofa to help her, but Mitch got there first. He held on to her. "Are you okay?"

"Uh, yeah. I guess I...just hadn't really thought about it like that." She looked up at him. "Someone wants me dead." She swallowed the tears building in her throat. She would not cry in front of this man. He already thought she was weak.

She closed her eyes for a second and then squared her shoulders. Opening them again, she gently pulled her arm from Mitch's grasp. "I have no idea who'd want to kill me. I've repossessed lots of items, but nothing worth killing for." She looked back at Mitch. "Do you have any ideas who's behind the bombing?"

"Yes and no," he said as he sat down on the arm of Gage's chair.

"Perhaps you could explain that a bit." Lacy sat down again on the sofa and Alex followed suit. Dex sat between them and resumed eating crackers and cheese.

"We don't know for sure. We know someone is after the prototype, and we were sure they were going to try and steal it. We know they hired a guy named Tolliver to try and intimidate Drake into selling it. When that didn't work, we thought you"—Mitch turned to Alex—"were the person Tolliver hired to take it."

"John Tolliver?" Alex asked.

"Yes," Gage said quickly. "Why? Do you know him?"

Alex grimaced. "Yes, unfortunately. John Tolliver is Monica Moore's ex-fiancé, the one I reclaimed the Matisse from. He's a real son of a bitch."

Alex reached out and grabbed a bottle of water. She opened it and took a long swallow. She was buying time. She had never revealed any of her clients' stories before. They weren't her stories to tell, but Tolliver was an asshole of the first order, and telling Monica's story might help with the current situation. Everyone was staring at her, waiting for her to continue. She shrugged and made a mental apology to Monica.

"John Tolliver is one of the meanest pieces of shit I have ever had the misfortune of meeting. Monica got my name from another client. She called my handler and begged for a meeting. Tolliver had come in and swept her off her feet. Wined and dined her, lavished gifts and attention on her, made her feel like she was the most interesting woman in the world. She was mad for him.

"She'd been married twice before, but neither one stuck. She thought she had finally found the man of her dreams. Turns out Tolliver was after her for her connections. The Moores know everyone who's anyone. Tolliver was trying to buy respectability. He does well enough in business to have the money, but he's a *persona non grata* with the 'in' crowd. Monica was going to change all that.

"Then she found out he was sleeping around on her. She was devastated. She had given him the Matisse her grandfather had given her. Of course, he refused to give it back. Once she dumped him, his new-found status with the 'in' crowd was terminated. They shunned him, so he made her miserable. He taunted her with the painting by hanging it in his office and humiliated her by posting some nude pictures of her on Instagram he had coerced her into taking. He hurt her in every way imaginable. I know she was afraid of him. She hired a bodyguard, but Tolliver must have paid him off.

"She came home one night, and Tolliver was waiting for her. I'm pretty sure he beat her. He blamed her for his sudden downfall. He's been trying to get accepted by the creme de la creme of monied society in New York for years, and he was so close. Anyway, she hired me to get the painting, which I did, and then I heard she ran off to Europe. Tolliver tends to stay on this side of the Atlantic."

Dex added, "I can confirm she's in Paris. Diana wished she would come back to the Hamptons for the summer but, so far, she's refusing."

"But how do you know him personally?" Mitch asked.

"He was livid after he discovered the Matisse missing. He called Monica and threatened her if she didn't tell him who took the painting. She caved and gave him the information on how to contact me. She called my handler and said Tolliver had threatened to kill me and swore revenge for humiliating him. Turns out he arranged a party to show off the Matisse when he went in to discover it missing.

"My handler told me about it, so I went on a threat assessment mission. I was introduced to him at a party, under an alias, and that was enough. He's a total slime-ball. He groped several women in the short time I was in the same room with him and managed to insult the rest. He's disgusting.

"I can easily see him threatening Monica to get Diana to use me, but I'm not sure that would be enough. Monica has gotten smarter where he's concerned and hired better security."

"I might have the answer to that," Dex piped up. "Diana let it slip that she had a short affair before her husband left her. I guess he'd been cheating on and off for years, and she finally wanted a bit of revenge.

"Anyway, he still doesn't know about that affair. Even though she's pissed at him for the moment, she still doesn't want him to find out about it. She's afraid he'll leave again. If Tolliver found out, he could have blackmailed Diana into setting you up."

"That sounds like Tolliver," said Alex. "I know he likes to pay people to keep him informed. Plus, he would have done serious research on Diana."

"So, what's our theory then?" Logan asked his brothers.

Gage leaned back in the chair. "Seems to me the theory is that Tolliver got Sterling to use Alex to get the car. He then set it up that he would have someone else steal the prototype at the same time so he could blame Alex for it. Anyone who knows Drake would know he would never let someone get away with stealing from him. He'd chase Alex to the ends of the earth for it."

Logan frowned. "It works as revenge for stealing the Matisse, but what about the bomb? And the guys shooting at Alex?"

"What if the bomb was meant to go off under the car?" Mitch said quietly.

"What do you mean?" asked Logan.

"What if Tolliver had someone on the inside and that person, knowing Alex was going to steal the car, planted the bomb on the driveway. If it was supposed to detonate as she was driving away, then everyone would assume Alex had the prototype, or at the very least she was part of the plan to get it. With her dead, we would have no one to question. Tolliver's inside guy would've had the time to steal the USB stick during all the excitement around the explosion. Then Tolliver gets revenge on Alex *and* the prototype."

Alex nodded. "Wouldn't surprise me if someone on Drake's payroll works for Tolliver. Drake would be the type of person Tolliver wants to keep an eye on."

Gage spoke up. "Makes sense. But why did the bomb go off when it did? She was already past it by the time it went off."

"I know. I can't figure out that part." Mitch rubbed his face with his hands and then jammed them in his pockets. "Wait. She fishtailed."

"What?" Logan asked.

"Dan came out of the woods and was running at her. She got distracted and fishtailed right there. She went over on the grass on the left-hand side."

Gage shook his head. "But if the bomb was meant to be set off by her driving over it, wasn't that one hell of a risk? Anyone could have driven down the driveway at any point and the bomb would have gone off."

Mitch said, "I've been sitting here thinking about it. Hear me out. What if the bomb had a proximity transponder? If the inside man put the corresponding transponder on the car, then only that car would set it off. It was supposed to go off when Alex drove over it, killing her and hiding the fact she didn't steal the prototype, but because she fishtailed the back of the car, she didn't drive directly over the bomb. When she swung back onto the driveway, the back of the car was then close enough, and it triggered the bomb."

"Except the prototype was in the car so that doesn't work either." Alex frowned. "They wouldn't want to blow up the prototype."

"The prototype was supposed to be in the safe, not the car, so the theory works. But if it's true, then only one person could be the inside guy." Gage stood up from the chair. "Dex, go talk to Jake and find out if he was on his way into the hospital or out of the hospital when he got shot at."

Dex got up and went to a door in the wall Alex hadn't noticed before and disappeared through it.

Mitch stood, too. "Dan was the inside guy. Tolliver is cleaning up his mess. He took a swipe at Jake because he was afraid Dan had talked to him. We need to get someone to the hospital to protect Dan."

Logan got up. "I'll call the police chief out there and fill him in."

"Logan, talk to Jake again. See if he ever reached Jason. He's been calling Jason to try and find out more about Dan, like why he wanted Dan to stay on after we took over the job. I guess we know," Mitch said. "I should have pushed harder, but Jason's been ducking us, which means he's in on it, too." He certainly hadn't seen that coming. Mitch closed his eyes. "Oh, fuck."

"What?" asked Gage and Logan simultaneously.

"Dan told me he was guilty, and I didn't believe him."

"What? What do you mean?" Alex asked. All eyes were on Mitch now.

"When Jake and I first went to see him at the hospital. He was just out of surgery and still pretty out of it. He said it was his fault. He apologized and said it wasn't supposed to happen that way. I assumed he was feeling guilty for getting hurt, but he wasn't. He was trying to confess, and I missed it."

Gage shrugged. "Jake didn't catch it either, so I wouldn't beat yourself up about it. He just got out of surgery. I don't imagine he was making too much sense."

Logan said, "I'd better go make that call to the Chief. The sooner we get a protection detail on Dan, the better I'll feel." He went through the same door as Dex.

"It's still not adding up to me, though." Alex looked up at Mitch. "How did Dan end up getting hurt?"

"We all thought Dan was running to help me stop you, which I guess he was, but for a different reason. He wanted to stop you from hitting the bomb because he needed to get the prototype out of the car. He heard Drake tell me it was in the car over the comms. My guess is, in the heat of the moment, he forgot exactly where the bomb was, and he went too close, so when you hit the driveway again and it went off, he was in the blast radius."

"Oh. I see... Did you guys say Jake got shot? Is he okay?"

"He's fine. Just a scratch." Mitch moved over to stand in front of Alex again. "But I'm afraid with all of this going on, we can't take the risk of letting you leave here. You're in too much danger."

"I see..." Alex mumbled again. Having Mitch this close to her was killing her concentration. Maybe it was finding out that someone had planned to kill her, or maybe it was because she was exhausted but, either way, she was losing the battle not to let Mitch's closeness affect her.

Her heart picked up its pace in her chest, and heat emanated from her core. She wanted to touch him, to run her fingers over his chest again. God, she wanted to rip his clothes off and take him right now. They said that a brush with death made people feel alive. Her whole body was tingling with the need to have Mitch Callahan.

She tried to shrink farther into the cushions, but there was nowhere to go. She tried to remind herself that he thought she was weak, that he had known who she was and had kept up the charade so he could have sex with her and humiliate her. But in that moment, she honestly didn't care.

Lacy rose from the sofa. "Alex and I need to go. I think we'll be fine on our own. These people have missed every single time. Apparently, they aren't good shots."

A little giggle escaped her lips. "I can see Tolliver trying to save a few bucks by hiring cut-rate henchmen."

"So, while we appreciate your concern, we'll be on our way." Lacy touched Alex's arm. "Let's go."

Alex stood up, which put her in closer proximity to Mitch. "Uh, um, excuse me."

"No."

Her gaze flew to his. "You need to move so I can leave."

"I can't let you do that." Mitch stood firm. "Think Alex, just for a second. If Tolliver went to all that trouble to kill you while he was getting the prototype, imagine how angry he is now. You thought he was pissed about the painting. Now he doesn't have the prototype he undoubtedly promised his client and you're still alive. His rage will be tenfold. He may have started with amateurs, but he's not going to continue that way. If I let you go, then I'm worried you won't make it back."

The seriousness of his tone got to her. Was he right? Would Tolliver be that angry? Yes. He'd be livid. And she'd be his first target. She had the prototype. "The guys in the park. You think they were there to kill me?"

Mitch shook his head. "I think they were there to kill the rest of us and get the prototype from you. Then they'd kill you."

A small shudder went down her spine. She did not want to die. Was she safer here? From Tolliver, yes, but being near Mitch was going to be hard. Heat started up her cheeks, but she willed it down. It was better for her to stay here, at least for tonight. Once she got the prototype back tomorrow, then she could get out—all the way out. Since Mitch and his brothers knew she hadn't hurt anyone and they would have the prototype, she would be free. "Okay, I'll stay."

Lacy did a double-take, but Alex just shook her head. "I need to be done with all of this. Once I give them the prototype tomorrow, I'm out and on my way to the other side of the world."

"I guess I can see your point." Lacy nodded slowly, "I, however, have some work to do so I'm going to head out. Call me first thing so I can go with you to get the prototype."

Alex smiled, reached over, and gave her friend a hug. "Thanks for having my back," she whispered. They pulled apart, and Lacy gave her a wink.

"Unfortunately, we can't let you go either, Ms. Carmichael." Logan had walked back into the room unnoticed.

Lacy whirled around to face Logan and then raised a hand to smooth her hair. Alex knew instantly Lacy was flustered. The hair thing was her tell. "I have work to do, Mr. Callahan. I cannot stay here."

"Call me Logan, please. We can provide you with a quiet, secure place to work, but leaving is simply out of the question."

Lacy's eyes narrowed slightly. "Excuse me? I will not be held against—"

Logan raised his hands in a surrender position. "I understand. However, we have had two shootings today, and although they don't seem to be good shots, there's a chance they could get lucky. I know you don't feel you are a target, but they shot at our employee, Jake, because he spoke with Dan. They've had plenty of time to discover exactly who you are, and as Alex's lawyer, you would also be her confidante. What's to stop them from scooping you up to question you about the prototype and killing you once they've gotten what they want?"

"I can assure you I'm not that easy to 'scoop'." Lacy's lips were crushed together in a thin white line. "I have managed to look after myself quite well in many different circumstances. I appreciate your concern for my safety, but it's unwarranted."

"I beg to differ, but regardless, I would think you would want to stay with your client and make sure she isn't being taken advantage of." Logan looked like he was trying to repress a smile, but triumph was clear in his eyes.

Lacy's face flushed crimson and she balled her fists at her side, but she acquiesced without a scene. Alex shook her head. If Lacy hadn't liked Logan before, now he was definitely on her enemy list. Heaven help him once this was all over. She'd rip him to shreds if she ever had the chance.

"Come, I'll show you a space where you can work without being disturbed." Logan gestured toward the elevator.

Lacy nodded but kept her back stiff. Logan hit the button, and the doors opened immediately. Alex wanted to call out to stop her friend from going. She didn't want to be left here with Mitch by herself. At least Gage was here. She swung around to locate him and discovered he must have left the room sometime in the last few minutes. She turned back to call to Lacy, but the elevator doors had already shut tight.

CHAPTER THIRTY

M itch saw the panic on Alex's face as the elevator
doors closed. She didn't want to be alone with
him. He wasn't sure it was a good idea to be alone with her
either. There was a lot to do, and he should be doing it, but
no one said anything to him, and he couldn't bring himself
to leave. "Are you hungry?"

"Wh—what?"

"Hungry? I noticed you wolfed down the cheese and
crackers." Alex's face flushed, and he mentally smacked
himself. "I meant, we didn't eat lunch, and it's getting on
dinner time. I could use some hot food. Would you like
some?" When she nodded, he walked over to the kitchen
area and grabbed the wall phone handset.

"Dex, everyone is sure to be hungry. Can you order us
some food?" He turned around and looked at Alex. "Chi-
nese okay?"

"Sure."

"Yeah, we're good with that. Do the usual thing, just
add more bodies." He hung up the phone and moved over
to lean on the island.

He had lots of questions floating around in his mind, but he didn't think she'd answer any of them. "If you're up for it, I'd like to review a couple of things." When she groaned, he said, "I know, I know. You want to be through talking about it, but the questions I want to ask are about different parts of your...caper."

She gave him a hard look but moved over to a stool and sat down at the island.

"Want another beer? That one has to be warm by now." He had his hand on the fridge door waiting for her answer.

"Sure, why not? Looks like I'm not going anywhere." Alex slumped a little on the stool, brushing the long black hair back from her face. She scratched her scalp. The wig was driving her crazy.

"You know, as much as I like your get-up, you can take it off if you want. It's not like I don't know your real name. Or your real eye color." He didn't dare mention he knew her real hair color as well. He remembered it clearly from the afternoon on the yacht when she was naked in his lap. Her hair "down there" had been blond.

"Just because you know my first name doesn't mean you can track me down. I have taken great pains to make sure my true likeness is nowhere to be found," she said smugly.

"I hate to tell you, but your stride is what will give you away if some law enforcement group goes searching for you." Mitch leaned on the island and took a sip of his beer. "The way a person walks is very distinctive, like a fingerprint. Different countries have been working on it for more than ten years. It's been tested in all kinds of places. Facial recognition isn't so great, and it can be easily confused. At least thus far," he amended as he thought of Drake's prototype. "But it's really hard to change the way you walk.

They can also use your ears if they have a picture to compare it to."

Alex frowned. "Still, no need for pictures of me to get out in the world."

"What makes you think we'd share that information?" Mitch asked.

"Why wouldn't you if someone asked?" Alex challenged.

Mitch bit back a retort. She didn't trust him. At. All. But could he blame her? Topic change. "How did you get into this business anyway?"

She took a sip of beer. "That's a long story."

"Well, we've got nothing but time at the moment."

She shrugged. "I had...an unhappy childhood." She was silent for a moment, and Mitch remembered what she had said about her parents ignoring her.

"I was left alone a lot, at least until boarding school. I met Lacy there, actually. She helped me. We were like sisters. Still are. But she wanted to go to law school after high school, and I had no such ambition. I didn't want to do any more studying. Books aren't for me."

Mitch started playing with the bottle caps. Did no one care about her or help her make decisions? Jesus, it hit him in the gut. She was truly all alone and had been for years. He had an intense urge to reach out and bring her close. He wanted to hold her and tell her everything was going to be okay. But she'd probably hit him if he tried.

"Anyway, I got a job working retail in an outdoor mall in Los Angeles. I worked at a kiosk. I noticed a pickpocket one day. He was good. Smooth. He would come several times a week and lift wallets from the people at the mall. It intrigued me.

"He noticed me watching him, but I never called security. We struck up a friendship, and he taught me how to find a mark and pick a pocket. I'm ashamed to say I did it a few times at the mall before I realized it just wasn't for me. I always felt this incredible guilt afterward, but doing it was so much fun. Anyway, I decided I would travel the world. I had no reason to stay where I was. I ended up bouncing around a while, Central America, Europe, that type of thing.

"One day, I found myself out of money and hungry. I could usually find a job or I'd meet other travelers, and we'd all share what we had, but I was on a dry streak. I ended up in Florence at an outdoor market.

"I cased it out and then made my way through. I managed to pilfer some fruit, bread, and I was going for some guy's wallet when he called me out. He didn't turn me in, but rather told me what I'd done was wrong and how I'd caught his eye. Then he took me over to the cafe in the square and fed me. We struck up a fast friendship, and he became my handler. We've been together ever since. I'd be lost without him."

"This handler then taught you how to steal?"

"Yup. He taught me how to plan jobs, what to look for, how to know if someone's conning you. And then there was self-defense training, some martial arts, and disguises. They were lots of fun. I had to learn how to develop different personalities, sort of like acting. Each character had a past and a personality. I had to memorize them all and keep them separate. It was a blast buying clothing that suited all of them. Each one has different taste. And then there were languages and cultural norms I had to learn. It was enjoyable to be sure. Still is."

"I'm a natural, so it didn't take a long time. My fatal flaw is that I can't get over the guilt of stealing things from people who don't deserve it." She paused, and a cloud passed over her face.

"Anyway, after a couple of things happened, I understood that what most people need is closure. They need to get through things, get over things, and just move on. So I became an Asset Repossession Specialist Extraordinaire." She held up a finger. "Don't say it!" He laughed, and she smiled then, too.

"My handler liked the idea, and he helped me develop the business. It's been great. I've done a lot of good work. Made a lot of people feel better about things. It's made me happy. Until now." Her face clouded over again.

"Now, I think it's time to retire. My handler has been after me for a while now to give it up and settle down. I think, after all of this, he might be right. It's time to get out while I still can."

"What will you do if you're not an"—he couldn't help himself, he had to say it—"an ARSE?" He started to laugh. Alex stood up, reached across the island, and whacked him on the arm. She tried to glare at him, but her lips tilted up at the corners. Soon she was laughing right along with him. Once he calmed down, he asked her again what her plans were now that she was retiring.

"Not sure. Never gave it much thought. I guess I'll go back to traveling the world. I always enjoyed it before. Now I can do it in any style I want."

He wanted to ask her about her handler, if he would be going with her, but he wasn't sure he wanted to hear the answer. He was saved by the bell, literally. The elevator dinged, letting them know that someone had come onto the floor. A lot of someones. Dex rounded the corner carrying a bunch of bags, and Logan appeared behind him carrying more. Then Gage arrived with Lacy in tow.

"Shall we eat in the dining room?" Logan asked.

"You guys have a dining room?" Alex's tone said she was surprised.

"It's across the hall." Mitch pointed to the other side of the kitchen where there was a doorway.

"Oh, I just assumed that was the bathroom," Alex said as she grabbed her beer and walked in that direction.

"There is a bathroom down here, three actually, along with four bedrooms. I'll take you on a tour later if you like," Mitch offered, and she nodded.

They walked into the dining room, and Alex stopped dead. Lacy, who was behind her, walked into her back. "Hey, why did you—?" She stopped speaking as well.

Mitch glanced over their heads to see what the holdup was.

Dragan was setting things up on the sideboard. As often happened when people saw him, they became startled like a deer in the headlights. Dragan must have sensed there was a problem because he turned around to look. Alex and Lacy were speechless.

"Alex, Lacy, this is Dragan. He's one of our specialists," Logan stated and then tried to usher the girls into the dining room. Dragan gave them a slow smile. Mitch saw Alex blink, and he tried hard not to sigh out loud. Women all found Dragan mind-blowing. It was somewhat beyond Mitch as to why, but Sloan had explained to him that Dragan was sex on a stick as far as women were concerned. Mitch didn't see it and said as much. Sloan shook her head and detailed it out for him.

Dragan, according to Sloan, was six-feet-five inches worth of hard-bodied hotness. With his slow smile, long dark hair, and ice blue eyes, he was the equivalent of catnip. And the way his voice sort of rumbled out of his chest, pure unadulterated sexiness. Add to that he's an ex-Navy SEAL and every woman dreamed of sex as soon as they saw him. At least that's what Sloan had said. Mitch found himself wanting to punch Dragan. Instead he pushed past Alex and Lacy, grabbed a plate, and began helping himself to dinner.

"Ignore our rude brother over there, ladies. Please grab a plate and get some dinner," Logan said. "Lacy, would you like something to drink?"

"I'd love a glass of white wine if you have any."

"I'll get it." Dragan moved toward the kitchen. "Do you have a preference for type of grape?"

"Uh"—Lacy blinked—"what do you have?"

"Why don't you come see? I think we might even have champagne if you're interested."

"Oh, count me in," Alex said, plopping her plate down on the table and following Dragan and Lacy into the kitchen. Mitch cursed under his breath and took a long swallow of beer. This was going to be a long night. He sighed. Suddenly, he wasn't hungry at all.

"You okay?" Gage asked.

"Yeah. Fine." He looked down at his plate. "Remind me later to get Jake to check the Ford for a transponder. We need to see if we're right."

"Already done," Gage said. "And you were bang on. There was a transponder on the back of the GT."

Logan sat down. "One mystery solved, but another one just came up."

"What happened?" Mitch asked.

"Dan's gone. The police chief went to the hospital to talk to Dan himself, but Dan was nowhere to be found." Logan looked down at his food and then pushed his plate away as well.

Gage looked at his brothers. "Do we think he left under his own steam or do we think he was helped along?"

Mitch frowned, but Logan spoke first. "You're thinking the only person who can actually link Tolliver to this is Dan."

Gage nodded. "What if Tolliver is cleaning up loose ends?"

"You're right. It makes no sense that Dan would run. His amnesia story would hold up, at least for a while. The doctor would back him up, saying it's possible. Why run now when he's still hurt and in pain?"

In the silence, Mitch could hear the girls chatting with Dragan in the kitchen. "They're going to come after her again. And the prototype. The sooner we get that back, the safer she'll be. We need to tighten security here tonight. Lock the place down. Those guys were amateurs today, but even amateurs get lucky. We can't afford to let that happen."

CHAPTER THIRTY-ONE

Dinner went by quickly. Alex noticed that all the Callahan brothers seemed distracted. She and Lacy chattered away with Dex, Zane, and Dragan. Various people came in, got food, and left again. There were too many to remember all their names. Callahan Security was much bigger than she had first thought. No wonder Mitch was worried about blowing this job. They needed to keep their reputation if they were going to make money to pay all these people.

"I'm gonna go down and get things rolling for tonight," Gage said as he stood from the table. "Logan, can you drop by when you're done here? We need to discuss a couple of things about the Gregson and Ferguson security jobs,"

"Sure. I'll be down shortly."

Lacy had begged off to do some work. Mitch went with her and Dragan back downstairs. Dex and Zane followed suit.

When Gage left with the others, Logan got up from the table and started cleaning up.

"I'll help." There was a lingering feeling of guilt in Alex's stomach. She didn't know why really. It wasn't like she asked them to protect her, but they were going out of their way to do it. And it would cost.

She wasn't interested in speaking with Mitch about it. Her feelings about him were still too new, too raw. Logan, on the other hand, struck her as more business-minded and pragmatic. Funny how a couple of hours ago she was pissed that she was stuck here. Now, gratitude was her top feeling. She'd never had to worry about people trying to kill her before. To her, doing her thing was just fun and harmless. It gave her clients a chance to get a little bit of dignity back, a bit of closure. Maybe it could be construed as dangerous, but to her it was more of an adventure. Tolliver had changed all that.

Alex finished clearing plates and carrying them to the kitchen. She started loading the dishwasher. Logan began putting away the leftovers.

"Um, I ah, appreciate all that you guys are doing. I know I gave you a hard time in the beginning but, um, no one's ever tried to kill me before." Alex kept her head down as she loaded glasses into the dishwasher.

"It's what we do," Logan responded as he scraped some noodles into a Tupperware container.

"But, well, you're not getting paid for this. I mean, keeping these people here tonight and everything."

Logan sighed quietly. "No, we're not, but we have an obligation to keep you safe so that we can get the prototype back."

Alex looked up at him sharply.

He cursed under his breath. "That's not how I meant it." He smiled slightly. "I'm just tired. Forgive me."

"I get it. It must have cost a fortune to put this place

together. Taking a hit for what happened at Drake's doesn't help your reputation any."

"No, it doesn't. Gage and I have been putting out fires all afternoon."

Alex finished loading the dishes. "That's my fault." The guilt that had been hovering landed squarely on her shoulders.

Logan leaned against the counter after he put away the last of the food. "Yes and no. You broke in so that gave Tolliver the chance, but we're pretty sure he's the one behind the bomb. I'm sure he would've figured out another way to go after the prototype. It just might have been a little less...flashy."

"I get it. His revenge plan to get me made your reputation take a bigger hit. I don't feel so good about this."

Logan reached up into the cupboard above his head and pulled down two mugs. "You want a cup of coffee?"

"Tea?" she offered instead.

He nodded. He pulled out a case and let her pick out the tea she wanted. Organic Earl Gray. Her favorite.

Logan picked out a green tea and then took the mugs over and poured boiling water in them from the hot water spout in the built-in coffee maker. Then he walked across the room to the seating area. He crashed down on the couch, and Alex sat down beside him.

"Look," he said, "it is what it is. Neither of us can change it now. Tomorrow we'll get the prototype back and give it to Drake. Hopefully, Drake will do right by us, and we won't lose any more clients."

"You lost clients over this?" The guilt just ballooned into a thousand-pound weight. This would be killing Mitch. She knew how important this was to him. She didn't want to think about why that mattered to her.

Logan hesitated. "Only two."

"But it's going to hit your bottom line," Alex confirmed.

Logan nodded. He took a sip of his tea. "I have no idea why I'm telling you all this."

"I bet you're the one who worries about the details."

Logan looked at her questioningly.

"My handler and I have a similar setup. He worries about finances and setting up the jobs. I worry about making the jobs happen. We both discuss planning, but even with that, it's my butt on the line so I get final say. I worry about it more than he does. You run the day-to-day around here so it's your job to be all about the bottom line."

"That obvious, huh?" He smiled briefly. "Anyway, it's not your problem."

"No, but it's kind of my fault. I want to pay your fees for today, tonight, whatever."

Logan shook his head. "You don't have to do that."

"I want to." Maybe it would ease the guilt that was crushing her. She kept seeing the worry written on Mitch's face when they discussed it last week. God, was it only last week? It seemed like a lifetime ago.

"I appreciate the thought, but it's not necessary."

"Would it be a conflict of interest with Drake?" Alex asked as she took her first sip of tea.

Logan tilted his head. "Hmm...I don't think so. To put it bluntly, we're keeping you alive so that we can recover Drake's missing prototype. More like it would be double dipping. It was our job to keep you from getting it in the first place. We're making good on the contract we signed with Drake. It's costing us more because of our mistakes."

"But Drake didn't tell you about putting the prototype in the car, so he should have to cover your expenses."

Logan laughed. "Drake doesn't see it that way."

"Well then, let me cover your expenses. Guarantee our safety until I retrieve the prototype tomorrow. I'll pay you for it." She put her hand on his arm. "Logan, please."

"Let me think about it." He frowned. "The bill would be substantial. I'm not sure you understand how much this type of protection costs."

She smiled. She knew for sure now he didn't know her full name. Her identity was still safe. "Try me." He named a figure, but she didn't even blink. Her family was worth billions. More importantly, she had made lots of money being an asset repossession specialist, and she had invested wisely. She hadn't touched her family money since she left home.

"Make you a deal. I'll pay you double that if, at the conclusion of this, you can guarantee that Tolliver won't try and have me killed again."

Logan blinked. "The asset repossession business must be far more lucrative than I had imagined."

She just smiled and held out her hand. "Deal?"

Logan put his hand in hers. "Deal."

"Now, if you can show me where Lacy is working, I can transfer you a retainer. Will fifty percent work?"

Logan got up and offered a hand up to Alex. They moved toward the elevator. "Fifty percent will do nicely."

A COUPLE OF HOURS LATER, Alex found herself at loose ends. She'd transferred the money and then chatted with Lacy for a while. Logan had come to say he received the funds. They'd closed the building down. All the windows and doors were covered. She couldn't see out. It made her claustrophobic.

She chatted with Dex and Dragan for a bit and played some video games with them on the big screen to distract herself, but she was too restless to stay put. She'd gotten a text from Leo, in code of course, but it said he was safe and back home with his nonna. She was eternally grateful for that.

She went back down to the second floor. The place had cleared out. A skeleton crew was left in place to manage the security of the building. Gage and Logan were in the boardroom going over something that they immediately stopped talking about when she walked in. She just said "hello" and left again. She hated being cooped up like this.

She wandered down a dark hallway, going by empty offices, until she came to one with a light on. Mitch was looking at something on his desktop. There was only a small desk light on and the light from his screen. She stopped outside his doorway and then turned around. She didn't know what to say to him. She wanted to deny what she was feeling. Being with Mitch was never going to happen. It was better if she just stayed away from him.

"Alex," he called softly.

She turned back around. "Uh, hi. Sorry to disturb you. I was just walking around. You know, bored. I'm not so good at being cooped up." She was babbling, and she knew it, but Mitch made her nervous.

Before it had been a game of cat and mouse. She had been in control.

The afternoon on the yacht came to mind. She'd thought she been in control, at least. Now, she had no illusions as to who was in control. She was up shit creek, and he was her lifeboat. She didn't like that, not one bit. She hated the fact that she was responsible for damaging his company's reputation as well. Normally, she wouldn't care, but this time, it was different.

"Come in, sit down." Mitch's hair was standing up a

bit, a sure sign he had been running his hands through it in frustration.

"I don't want to disturb you."

"I could use a break." He got up from his desk and gestured toward the couch. He picked up a remote from the coffee table in front of the couch and hit a button. She grimaced, thinking he was turning on a TV. She didn't see the gas fireplace until she was in the room.

"Oh, nice. I love fireplaces."

"Me, too," he said, "but don't tell my brothers. I almost have them convinced I picked this office because it's smaller than theirs. Would you like some water?"

"Sure," she said as she sat down on the opposite end of the couch and watched the flames dance on the hearth. Mitch went behind the sofa to his desk and then came back with two bottles of water. "They're room temperature. I hope that's okay."

Alex nodded. "I've been thinking," she said, giving Mitch a quick glance, "it was Tolliver that day on the yacht, arguing with Drake, wasn't it?"

"You were watching, huh?" The corners of Mitch's mouth turned up slightly. "Yes, it was Tolliver. He was trying to buy the prototype. Drake was pissed that Tolliver even knew about it. He started grilling Tolliver about where the information came from, but Tolliver wouldn't talk."

"I couldn't see his face. Otherwise, I would have known him instantly." She pictured Tolliver. Tall, dark slicked-back hair with a receding hairline. Dark eyes that were a little too close together for her taste and a smile that always seemed like a sneer. A small shudder went down her back. "He's so grotesque."

"My turn," Mitch said. "It was you in the casino on the mezzanine, wasn't it? You were wearing a black dress and a black wig. Not this one. The wig wasn't quite as black and a bit shorter. And it was you on the balcony in Venice. I liked that dress much better. It showed off your…assets."

She laughed. "Sharp eye. Yes, it was me. Doing recon in the Casino. You made me laugh. The takedown of the lady in red was epic."

He feigned innocence. "She should know better than to come running at someone surrounded by security. How was I to know she didn't have a weapon?"

She laughed. "It was pretty harsh. You could have been nicer."

Mitch shrugged. "Maybe, but it wouldn't have been nearly as much fun."

"And yeah, it was me in Venice. You weren't supposed to be on that balcony." Alex scratched her head again. She couldn't wait to take the wig off and dig her nails into her scalp.

"Neither were you." He grimaced. "Just take the damn thing off. I know it's bugging you."

"I'm okay." She scratched again.

Mitch rubbed his face with his hands. "You owe me a favor."

Alex arched an eyebrow at him. "Pardon me?"

"The dance bar. I was better than expected, so you owe me a favor."

"Really." She sized him up. "And suppose I went along with it. What would the favor be?"

"Take off your wig, the jewelry, the make-up, and let me see the true you," Mitch challenged.

"Why would I do that?"

"To humor me. I want to see what you really look like."

She shook her head. "There are too many cameras around here. I've gone to great lengths to make sure no one has my image."

"What if I promise to not share your image with anyone?"

She bristled. "Your credibility is questionable at the moment." She was still having a hard time with what she thought of as his betrayal.

His face hardened, and he rose from the couch. Running his fingers through his hair, he started to pace back and forth behind the couch. "I never meant to hurt you. Friday, on the yacht. I wasn't planning on having sex with you. I...was just happy you called. After what happened at the club, I didn't think you would."

"I had to. You were... I had a job to do." She'd almost confessed that she was planning on using him to get into the party. Guilt washed over her. Here she was mad at him for doing to her what she had been planning on doing to him.

"Look." Mitch stopped pacing and touched her shoulder until she looked at him. "It was my job to track you down and find out what you were after, but once we started talking, once we started getting to know one another, all that went out the window. Friday was all real. It was all me. I wanted to be with you, the real you, the you that told me about your parents. I wasn't trying to use you or humiliate you."

She knew he was telling the truth. It was in his eyes. They were worried and sad and tired. She just wanted to grab him and hold him tight. She knew in that moment that he was being real with her. She had been humiliated on the yacht, but it stemmed from fear. She'd relaxed and opened up. She'd been herself, and it had scared her.

It still scared her. Her racing heart was proof of that. She opened her mouth to speak, but closed it again. What could she say? How could she tell him it was real for her, too? Too real.

She took a deep breath and started pulling off all the jewelry she was wearing. She put it on the end table next to her. Then she took a handful of tissues from the box on the table and poured some water from her bottle on them. She wiped her face until the makeup was gone. She took out the contacts and threw them on the used tissues.

Finally, she pulled off the wig and then undid the pins that were holding her hair up. Her waist-length, blond hair slowly unraveled. Then she stood up and turned around to face Mitch. He wanted the real her. Well, here she was.

CHAPTER THIRTY-TWO

M itch stared—mouth open stared. Alex was extraordinary. There was no other word. He'd seen her eyes before, but now they glowed like emeralds. Her skin had a luster he'd never seen before. The dusting of freckles over her nose and cheeks just made the red of her lips more prominent. Her hair was stunning. He'd never particularly been a long-hair man, but he was blown away by hers. It was like spun silk shining in the firelight. All he could think of was how much he wanted to run his fingers through it.

"You are so beautiful. Your hair is...exquisite."

"Thanks," she said softly. "This is the real me. Alexandra Buchanan. That's my whole name. Being Alexandra Buchanan is hard. I got tired of life being hard, so I created a whole persona around Alex Morgan, thief, and I've lived it for a long time now. But you're being real with me, so I want to be real with you."

Mitch's chest constricted. He wanted to gather her into his arms and never let her go. He wanted to take away all the pain and loneliness. "I understand how hard it is to be without your parents. I was devastated when my mother died. I still miss her a lot. It must have been incredibly difficult for you being an only child and having your parents ignore you."

Alex let out a bark of bitter laughter. "You don't understand." She shook her head. "My parents didn't just ignore me. My dad liked my mom's money, and when that wasn't enough anymore, he left. My mother was devastated and never got over it. She vacillated between blaming herself and blaming me for him leaving."

"Oh, honey. That must have been tough. I'm sorry you were so lonely." Mitch ached to touch her and soothe away all of the hurt. He reached for her but she moved away.

"You wanted to see the real me? There's more. Lots more." Alex's voice had a hard edge to it. It was the type of edge Mitch's superiors used when they were about to deliver a harsh dressing down. He tried to brace himself for what was coming.

Alex turned to face him. Her eyes were hard and her lips were in a thin line. "My mother committed suicide, and it was a huge *relief*. Did you hear me? It was a *relief*. No more yelling and screaming and, best of all, no more accusatory silence."

She paced in front of Mitch's desk. "I was happy at boarding school. Happy to be away from her constant emotional torment.

"The day the letter from my mother arrived, I waited until classes were over and went to my room. I remember my hands trembled as I opened the letter. I kept wondering if maybe she'd finally noticed I wasn't in the house anymore. Maybe she actually missed me. But the joke was on me." The bitter laugh was back, but this time it turned into a sob.

Mitch watched as Alex gathered herself. It was killing him to see her suffer like this, but he knew she needed to get this out.

Her shoulders straightened. "The letter was only two pages. My mother apologized for blaming me for my father deserting us. See, she had tracked down my father and asked him why he left. He told her it was *her* fault. She just wasn't enough for him. *She* had driven him away." Tears glistened on her cheeks. "Then she said there was no help for it, she just wasn't good at being a wife or a mother. She wished me better luck in life and love. And that was it."

Mitch's chest ached like he'd been hit with a rubber bullet. Pain was etched on her face. If her mother was still alive, he'd have killed her himself. He reached out to pull her into his arms again, but she still resisted.

"They found her body in bed. She'd taken a bunch of pills. I remember when the headmaster told me. All I felt was relief, but that was the last quiet moment I had.

"The service, the funeral, what a circus. The press was everywhere. There wasn't a moment when I didn't have to be dressed appropriately or say the correct thing, lest we, the mighty Buchanans, would be portrayed as less than sympathetic in the media.

"I decided on the day of my mother's funeral that once the circus died down, I would leave, I don't know...*Poof*, just disappear. Create a whole new me." She turned to look at him. "And that's when Alex Morgan was born."

Mitch frowned. "I'm confused. Why was the press interested in your mother?"

Alex sighed. "Because my mother was Cynthia Buchanan."

"Jesus Christ!" Mitch fell back against the couch. It was the second time in the last half hour that he'd been totally blown away. Cynthia Buchanan was one of the richest women in the world. Her family, Alex's family, were infamous. It was like being a Kennedy or a Kardashian. No wonder she ran from them. Nightmare wasn't a strong enough word.

"You wanted the real me," Alex said, "there it is. It's not pretty, but it's true." She stood in front of Mitch's desk. "I think I'll go find—" She started walking to the door.

He reached out over the back of the couch and grabbed her arm. "Don't go."

Alex looked down at him. "It's probably better if I go. My life is complicated enough."

"Stay with me. I don't care who your family is or that you're a thief. I care...about you. Stay." She had to stay. He needed to hold her. He wanted to see her like she was on the yacht, wild with joy and abandon. He wanted to give that to her.

She looked toward the doorway and then back at Mitch. She gave her arm a gentle tug. He reluctantly let go. He couldn't force her to stay, but he wanted to. Badly. He cared about her. Hell, who was he kidding? He was falling in love with her. His chest was hurting as he watched her walk toward the door. He stood up and desperately tried to think of something, anything, that would make her stay but his mind was blank. He closed his eyes and heard the door close with a soft click.

Then there was a second click. His eyes shot open. Alex was standing there, leaning on the door. "I didn't want to be interrupted. Exposing my girls to the world was a one-shot deal. I'd rather keep them private if that's alright with you."

In one step, he was on her and had her pressed against the door. "More than alright," he whispered. He slanted his mouth over hers, claiming her as his. She was his. His thief. His woman. He ran his hands down her back, cupped her ass, and hauled her against him. He molded his body to hers as her tongue twisted around his. He needed skin to skin contact like a drowning man needed a lifeboat.

Her hands started tugging at his jeans. It was too much. If she even touched him, he would lose control. He broke off the kiss and grabbed her wrists. He put them above her head and encircled the fine bones with one hand.

"What are you doing?" she asked, her breath coming in gasps. "I want to touch you.

"No. Not yet," he mumbled as he dropped kisses on her collarbone. As he used his tongue on the hollow of her neck, she inhaled sharply. He did it again and again until she was writhing against him.

He slipped his free hand under her T-shirt and bra and cupped her breast. He stroked the nipple with his thumb. Claiming her mouth again, he kissed her hard, his tongue dancing with hers. He deepened the kiss as her hips ground against him. She lifted one leg and wrapped it around his hips, trying to bring him closer. He dropped her wrists and picked her up. He carried her back to the couch and set her down. Then he lowered his weight on to her slowly.

"Can you breathe?" he asked with a smile.

"I'm out of breath, but it has nothing to do with you crushing me." She claimed his mouth and fisted her hands in his hair. She wrapped her legs around his waist, bringing his hard-on in direct contact with her core.

He could feel the heat through her leggings. She started rocking her hips against him. She found the hem of his shirt and pulled it up. He shifted his weight and finished taking it off. It landed on the floor next to the couch. Her T-shirt and bra soon followed.

His body touching hers was heaven. His hands cupped her breasts as he kissed his way down her neck to the valley between her breasts. She arched up against him. He playfully tugged at her nipple, and when she moaned and protested that he was driving her crazy, he claimed the sensitive nub with his mouth. His tongue, alternated between swirling and sucking. She called out his name. She was his. His alone.

HIS TONGUE WAS DRIVING her to the edge of reason. She needed him to stop. She needed more. She'd never experienced anything like this. His skin on hers was exhilarating. She arched her hips and rubbed against him. She reached down and fumbled with the button of his jeans. She ached to touch him.

He brought his hand down and tried to brush her hands away. "No." His voice was rough.

"Yes." She kept fighting to get the button undone.

"No. If you touch me, I won't be able to stop. I want to see you come first."

She loved how his voice rumbled out of his chest. His eyes were smoky gray and his breathing was irregular. She loved that she did that to him. "Mitch, I need to touch you. I didn't...we didn't get to do that last time." She fisted her hands in his hair and locked eyes with him. "I want to feel you inside of me. I want to come with you inside of me. Do you understand?"

His smoky eyes glowed with a feverish light. He growled something unintelligible and got up swiftly. He took a condom out of his wallet and then shucked the rest of his clothing in seconds. He covered her with his body again and then claimed her mouth in a scorching kiss. She could barely breathe. His hands pushed down her leggings and her silk thong. She helped him until her clothes were next to his on the floor.

His weight excited her beyond anything else. She arched her hips up and wrapped her legs around him, rubbing her silky folds against the length of his cock. When he groaned, she did it again. The pleasure from that limited amount of contact was exhilarating.

His hands gripped her ass and brought her closer. She angled her hips so he could slide inside of her, but he pulled back. "Mitch?"

"Don't worry, honey, we can both have what we want." He moaned again as she rubbed against him. He shifted his weight until he was kneeling on the floor and had her thighs over his shoulders. She bit her lip with anticipation.

When he blew on her hot center, her hips jerked in response. A grin lit his face.

"Mitch," she gasped as he leaned down and captured her with his mouth. His tongue swirled, and she moaned. He put one finger inside her and moved slowly. It wasn't enough. Her hips strained upward to his mouth. "More," she demanded, fisting the sofa cushions to keep from screaming. Mitch alternated between licking and sucking while thrusting his fingers. He lapped and rubbed until her breath came in pants. She yelled his name as her thighs tightened and her body clamped around his fingers. She shattered as her orgasm exploded through her.

She peeled herself down off the ceiling. Her body was boneless until she saw Mitch's smoky gray eyes watching her. Her core instantly tightened. She still wanted this man. "My turn," she purred and sat up. She pulled him up to the sofa and climbed on top of him. She kissed his neck and worked her way down his chest. She teased his nipples, first licking and sucking and then nipping them. She loved the animalistic growls he made. She moved farther down until her mouth was level with his cock.

She let her tongue touch the very tip, then slowly she drew more and more of him into her mouth, sucking and twisting her tongue around his shaft as she went. His growling got deeper and rumbled out of his chest.

His voice was rough. "You're killing me." His hips started to move, but then he grabbed her and pulled her back up. "I want to come inside of you." His eyes were two pools of gray silk. He captured her mouth with another scorching kiss. She moved until her overheated core was hovering above his hard cock. She gave him a slow smile. He reached out and grabbed the condom. Seconds later, she lowered herself slowly down on top of him. Inch by inch of exquisite madness.

She tilted her pelvis and started moving. Mitch groaned and grabbed her hips. He moved her more quickly up and down the length of his shaft. The delicious pressure was building inside of her. "Faster. Harder. More," she demanded as she arched her hips to allow him to go deeper. Mitch matched her every move. "Oh, God, yes Mitch," she yelled as he drove a final thrust inside her and they both went crashing over the edge.

She fell onto his chest and lay there panting as she tried to recover. Mitch's breath was coming in gasps as well. His arms circled around her. As she lay there with her head on his chest, listening to his heartbeat return to normal, she admitted to herself she had fallen for Mitch. Hard. He was magnificent, and in so many ways her perfect match.

She swallowed the tears that were building in her throat. There was no life for her that ended in happily ever after. She could never escape her family name and all the attention that brought, but she could keep moving and maybe outrun it a while longer. She didn't want to think about leaving or what that meant. She brushed those thoughts aside and lifted her head to meet Mitch's gaze. "Round two?"

CHAPTER THIRTY-THREE

A lex woke with a start. It took her a second to realize the weight on her waist was Mitch's arm. He'd held her to his chest all night. She took a deep breath. His musky scent made her want to snuggle down with him forever. She closed her eyes, but they popped open again almost immediately. She didn't have that luxury.

She ever so slowly moved Mitch's arm and slid off the sofa. She gathered her clothes, her wig and jewelry, and then stood up. Not wanting to wake Mitch, she moved over next to the door and got dressed. She slapped the wig in place. She reached over and grabbed her jacket off the back of the sofa.

She took another deep breath and steeled herself to walk out the door. Last night had been magical, beyond anything she'd ever experienced. When she glanced over at Mitch, it was almost her undoing. A wave of love so fierce crashed over her. She leaned against the door and blinked back the onslaught of tears.

If there was ever a place she could stay, or a person she could stay with, it was now, here, with Mitch, but she didn't have the luxury of staying in one place. If she stayed, life would become a circus again. Paparazzi were far worse now than when she disappeared years ago. She would be back in the spotlight, and Mitch would end up there with her. Everyone had forgotten about her. And it was better that way.

She brushed a tear off her cheek. Quietly, she slipped into the hallway and closed the door again. Time to get on with it. She glanced at her watch. Five forty-five a.m. Eddie should be back at his spot by about six, six-fifteen. She moved down the hallway to the main corridor and then took the stairs up to the fifth floor. She passed by a bedroom and saw Lacy still asleep. There were two twin beds, so she assumed that's where she was supposed to have slept. With the building shut down, Lacy must have guessed that she had fallen asleep elsewhere. Alex went to one of the restrooms so she could clean up.

Swank wasn't a strong enough word. The whole bathroom was done in marble with glass fixtures. It was old world with a bit of modern thrown in. The showers were oversized. The vanity ran the length of one wall and was fully stocked. It had everything from Q-tips to disposable toothbrushes. There were even mini deodorants for both men and women.

Color me impressed. She quickly grabbed a towel from the cabinet at the end of the wall and got undressed. She took a speed shower, but did take a couple of minutes to wash her hair. The shampoo and conditioner smelled divine. She was going to have to ask Logan about them.

Fifteen minutes later, she was dressed, wig in place, ready to go. *And* she had clean underwear. She'd washed out her thong in the sink and dried it using the intense hand dryer. Logan was a god, she decided.

She left the restroom and went in search of someone to

let her out of the building. No one was around in the
kitchen, so she went down a floor but it was empty as well.
She went back down the stairs to the third floor and was
reaching for the door handle when the door opened.

"Oh. You scared me."

Zane smiled. "Sorry." He moved into the stairwell.

She hadn't realized how big he was, but now that the
two of them were sharing the landing, it became obvious.
His brown hair was a bit messed, like he'd gotten up
quickly but his deep brown eyes were wide awake and
studying her closely.

"Can I find something for you?" he asked.

"What makes you think—" She snapped her fingers.
"The cameras."

Zane just kept his smile in place.

"Okay, so I need to leave the building." She shot Zane
a megawatt smile. "I have to go meet someone."

Zane shook his head. "Sorry, I can't let you out until I
get the word."

She nodded. "I totally understand, I do, but you see, I
have to get the prototype and have to meet someone to do
it. So, if you could just let me out, I'll be on my way."

Again, he shook his head. Alex did her best to keep her
temper in check. She casually put her hands behind her
back and crossed her fingers. "Look, I promise I'll come
back with the USB drive." She wasn't coming back, but
she would make sure Mitch got the prototype. She just
couldn't come back and go through a long good-bye.

"I understand." Zane stood there staring at her.

"You understand so you're going to help me?" she
asked hopefully.

"No. I understand, but I can't help you."

Alex ground her teeth. She heard a door open above
her and footsteps coming down the stairs. A second later

Logan appeared. He looked like he just stepped off the pages of GQ. How did he do it? He probably had a well-stocked closet to go with his well-stocked bathrooms.

"Morning," he said. He sounded very cheery and chipper.

"Morning," she replied. Zane merely nodded.

"Did you sleep well?" Logan asked.

She looked for any meaning in the question, but his face was benign. "Fine. I was wondering if you could help me out. I need to leave to get the prototype. Could you let me out of the building?"

Logan blinked. "Have you spoken to Gage or Mitch about it?"

"No. I didn't see them. They're probably still asleep." She sensed she was about to get turned down. "It's a bit time-sensitive. I really need to go if I'm going to get it back."

Logan frowned. "I can't let you go without protection. We need to formulate a game plan on how to retrieve it and keep you safe. As a matter of fact, I think it's better if you don't leave here at all. The guys will go get it and bring it back here."

"Uh, that won't work." *Shit.* She didn't want to still be here when Mitch got up. "Uh, I have to talk to someone to get it back. They won't give it to you."

"Are you sure?" Logan frowned again. He nodded at Zane. "These guys can be very persuasive."

She glanced at Zane. He was casually leaning against the wall with his arms folded across his chest. His brown eyes met hers. "Um, yeah, well my person still won't give it up so"—she twisted the long hair of her wig—"Zane could come with me. Dex, too, if that makes you feel better." She was getting desperate now. Any second Mitch would wake up.

Logan studied her face for a second and then turned to Zane. "Do what the lady says. It's her dime." Zane nodded and pushed off the wall. He opened the door to the third floor and disappeared.

Logan turned back to Alex and took a step toward her. Locking his stare on her, he said, "I'm not sure what your game is or why the big change from last night when you wanted us to keep you safe, paid handsomely for it, in fact, but we'll play it your way. You're the client. The guys will keep you safe as best they can, but you have to give us the prototype. If you try to run with it or hide it or sell it or anything besides give it to Zane or Dex, I will hunt you down to the ends of the earth. Are we clear?"

A chill went down her spine. He might be the lawyer in the family, but she had no doubt he could be just as deadly as his brothers. He was scary as shit.

She swallowed and licked her lips to get some moisture back in her mouth. "Deal," she said and stuck out her hand. He grabbed it and held it hard.

Zane came back into the stairwell with Dex right behind him. Both nodded at Logan. "We're good to go," Zane said. Dex merely nodded at Logan and gave Alex the once-over. Gone was the chatty, friendly guy from last night. Maybe he wasn't a morning person. She really didn't care. As long as she got out of the building ASAP and finished this, he could stay silent forever.

They went down the stairs to the lobby. Zane leaned over the desk and hit a few buttons on the computer there. He murmured something, and she realized he must be wearing an earbud. A few seconds later, the steel door slid back silently, and sun poured in through the glass doors.

Alex tried to block her eyes, but she wasn't fast enough, and she was blind for a few seconds as her eyes adjusted to the light. *Mistake.* She should have been prepared for the light. She was definitely off her game this morning. She even stumbled a bit, and Zane bumped into her. She dropped her jacket. He quickly bent down and picked it up for her.

Focus. She needed to get her head in the game.

Zane unlocked the doors and checked the street. He nodded, and then Dex gestured that she should follow. They got into a waiting SUV. She hadn't seen the driver before, but the guys referred to him as Gunnar.

He was a hulk of a man. He looked cramped sitting in the driver's seat of the SUV. *Great.* She had no doubts she wouldn't be able to escape if he got a hold of her. Best make sure that didn't happen.

They rolled down the street, and Gunnar said, "Where to?"

She took a beat. This was it. Should she try to lose them? Do everything herself and then mail the thumb drive back to them? It's what she would normally do, but it would take a herculean effort on her part, and for the first time in a really long time, she wasn't sure she'd be successful. She had to try. She wasn't giving up Eddie. She didn't want him to be stuck in the middle of this mess. "Head toward 14th street."

The drive was made in silence. Gunnar did some fancy moves to see if they were being followed, but it looked clean. She put on her jacket. She didn't want to leave anything behind.

They were rolling down Park Avenue South when she saw her opportunity. There was a mass of Asian tourists on the corner and the light had turned red. The thing about BMWs was that the door handle had to be pulled twice to actually open the door. The first pull unlocked it and the second opened it.

Alex coughed to cover the sound of her first tug on the

door handle. She waited a beat. At the same time the light turned green, she pulled the handle a second time and shot out of the SUV into the crowd.

She heard the yell behind her but she kept running down 19th street. Halfway down the block, someone was coming out of a building. She grabbed the door just as it was about to close and shot through, pulling it tight behind her. She saw Zane through the glass but turned and ran. She went through the lobby and toward the back of the building. Frantic, she looked around.

There was a door in the corner. She pulled it open. There was only one way to turn, so she went left. She jogged down the hall until she found the door to the alley.

She flew through it and down the narrow passage way. At the corner, she quickly ducked her head around it and looked in both directions. *Nothing.*

She hightailed it across the street and banged on the gray door of the building. She banged again, frantic to get in before Zane came through the alley or the SUV came down the block.

The door opened, and Ralph's thickly lined face popped out. "Girl, there is no need to make so much noise."

"Ralph! Thank God!" She ran inside and Ralph closed the door after her.

"What kind of trouble have you gotten yourself into this time?" He hitched up is tool belt and he shook his head.

"Ralph, no time to explain. I gotta meet Eddie in the park. Thanks for opening the door."

"Anything for you, doll. Maria misses you and those amazing cookies you sent." A grin split his face. "I might miss the cookies, too." He cackled as he rubbed his belly through his overalls.

"I promise to send you some more, but you gotta let me out the front door, okay?"

"Well, come on then, girl." He led the way down a series of hallways and opened the door at the front.

She cautiously stuck her head out and checked for the guys and the SUV. Nothing. She moved into the street.

"Thanks, Ralph." She leaned up and kissed his weathered cheek. "Cookies are on the way to you."

He smiled again. "You take care of yourself now." He patted her shoulder and then closed the door.

As she crossed the street, she thanked her lucky stars that she'd spent time cultivating friends around the square. It was a great spot to disappear with all the tourists, cabs and the subways right here. She'd met Eddie, who'd introduced her to Ralph and others. She had friends or assets in most of the buildings around the park.

She made her way over into Union Square Park, keeping her head on a swivel for anyone who might be looking for her. Once this was done, she was home free. Her heart squeezed in her chest. She didn't want to be home *free*. She wanted to be home with Mitch. She mentally gave herself a shake and picked up her pace.

CHAPTER THIRTY-FOUR

"Mitch!" Gage called as he threw open the door to Mitch's office. Mitch went from a dead sleep to sitting bolt upright on his couch. He blinked rapidly. He'd been asleep. Dead asleep. He hadn't slept like that in—

"Mitch. Focus. Now. We need to talk."

Mitch, recognizing the urgency in his brother's voice, threw the blanket off that he'd pulled over them last night. Alex. "Where's Alex?" he demanded.

"Seriously?" Logan said as he walked into the room behind Gage and got an eye full of Mitch naked. "I can't un-see this."

"Alex is…fine. You don't have time for a shower," Gage said.

Mitch cursed under his breath. Logan held out a cup of coffee.

"Mitch grabbed it and took a gulp. The jolt of caffeine had his system humming. "Thanks." Mitch nodded to Logan, and Logan nodding back, walked out of the room. Mitch could hear him answering his phone.

"What's going on?" Mitch asked.

Gage frowned. "Jake just called. Two bodies were pulled out of the sound this morning. They were spotted by early morning fisherman."

"And?" Mitch asked.

Gage looked grim. "Dan. He looked like someone had worked him over pretty bad."

"You think Tolliver had his boys clean up his mess? Stop anyone from linking him to the bomb?"

Gage shook his head. "The other body was Tolliver."

"The client." Mitch said, "Tolliver made a mess of things, so the client was the one cleaning up loose ends."

Gage nodded in agreement. "That's what we're thinking."

"How was it done?" Mitch asked.

"Double-tap to the back of the skull." Gage took a sip of his own coffee.

"Damn." Mitch grimaced. "Professional. These aren't the amateurs that Tolliver was using."

Logan walked back into the room and threw clean underwear and a T-shirt at Mitch. He looked at Gage. "Did you fill him in?" When Gage nodded, he said, "Good, because you two need to get moving if we're going to make sure Alex stays safe."

The room went still. Mitch froze. "What do you mean? Where's Alex?" His voice was dead calm, but inside, his mind was screaming.

Logan glanced at Gage then back at Mitch. "Alex left earlier to retrieve the prototype."

Mitch very carefully put down his coffee cup on the end table. Then he started advancing on his brother. "You let her go with people trying to kill her?" He moved so fast Logan didn't even see it coming, but Gage did, and he stepped in front of Logan. Mitch's blow glanced off Logan's chin. He rocked back on his heels but came forward again with his hands up and ready to go.

Mitch stood there, grinding his teeth, clenching and unclenching his hands. He wanted to pound Logan into the ground. How could he let Alex go when someone was trying to kill her? He stared at Gage, but he knew Gage wouldn't give an inch. Gage always protected Logan. Always had his back. "I need to find her."

Mitch tried to push past his brother, but Gage held him. "Zane, Dex, and Gunnar are with her. She was fine as of a couple of minutes ago. If you'll stop being an ass, we'll go get her and bring her back."

Mitch relaxed and stepped back. Gage let him go, but he stayed close to Logan in case Mitch changed his mind.

"I didn't have a choice. I had to let her go," Logan spoke in quiet, authoritative tones. His lawyer voice.

"If you spin some shit about kidnapping, I swear I'll—"

Logan talked over him. "She's a paying client, and if the client wants to go, we have to let her go."

"What do you mean, she's a client?" Mitch roared. "Are you charging her for this?"

"She came to me and wanted to pay. She felt guilty because we lost clients over the bombing. She offered to pay. I refused several times. In the end, I gave in because we need the money. More than you know. She saved our asses, if you want the truth of it. As a matter of fact, she owes us the rest of the money for last night and the same again because Tolliver is dead. She offered to pay double if we could guarantee that Tolliver would never get to her again."

Mitch was stunned. His brain couldn't wrap itself around what Logan had said. Alex, his thief, his woman, had bailed his ass out. She had his back. His SEAL buddies always had his six, but no one had ever personally had his back. Until now.

He pushed past Gage and Logan. "Come on. We've got to go. Now!"

UNION SQUARE PARK was more of a parkette in her opinion, but in New York, green space was green space. It took up about a city block, or maybe a little more. The greenery was divided into patches and fenced. It was a combination of grassy areas and flowers and trees.

The green part of the park was shaped like a fish with its tail being the flat 14th Street side where they often held rallies. There were several statues around the park, a flag pole in the center, and another big statue at the tail of the fish. She'd never read any of the plaques and had no idea about the statues, but it was a nice little bit of green in the city.

There were park benches so people could enjoy the view and catch a bit of sunlight. The end of the park on 17th street was clear of gardens and was where the popular greenmarket was set up.

Alex looked around as she entered the park before starting down the cement walkway. It looked like a normal morning to her. Nothing stood out as being off. People passed her in droves, heading for the subway station. There were a couple of different coffee carts on the street. The one by Barnes and Noble on 17th had a line. It was just a normal Monday in New York City.

She walked to the far side and turned left down the walkway that followed the curve of the gardens. There was a homeless man sitting on the ground, leaning on the fence in front of one of the flower patches. He had all his stuff piled up in various garbage bags, boxes on his left, and his dog on the right. There was an old straw hat in front of him with a small sign that said *please help me feed my dog.* Alex stopped in front of him. "Hey, Eddie."

"Hey girl, is that you? You back so soon? How you doin' on this fine day?" His face was prematurely aged from his years outside, and his blue eyes were faded in the sun. He was wearing several layers of old clothing. The top layer was an old pale pink shirt that used to be red and a pair of gray work pants. Both had holes and tears. His smile showed teeth that had seen better days, but it was infectious, and she smiled back.

"I'm hangin' in there, Eddie. How's Bandit today?" The dog wagged his tail at the mention of his name.

"He's doin' okay. He got to chew on some bones from the restaurant on the corner last night so he's feelin' pretty good. They try and save him a little something when they can."

"That's nice, Eddie." Alex dug a twenty out of her pocket and dropped it into his hat.

"You don't need to do that, girl." Eddie grinned. "But I thank you kindly."

"So, Eddie, I need my bag back. Have you still got it?"

"Yes, ma'am." He turned and dug around in one of his garbage bags until he came out with her backpack. She went down on her haunches and reached out to take it from him. Bandit jumped on her and, as she fell, she heard a voice say, "Stay exactly where you are." She looked up but had to raise her hand to her eyes to block out the sun.

There was a bull of a man standing above her. He had on jeans and a dark shirt with a black windbreaker over it that was open at the front. He pulled his jacket aside and showed her his gun.

"I've gotcha, Bandit." Eddie was hunkered down on the sidewalk shielding Bandit with his body.

"What do you want?" Alex asked.

"Give me the prototype." He was wearing sunglasses, but Alex didn't need to see his eyes to know he was serious.

"Um..." She licked her lips.

"I know you have it. Give it to me now, or the old man dies." He turned the gun on Eddie.

Alex's heart was slamming into her chest. It was hard to breathe. She couldn't let Eddie get hurt. She'd never forgive herself.

"Okay. Okay," Alex said, and she reached across to grab the backpack from Eddie.

"I don't think so." She immediately recognized the voice that hit her ear.

Mitch was standing directly behind the guy with the sunglasses. The man stiffened and started to turn, but Mitch did something she couldn't see and suddenly Sunglasses stopped moving.

"Alex, I want you to get up and walk over to Zane." Mitch's voice was calm. He tilted his head to his left where Zane was standing about twenty feet away. *How did everyone find her?* Her jacket. *Shit.* Zane must have put a tracker on her jacket. But how did the other guy find her?

Now wasn't the time to think about it. She reached over and took the backpack from Eddie. She opened it and started rummaging around.

"Uh, Alex, just take the whole thing and go, please." Mitch's voice had an edge to it. She looked up. There was another man dressed similarly to Sunglasses in the park who was heading directly toward them.

Suddenly, she could hear sirens, a lot of them, getting closer. The guy with the sunglasses moved quickly to his right and Mitch responded. The guy brought out his gun but Mitch knocked it out of his hand. There was a scream when the gun hit the pavement, and people started running.

She dug around some more. "Come on, come on. Where is it?"

Her fingers closed around a smooth cylinder. She pulled it out and looked. The case for the thumb drive. She turned, looking for Zane, but he was fighting with the other guy.

She glanced over at Eddie, who flicked his eyes toward 14th street and then winked at her. The sirens were right on top of them. If she didn't leave now, she'd be the star in this new circus.

She handed Eddie the thumb drive. "Give this to the guy with light brown hair and gray eyes. Tell him..." What?

"Go." Eddie nodded toward the street.

She hopped up and slung the backpack over her shoulder. She started running. She past the flagpole and the big statue. She was running flat-out when a man wearing all black and a black ski mask popped up off to her left, gun pointed at her gut. She slid to a stop.

"Get in."

She looked over, and there was a black SUV with blacked-out windows at the curb. She opened her mouth to scream when the guy with the gun suddenly twirled in a circle and hit the ground.

She whirled around and saw Mitch standing back by Zane, gun pointed in her direction. She turned back toward the SUV. The guy was being dragged across the sidewalk by two other men dressed the same way. The door of the van opened, and they threw the guy in and followed him. The van door slammed and screeched away from the curb.

She heard her name. Mitch was coming her way, but

he stopped. The cops were behind him, telling him to get on the ground. Mitch and her eyes locked for a beat. She wanted to go to him, but if she did, it would be a bigger nightmare. Her heart was shattering into a million pieces. Her legs were heavy as concrete. It was now or never. She loved Mitch, but being with him would make his life a living hell. She just couldn't do that to him. She turned away and melted into the crowd that was forming.

CHAPTER THIRTY-FIVE

S he zigzagged across the city for several hours after the shooting, making sure she wasn't tailed. She had taken off her jacket immediately after leaving Union Square and bought new clothes, ditching the old ones in various garbage cans as she walked. She wasn't sure how the gunmen had found her, but the only logical thing she could come up with was they somehow had an "eye" in the sky.

A drone made the most sense, but how they'd managed to do that without the whole world knowing was beyond her. New York had very tight security. But if it had been a drone, then they'd been watching the building and then tailed the SUV. They would've been able to see where she'd gone. She glanced up but then quickly put her face to the ground. No sense in making it easier for them if they were still watching.

Mitch. She tried to convince herself she'd done the right thing. That Mitch was better off without her. Logan would get him out of whatever mess he might be in because of the shooting. She was confident in that.

She'd wire the rest of the money to the company as

soon as she got back to her apartment, so the company would be good, at least for now. Drake would be happy that he got his prototype back so, yeah, Mitch would be fine.

But she wouldn't. Her career as a thief was over. She almost caused Leo to get caught and herself to be killed. It was definitely time to retire. She just had no clue where to go or what to do.

She'd spent years creating the life of Alex Morgan, Asset Repossession Specialist Extraordinaire. Now she was just Alex. Her heart hurt when she thought about Mitch. He'd shut down when he realized she was walking away. His face went blank. It killed her to know she had hurt him. She loved him. She knew it in her very marrow, but he was better off without the circus, and if she stayed in one place too long, she would be discovered.

She took some time to watch her street, and when she was satisfied she wasn't being followed, she went into her building. She waited with a small group of people for the elevator. The ride up was long and slow. People were talking about the shooting in Union Square. She didn't want to hear about it, just wanted off the elevator.

Finally, she got to her floor and moved quickly down the hallway to her place. She unlocked her apartment door, stepped inside, closed the door, locked it, and then turned around and leaned against it.

The adrenaline had worn off long ago, and now the exhaustion set in. She wasn't sure her legs would carry her to the couch. She took a deep breath, closed her eyes, and leaned her head back on the door.

"Did you think I wouldn't come after you?" he growled. Her eyes flew open. Mitch was sitting on a stool, leaning on her kitchen island.

"How— Where?" She stopped speaking. She was incapable of making a complete sentence.

"I'm just that good." His smile was smug.

Her eyes narrowed. "Logan. He tracked me down, didn't he?"

The smile disappeared, and Mitch's expression got serious. "What did you think you were doing?" he demanded.

"Don't," she yelled as she pushed off the door. "Don't you start with me." She moved across the room and wagged her finger at him. "I would have gotten away from the guy with the gun, no problem. I was about to do so when you shot him. I don't need you to take care of me. I am perfectly capable of doing it myself." She stood in front of him with her hands on her hips.

"I was talking about leaving me. Did you really think I would let you walk away after last night?"

"I… Mitch, we don't work." Her hands fell from her hips, and she turned away to walk to the windows.

"The hell we don't. We were working just fine last night and early this morning."

The heat rushed up her cheeks, but she pushed it back down. "That was just sex. It wasn't—"

"It wasn't what? Important? Real? What are you going to say? Because it was both of those things. It was me being me and you being you, and it was fantastic. I don't care who your family is. I care about you. The real you. The one that loves a challenge and rises to it every time. The brilliant, beautiful thief, who makes my life hell but makes me better at my job because of it. I love your laugh and your smile. I love the way you dance and the way you fit perfectly with my body and in my life."

"But I don't," she said. "That's what I'm trying to tell you. Oh yeah, it will be great for the first few months, and then someone will figure out who I am and the circus will start. Paparazzi will follow us, me and you, wherever we go. There's no privacy left. How will you work?

"Then you'll get angry and resentful because your life is no longer your own and you can't do what you used to do." Her voice caught in her throat. "The money won't be enough anymore. You'll end up hating me. And I don't want that Mitch."

Tears started to roll down her cheeks, but she didn't stop them. The emotion was too great. She didn't have the energy to hide it anymore. "Mitch, I love you and I never want you to hate me. I love you too much."

Mitch got up off the stool and walked over to stand directly in front of her. "You need to listen to me, and listen good. I will never hate you. We are stronger together than we'll ever be apart. I need you in my life. I need to know that you have my back. I don't care about the money or the circus or anything else. It's you I want.

"If it all gets too much, we can run away to an island somewhere and live off coconuts as far as I'm concerned. But know this, I love you and I will not let you go. Not now. Not ever. You are mine. My woman. My thief." He slanted his mouth over hers, claiming her lips and her heart with a scorching kiss.

EPILOGUE

"Where are they?" Logan demanded as he paced back and forth in the conference room. "I don't have time for this, Gage."

"Relax, Logan. They'll be here. They're only fifteen minutes late." Gage rocked his chair back on two legs.

"But they're always late. My God, they're like bunnies. Can't they limit their sex life to nighttime like everyone else?"

Gage grinned. "Someone sounds jealous. Need to get laid, Logan?"

"Fuck off," Logan snarled.

Gage just laughed. "You're proving my point."

Logan threw himself into his chair. "Let's just get started. Mitch and Alex can catch up whenever they come up for air."

Gage put his chair down and slid a file across the table at Logan. "We still have no clue who hired Tolliver or how they found out about the prototype. I spoke with Drake again after I reviewed everything via encrypted email with his programmer. I can't figure out the leak from that end, but there has to be one. He still won't tell me where she is, and he's insisting she's safe."

"What does he want us to do then?" Logan was frowning as he tried to read the file.

"He wants Mitch and Alex to go to Europe and take over his security there. He's had a couple of weird things happen, and Mitch is the only one he trusts. I guess he'll put up with Alex if it means Mitch will come, although he's not pleased about it." Gage grinned. "A hundred says she'll win him over inside of a week."

Logan shook his head. "No way. That's a sucker's bet. She's too charming. Even Drake will end up liking her."

Logan frowned again. "What am I looking at, Gage? I don't understand it."

Gage leaned forward and took the top piece of paper. "That's because it's in code. The night of the shutdown, Lacy Carmichael was working here. She sent a series of coded emails. That's what you're looking at. They mention the prototype. We haven't entirely decoded everything, but it seems like whoever she's emailing was very interested in it."

Logan looked at his brother. "Are you thinking whoever she sent the emails to could be the buyer?"

Gage shrugged. "It's possible. She could have told Tolliver to make Monica use Alex."

Logan was skeptical. "But they're best friends..."

"Yes." Gage went silent.

Logan eyed his brother. "What aren't you telling me?"

"We've picked up some chatter about the prototype. It's no longer the secret it once was. The chatter says something big is going to happen soon, and the Bahamas have been mentioned. We're not sure how it fits in but, coincidently, Lacy Carmichael is heading down there this weekend."

Logan nodded. "And you're going to go down and keep an eye on her."

"No." Gage shook his head. "You are."

"Me? Why me?" Logan was dumbfounded. He was the CEO. He oversaw running the daily business. Ops were not his thing.

"Obviously, Mitch and Alex can't do this, plus they're needed in Europe. I have to work with Mitch on Drake's security plan, but I also have a couple of things I have to check out. We need Dex, Zane, and Dragan to hold down the fort here and do some minor jobs we have coming up. Look, she's probably going down to Nassau to lie on a beach and soak up some rays while drinking rum punch. You could use a little of that yourself. Maybe even get laid." Gage stood up. "I've gotta go. We'll chat later," he said as he headed out of the room.

"Wait. Mitch and Alex were never supposed to be at this meeting, were they?"

Gage's laughter floated back to him. "Your flight leaves in three hours. Sloan has all the info."

Logan sat at the boardroom table looking down at the gibberish on the papers in front of him. Maybe his brother was right. Maybe he did need a bit of R&R. He could use some sunshine and rum punch. Hell, he'd like to get laid. Gage was right—it had been too long. But the more he tried to convince himself that this was a good idea, the more he knew in his gut it was going to be a nightmare.

DID you enjoy Break and Enter? If so check out the next book in the series, *Smash and Grab*. Keep reading for sneak peek, or Grab Your Copy Here

KEEP READING FOR A LOOK AT
SMASH AND GRAB

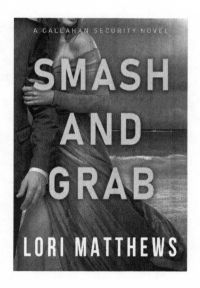

Can't get enough of the men of Callahan Security? Keep reading for a sneak peek at Logan Callahan's story, which takes place in the exotic Bahamas.

Logan Callahan knows he's out of his depth. As CEO of

Callahan Security, he thrives on balance sheets and bottom lines. But there's a huge difference between running a company and running for your life. Unfortunately he doesn't have a choice. The woman he came to the Bahamas to investigate was kidnapped and he was taken right along with her. He knew the sexy lady lawyer was trouble. He just had no idea how much.

Taken again. Lacy Carmichael was not new to the Kidnap and Ransom game but usually she managed to talk or fight her way out of it. After all, when your father was one of the largest arms dealers in the world, danger comes with the territory. Since Logan was grabbed with her, she'll have to reveal all her secrets in order to save their asses.

Logan is hesitant to trust Lacy but a power grab by her father's enemies removes his choice. If only she wasn't so damned smart and sexy, staying neutral would be easier. Searching for a way out of the mess, and fighting their mutual attraction to each other, will take all of Logan's and Lacy's skills. Unfortunately, deception and betrayal by those they trust the most has changed the rules of the game, and they find themselves battling for their lives and their love.

SMASH AND GRAB

"I'm not going, Markus," Lacy Carmichael hissed as she tugged her arm from the large man's grasp.

She took a step back and glanced around the party to see if anyone had noticed. It was packed, and the beat from the music was vibrating in her chest. "Like I told you when you called, I'll meet my father on Monday. He expressly told me not to come to see him before then. If he wants me to come now, he's going to have to call me and tell me himself. I'm only following orders."

She straightened her dress. "Now," she said above the noise, "I'm on this yacht to enjoy myself, not to discuss business." With that, she turned on her heel and disappeared into the crowd. She glanced over her shoulder to see if Markus followed and smashed right into someone, a man's chest to be accurate.

Looking up, she almost choked on her champagne. "Logan, what are you doing here?" she sputtered. Of all the people she could have run into on a yacht party in the Bahamas, this was about the worst-case scenario.

"It's nice to see you too, Lacy." A small smile played at the corners of his mouth as he wiped champagne from his chest.

He looked amazing. His dark hair was a little long, and the moist Caribbean air was making it curl more than usual. One lock tumbled over his forehead, and she started to raise her hand to push it back but caught herself.

"Is everything OK?" His blue eyes, so piercing, glanced over the top of her head, but when she whipped around, there was no sign of Markus. Thank God.

She should have been ready for his next question, delivered seconds after the first one, but somehow she wasn't.

"Who was that man you were fighting with?"

This time she did choke. She coughed and coughed. Logan, concern written on his face, drew closer, but she waved him off.

"Sorry," she croaked. "Went down the wrong pipe." She coughed a bit more. "Ah, nobody." She ran a hand over her own hair, smoothing down any wayward strands. "It's nice to see you, Logan. I'm just surprised you're here in Nassau. I didn't know Callahan Security had clients in the Bahamas...unless you're on vacation? Being the CEO of your own company has some perks, eh? Are your brothers with you?"

She bit the inside of her cheek to stop herself from rambling and tried to make her expression as neutral as possible, but she'd always felt Logan could see right through her. It wasn't something she was willing to admit to anyone else. She knew his former associates had nicknamed him "Lucifer" for that very stare which, rumor had it, could see right into a person's soul. Not to mention he was a devil in the courtroom if the case ever got that far.

"Callahan Security doesn't have clients here, and I left

Gage and Mitch in charge in New York. A bit of a risk, I admit." He smiled. "Actually, I have some business to attend to for my old law firm. They flew me down."

He had finished wiping his chest, and now he gave her the once over, even studying her arm where Markus had grabbed her. "You sure you're all right?"

"Um, yes. Fine." She started to bring her hand up to fix her hair again but stopped herself. No need to let him know how much he rattled her.

"What about you?" he asked. "What are you doing in the Bahamas and, more specifically, at this party? Do you know the Dobsons?"

"The who?" She had been distracted by his cool blue eyes checking her out. The smile was back, threatening the corners of his mouth again.

"The Dobsons. This is their party. They own the yacht."

"Right. The Dobsons. Well, actually, I was invited by an old college friend who's here in town. He asked me to drop by."

Logan glanced around as if looking for the person in question.

"Oh, he's around here somewhere." She pretended to look for him. In reality, she had been invited by a woman she met by the pool at her hotel. She wouldn't normally say yes to something like this, but life had been stressful of late, and she just wanted a chance to dress up and go to a party without the hassle of having to talk to anyone. Now she very much regretted her decision to party crash.

She saw Markus coming up from below. He was talking on his cell. Holding up her empty champagne glass, she said, "You know, I think I'll go find some water. Great to see you!" She quickly turned and fled. The last thing she wanted was for Logan and his super-stare to see her and Markus arguing again.

She made her way through the crowd to the railing and leaned over the side of the yacht. It was a perfect Caribbean night. The breeze was warm but not hot. The boat was decorated with twinkly lights along the railings and lanterns hung high up across the decks. They had even turned on the lights by the water so the hull was illuminated. She saw a fish swim alongside the yacht and then disappear into the inky water.

She peered up at the night sky. The bright light on the yacht made it difficult to see the stars. She made a mental note to look up once she left the yacht. The pier and the parking lot weren't well lit so she might be able to see the brilliant white dots in the heavens, if there were any visible.

Rolling her shoulders, she tried to ease some of the tension in her neck. Some vacation. She wanted a weekend to decompress from work, which had sucked lately. Well, it always sucked. The truth was, she wanted out. Out of being a lawyer. She had enough clients to make a good living, but she just found the whole thing boring. And there was her father...but she wasn't going to think about that. This was her weekend off. She wanted to enjoy it.

She glanced up, spotted Markus again, and then breathed a small sigh of relief when he disappeared around the bow of the yacht. She wasn't surprised he found her at the party. Her father had eyes everywhere. It was weird though, that her father hadn't contacted her directly to tell her he wanted her to come home. Why send one of his henchmen? He knew she wouldn't go with Markus unless he called her. She was following his instructions. The whole thing was off somehow. Come to think of it, Markus was acting weird, too. Nervous.

She exchanged her empty glass of champagne for a full

one from a passing waiter and took a large sip. One for the road. It was time to abandon ship. This wasn't the way she'd wanted to kick off her weekend break.

She caught a glimpse of Logan through the crowd. Logan Callahan. The man who always had made her knees weak. From the moment she saw him across a board-room table, she'd been hyper aware of him. She'd been a newly minted lawyer and thought she knew a thing or two. He quickly ground her into dust.

She'd never forgotten him, or forgiven him for that matter. Still, their interactions had made her a better lawyer. She had been much better prepared the next time they'd met. She even scored a point or two on him.

Since then, she'd improved greatly, and now she was pretty sure he saw her as a worthy adversary. Or at least he had until he quit and started running Callahan Security with his brothers. She didn't want to think about her weekend with Callahan Security. It was part of the reason she needed this weekend off.

She prided herself on being a very capable and strong woman. She knew she couldn't have gotten far in life—her life, specifically—if she didn't have her shit together. But Logan always threw her for a loop. She'd gotten better at hiding it but, still, the moment she saw him, she turned into an idiot. Case in point. She'd just spilled her drink all over him.

Keeping one eye out for Markus, she worked her way across the length of the yacht and down the stairs to the deck below. As she neared the gangplank to get off the boat, she heard a splash and then a scream. The world seemed frozen for a second before people rushed to the railing. The partygoers were yelling, pushing, and shoving, and someone yelled, "Call for an ambulance!"

Dread washed over her as she elbowed her way to the rail. Her stomach lurched at the sight of what lay below.

A body bobbing in the water.

No need for lights and sirens. Markus floated face up, giving her a perfect view of the hole in the middle of his forehead.

Panic engulfed her, and she white-knuckled the railing. *Just breathe. Just breathe.* She kept repeating the mantra until everything stopped spinning. She scanned the crowd. Most people were still peering down at the body in shock, but some were already making their way off the yacht. That seemed like a grand idea to her. While she and Markus had been acquaintances and she was sorry he was dead, it wouldn't do her any good if she got caught up in whatever mess he was leaving behind.

As she turned, something caught her eye, so she stopped to scrutinize the deck above. Logan was standing there watching her. Their eyes met. A shiver ran down her spine. Then some panicked partygoer slammed into her, and the spell was broken. By the time she righted herself and looked up again, Logan was gone.

Sirens in the distance made goose bumps raise on her arms. She made her way to the gangplank, pushing through the crowd. Being gone by the time the cops arrived would be best. It was never good to chat with the cops with her father on the wrong side of the law.

As she hit the pier, the mass exodus created a logjam of bodies heading the same direction as she was going…to the parking lot. Strobing lights on the arriving cop cars lit the sky, rendering any chance of seeing stars moot.

Glancing around, it appeared the best way out of there was to walk left and back down the pier along the side of the warehouse, away from the parking lot. The pier extended maybe twenty feet past the end of the warehouse.

She tried to pull up a mental map of the area. Wasn't there a boardwalk on the far side of the warehouse by the other end of the parking lot? If she traveled around the warehouse, she should be able to get to the boardwalk. She would only be exposed as she covered the last bit of parking lot. There were a couple of hotels if she remembered correctly. She could grab a cab.

Changing direction, she worked her way through the crowd. She finally broke free and hustled down the pier, sticking close to the warehouse so she would be in the shadows the whole way. The shock of seeing Markus floating lifeless in the water was starting to wear off, leaving dozens of questions in its wake.

Behind her, cops were ordering people back onto the yacht, so she picked up her pace. There would be plenty of time later to theorize about what had happened. She rounded the corner and broke into a light jog along the far end of the warehouse. Not easy to do in high heels, but desperate times called for desperate measures.

It was dark, and she stumbled, but caught herself. She glanced upward and realized there were no stars. So much for the perfect Caribbean night.

Coming to the next corner, she peered around it, making sure there were no cops. She stuck close to the warehouse as she worked her way back down the pier. She was almost halfway down the side when a cop came around the corner of the warehouse from the parking lot. She stopped jogging and quickly hid behind some pallets that were stacked on the pier next to the warehouse. The cop walked directly toward her, and she shrank back into the shadows.

A hand covered her mouth. All the air left her lungs. Struggling to breathe, she started to fight off her attacker.

"Stop struggling, or the cop will find us," a voice breathed in her ear. She froze. Logan took his hand away from her mouth and pulled her deeper behind the stack of pallets. Her pulse skyrocketed. Being pressed against Logan wasn't helping. Electricity danced across her skin.

They stood frozen as the cop came closer. He took out a flashlight and moved the beam around the pier. The light didn't penetrate the pallets, and the officer walked back the way he'd come.

As soon as he was out of earshot, Lacy turned to face Logan. "You scared the shit out of me!"

"I didn't want you to yell and let the cop know where we were."

She couldn't see his face in the shadows, but she had a sneaking suspicion he was laughing at her again. "Whatever. I need to get out of here." When she took a step forward, Logan followed her. She glanced at him, "What are you—?"

"Looks like we both want to get out of here, so why don't we talk later and just keep moving now, hmm?"

It was tempting to argue, but she nodded and started walking toward the end of the warehouse. Logan was the last person she'd expected to find hiding out on the pier. He was a top-notch lawyer. Squeaky clean. The fact that he was lurking in the shadows tonight was interesting. Very interesting.

When they came to the end, Logan glanced toward the yacht. "The cops have the area cordoned off. Looks like they're questioning people."

Lacy took a quick look and confirmed what he'd said. She immediately swore.

"What?" he asked.

"Peter Trenthom."

"Who?"

"The guy in the suit standing next to the gangplank. He's probably the lead detective on the case."

He cocked an eyebrow. "And how do you know so much about the police in the Bahamas?"

"It's a long story. Let's just say, my employer has had some legal issues in town." She peeked around the corner again, trying to figure out her best move.

If Trenthom saw her, it would be game over for sure. He knew both she and Markus worked for Armand Fontaine. She would be questioned. If he found out she had been arguing with Markus, she might have to spend the night at the station. She wanted no part of that. Very few people knew that Armand Fontaine was also her father, and she'd prefer to keep it that way.

Logan eyed her. "What are you thinking?"

She turned her head toward him. It was hard to see his features in the small bit of ambient light, but she the intensity of his gaze warmed her.

She licked her lips. "The boardwalk is just over there, so I think we should make a break for it and hustle toward the hotels that are down the beach." She started forward, but he grabbed her arm and hauled her back.

"Let's take a moment to think about it." He held her arm as he scanned the area, the contact making the butterflies in her stomach take flight. She tried to pull away gently, but he held fast. Her heart started to beat a bit faster.

"If we walk across the parking lot to the boardwalk entrance, we're bound to be seen," he murmured, more to himself than to her.

The scent of Logan carried on the breeze, surrounding Lacy. He smelled distinctly male, mixed with citrus and a hint of salt air. The heady aroma was clouding her thinking and making her conjure up all kinds of inappropriate thoughts. She swallowed hard. "Well, do you have a better plan?" she asked as she tugged her arm again, anxious to be free of his touch. This man was friggin' kryptonite, and she was losing the ability to concentrate.

"As a matter of fact, I do." He let go of her arm and wrapped his arm around her shoulders, pulling her close. Startled, she gasped and glared up at him.

"Just follow my lead." He walked them out from behind the building and turned *toward* the yacht.

"What are you doing?" she asked in a fierce whisper. *Was he crazy?* She heard someone yell, but Logan didn't pause. He lowered his head closer to hers. "Keep walking."

The yell came a second time. Logan whipped her around, placing himself between her and the police by the yacht. He bent down and swiftly captured her mouth with his. She opened her mouth in surprise, and he deepened the kiss. She put her hands on his chest, ostensibly to push him away, but they had a life of their own. They fisted his shirt and pulled him closer. She was so wrapped up in him, she barely noticed someone was still yelling at them.

He suddenly broke away from her and turned his head. She was trying to get her bearings. Was he talking to someone? The world snapped into focus. There was a uniformed officer standing just to her right.

"Sorry, officer," Logan said. "We didn't hear you." His aw-shucks smile was almost convincing enough to fool her. "What's going on over there? Did someone get hurt?"

Her heart was pounding so hard she was sure he could feel it. That kiss had been so amazing and crazy and *ohmygod* good. Her body was still crushed against his, and the closeness was killing her concentration.

The officer hesitated and then took in her cocktail dress and his suit. "You need to come with me."

"We'd be happy to come, officer. We were just walking over to the party when we saw all the commotion. We took a bit longer getting ready than we'd planned." He winked at the cop.

Heat crawled up Lacy's neck. Was he for real? Did he just wink? Mortified didn't begin to cover her consternation.

"You haven't been to the party?" the cop asked.

"No, we were on our way. What happened? Are the Dobsons alright?"

The officer gave Logan the once over. "Do you know the Dobsons?"

"Yes. I went to law school with their son, Peter." He turned to Lacy. "Maybe I should go and see if Peter needs help."

Just then a second police officer arrived.

"What's going on?" the new cop asked.

"These two say they were just going to the party," the first officer said.

"Yes, officer," Logan agreed. "We were late getting here. I understand there's been a problem. As I was telling this officer, Peter Dobson and I went to law school together. I thought I might go over and offer my services."

"Ah…" The second cop hesitated. "I don't think that will be necessary, sir. It's better if you leave. I'm sure the Dobsons will be in touch if they require your assistance."

"If you're sure," Logan said. "I'd feel badly leaving Peter in the lurch. Maybe I—"

"No, sir. I'm afraid I'm going to have to ask you to leave." The officer pointed to the boardwalk behind them.

Logan turned himself and Lacy slowly as he said, "OK. We'll go."

"Thank you, sir. Have a good evening."

Lacy let out the breath she'd been holding. That had been close. Too close.

You can buy Smash And Grab Here

A NOTE OF THANKS

YOU READ MY BOOK. You read the whole thing! I cannot thank you enough for sticking with me. If this is the first book of mine you've read, welcome aboard. I certainly hope it won't be the last! If you are already a fan then I can only say, thank you so much for your continued support! Either way, you have made my day, my week, my year! You have transported me from writer to *author*. I feel so special! You have made my dreams come true. Genuinely, truly, you are a fairy god-parent. So thank-you!

Now, I'm hoping you love this new-found power of making dreams come true and you want to keep going. The next book in the Callahan Security series is called ***Smash and Grab***. You can get it here: My Book. I will be eternally grateful if you buy a copy. You will be fulfilling your destiny as a wish granter. (Is that even a thing outside of genies and fairy god-parents?)

If you would like to try your hand at being a super-hero, you can always help make me a bestselling author by leaving a review for ***Break and Enter*** on Amazon, (My Book) or **Goodreads** (https://www.goodreads.com/

book/show/50617424-break-and-enter) or **Bookbub**, (https://www.bookbub.com/books/break-and-enter-by-lori-matthews). Reviews sell books and they make authors super happy. Did I say thank you already? Just in case I forgot, thank you soooo much.

And now that you are reveling in your superhero status, I would love it if you would stay in touch with me. I love my readers and I love doing giveaways and offering previews and extra content of my upcoming books. Come join the fun. You can follow me here:

Newsletter:
Signup Form (constantcontactpages.com)
Website:
www.lorimatthewsbooks.com
Facebook:
https://www.facebook.com/LoriMatthewsBooks
Facebook: Romantic Thriller Readers (Author Lori Matthews)
https://www.facebook.com/groups/killerromancereaders
Amazon Author Page:
https://www.amazon.com/author/lorimatthews
Goodreads:
https://www.goodreads.com/author/show/7733959.
Lori_Matthews
Bookbub:
https://www.bookbub.com/profile/lori-matthews
Instagram:
https://www.instagram.com/lorimatthewsbooks/
Twitter:
https://twitter.com/_LoriMatthews_

ALSO BY LORI MATTHEWS

Callahan Security

Break and Enter

Smash And Grab

Hit And Run

Evade and Capture

Catch And Release

Cease and Desist (Coming Soon)

Coast Guard Recon

Diverted

Incinerated

Conflicted

Subverted

Terminated

Brotherhood Protectors World

Justified Misfortune

Justified Burden

Justified Vengeance

Free with Newsletter Sign Up

Falling For The Witness

Risk Assessment

Visit my website to sign up for my newsletter